WHERE YOUR TREASURE IS

M. LIZ BOYLE

M. LIZ BOYLE

Contents

1

Of all the skills I'm proficient at, tripping tops the list. It wouldn't be so bad if it was isolated to tripping over objects, like the metal pail that is going to leave a dent in my left shin as I hobble toward the phone. That pales in comparison to some of my life decisions.

A minute ago I was dutifully cleaning gear outside when the phone in *abuelo*'s office rang, and knowing the guys were busy, I sprinted for it. And tripped.

I recover, hanging up an armful of dive masks on the rack on my sprint through the aisles. I politely dodge a clump of customers to get to the phone, so now I probably sound too breathless to be working at the dive shop like the responsible adult that I'm supposed to be. "Ruby Sunset, Ruby speaking." I move the phone away from my face long enough to take a much needed breath. My name should give enough evidence that I do belong here. That I can in fact make grown up decisions.

"Hi," a female voice responds. "Do you give scuba tours to people who have never scuba dived before?"

"All the time," I say. I lean my head out of the office and give an 'I've got this' smile to my brother. He nods and turns his attention to the next customers at the counter. Memorial Day rush.

"Okay. How do I book one?" She's polite, so I open up the scheduling app on the computer. If she was rude, I'd be rude too. One of my many faults, or so I'm told. I talk her through the usual million steps to sign up for a diving tour, take down her credit card information to reserve her spot, and when I think the conversation is wrapping up, she asks, "Um, are you the same Ruby that works at the aquarium?"

Yes, but how does she know? "Yes, I am. Were you there recently?"

"Yeah, I took one of the plane tours yesterday. The pilot, Brett, mentioned you."

"He did?" I've known Brett for years, and apparently he's a distant relative because I've seen him at family gatherings before. I always assumed he was nothing closer than a cousin's cousin by marriage or something. *Abuelo* and *mamá* always talk to him at family gatherings, but I don't think Brett likes me at all. His wife is nice, or at least she seemed to be when I met her at the company picnic. Brett usually looks at me with an expression like he smelled a dead skunk, so I'm surprised that I would come up in conversation.

"An offhand comment. He said something about your family's business."

Brett is plugging our business now? That's unexpected. "I've flown with him on a couple rescues."

"That's what he said. Then when I was watching a dolphin show, the announcer told the audience to wave to Ruby. You were carrying pails of fish to the trainers."

"That was me." Good thing the bosses teach us to always smile at the audience. They're paying customers, and you never know the impact you'll have on their vacation, to summarize what Jerome says.

"You must know everything about the ocean," the woman comments. "Working at a dive shop *and* an aquarium."

I laugh lightheartedly. "Well, the ocean is definitely my stomping ground, but I've got plenty to learn."

"You know more than me. This trip is my first time seeing an ocean."

Wow, really? I can't imagine not smelling saltwater with every breath and always having the waves as the background music to my life. "I hope you're enjoying your first trip. You'll love the dive tour tomorrow. It's my favorite way to see the ocean."

"Thank you. I can't wait." Her voice makes me picture a bubbly lady, forty-five years old, a bouncy ponytail with its first gray hairs concealed by a few cutely placed hair wraps done at one of the tourist shops. She looks the part on her whirlwind weeklong trip, tirelessly packing her days with everything she's dreamed of doing at the beach.

"I'm glad you chose our shop."

"Thank your pilot friend for the recommendation." We say goodbye and I jog to the front door, opening it for *abuelo* who is carrying a couple air tanks, a wetsuit, and a pair of fins.

"*Gracias*, Ruby." *Abuelo* is the combination of strength and experience. He has the weathered look of a guy who has endured hurricanes, yet he also possesses the gentle *abuelo* touch that has cared for injured ducklings. I've seen him scare off a bull shark, and I've seen pictures of him holding me and the twins as newborns. He's the real ocean expert, and nobody ever offers to carry a big load for him because he doesn't need it.

"Good dive?" I ask him.

He looks down at his armload and shifts the tanks, then continues walking. I let the door close and follow him toward the back of the store. "Mmhmm."

Mmhmm? That is not a usual *abuelo* response. He's not one to talk anybody's ear off, but he isn't one to walk past me and avoid conversation either.

Abuelo sets down his tanks and fins behind the counter and glances at me. My brothers August and Axel are still busy with customers. *Abuelo* checks his watch and looks distracted. Maybe even worried.

"Want to dive this weekend? For fun?" I haven't dived for fun in over a year. These days I dive all the time at the aquarium, and I still lead the occasional Ruby Sunset tour in the reefs, but diving for fun ended almost a year and a half ago. It's not that I don't enjoy diving. Diving is part of who I am. I much prefer diving over talking to customers or answering tourists' questions. I love diving, but it isn't fun anymore. It's lonely. When I let my dreams of *Dos Hermanos* sink, diving lost its meaning.

"Diving for fun? That sounds more like my Ruby." *Abuelo* spins around and looks at me, his eyebrows lowering. "Where are you thinking?"

The answer I was looking for would've been a smile and him saying there's nothing he'd like better to do this weekend. I feel my face fall at his lack of enthusiasm and I shrug. "A fun coral reef or something. Unless you have a suggestion?"

Abuelo shifts his eyes to survey the customers, my brothers, the aisles of the store. Five awkward seconds tick by, and then he looks back at me. "I'm glad you want to have fun again. Right now I need to make a phone call. We can talk diving later." He squeezes my shoulder, steps into his office and closes the door behind him. Something is definitely up.

"Here we are," *abuelo* says as he idles the boat motor down. "Amber Key Reef."

After *abuelo*'s mysteriously timed phone call, he talked to me again about diving and we made today's plan. The twins are along too, so it takes me back to when the boys were teenagers and I was still learning to dive. I've always done more diving with *abuelo* than with my own parents. August and Axel usually begged him to leave me home. *Abuelo* won out more often than not, so I got to tag along, at least until they got secretive and searched for a big, famous wreck when I was a teenager. During that time I got to fly with *mamá* quite a bit, which was cool, even though I would've rather been hunting for the wreck with them. *Abuelo*'s vessel, *Abuela*, rises with a wave, bringing me back to the present.

The sun warms my bare shoulders and the breeze makes my shoulder-length hair dance. August lowers the anchor, Axel begins checking our regulators, and *abuelo* eyes a map of the seafloor. I inhale the salty air and look at the expanse of deep blue stretching beyond the horizon. Florida, the ocean, and diving are as much a part of my life as the air I breathe. It's been too long since I've been out here with my *abuelo* and brothers. It'd be nice if *mamá* and *papá* were here too, but I'll take this. August meets my eyes and I smile at him.

Abuelo motions that we should crowd around him and the map. "This reef is a good one to dive. Haven't been here for a few years. It'll give us an excuse to check up on the health of it." Everybody nods, knowing that *abuelo* will keep a detailed report of the dive. "August and Ruby, you're on standby first. Axel and I will have forty minutes of bottom time."

August and I nod, and he hoists the red and white dive flag on *abuelo*'s vessel. I don't mind having forty minutes to catch up with my brother at all. *Abuelo* and Axel prepare to go down, and August and I watch them go through the BWRAF buddy check, the double and triple check of their BCDs, weights, releases, air, and final OKs. Sometimes all the safety checks in the world won't do any good, but I've been taught to do our part to be safe. We stack our fists on top of each other's, a tradition we've done as long as I can remember, and on three we say, "*Conquistadores.*" Don't overthink it. I'm pretty sure the boys came up with it when they were little, and it's just our family's dive christening procedure.

Abuelo and Axel flip backwards off the end of *Abuela*, and August starts a timer so we know when they should be up by. I grip the top rail with my hands and will my Mexican skin to get darker in the sun. Wetsuits and diving don't exactly make for a great tan, so I'll take advantage of these forty minutes of sunshine. August joins me, leaning forward with his forearms propped on the top rail.

"How's Ruby Sunset doing?" I ask. It stung when my brothers officially took over the family business and fired me. Not fired exactly, but demoted me to a contract worker. Less than a part-time employee. I was already working plenty at the aquarium, but it wasn't about the hours or the money. Being told I no longer had an important part in the business that shares my name, the business where I literally grew up, was a punch in the gut.

August knows all this and he gives me a sympathetic smile. "We're very busy. Taxes are robbery, but the new CPA is helping us."

"The new CPA," I say with a waggle of my eyebrows. "As in Stacia? Your girlfriend?"

August grins and dips his head. "She's a good CPA. All the small business owners I asked said she's been really good for their companies."

"And she likes your goatee and backwards baseball cap?" I tease.

August laughs and nods. "We've been dating for a few months."

"Is that all?" I thought it was longer.

August grins again. "Seven months, to be precise."

I smile and look back to the horizon. "I'm happy for you."

August goes silent and I know exactly why. I was in love once too. I hope August has a better run than Tanner and I did. August gives me a minute to have a pity party, and then I restart the conversation. "Hey, *abuelo* seems really distracted lately."

"Oh?" August's tone makes me snap my head to look at him. In that one-syllable word, he conveyed both fake confusion and surprise.

I feel one of my eyebrows dart up. "You know what's up."

August puffs out his cheeks and slowly exhales. His eyes shift right and left and he even looks at his diving computer on his wrist to check the time.

"You're a horrible actor."

"You just get right to the point. Every time. And so fast. In two seconds you went from grieving Tanner to accusing me of knowing a secret."

"Is there a secret?"

August flips his face to the sky and rolls his eyes in exasperation.

I let a full two minutes tick by and then I loudly tap my toe on the deck.

August looks at me and says, "I think there's a lot of stress right now with the nautical grant."

"That's the lamest answer you could've come up with." There's always stress regarding which treasure divers will receive the nautical grant to afford the niche hobby of scanning the seafloor for valuables.

August laughs, breaking the tension.

"Whatever. Keep your secrets." I shrug, the familiar feel of deflation settling inside me.

August leans over the boat rail again. "How is the aquarium?"

"It's good. I'm learning a lot. The high-ups think I should apply for the apprentice aquarist program."

August nods. "There could be job security in that."

"Since there's none in the family business?" I don't attempt to mask my frustration.

He turns his head and looks me square in the eyes. "It's not that simple. Come on, I'm not Axel. Can you pretend you like me? Like usual? Let's just catch up."

I swallow. Something is up with the men in my family. August and *abuelo* are the men I connect with the most. If I can't crack either of them and get to the bottom of the family tension, I'm sure not going to get anything out of Axel or *papá*. Not that I would bother trying. As much as I want to push August more, I'd rather have peace. For now. So I sigh, meet his gaze, and say, "How are *mamá* and *papá* doing?"

August looks back to the water. "*Papá*'s good. You talk to *mamá* more than I do." Is it normal or strange that two people married for so long have both completely separate and joined lives? Whenever I talk to one parent, it's like I've talked to both, but then again, talking to only one parent is only half the story. Oh well. It gives us siblings something to talk about.

"*Mamá*'s good." I watch the water and take a breath. "You think they'll ever move back here?"

August nods. "Yeah, I think so. Not sure when, but someday." It really bugs me that they moved away. It shouldn't be a big deal since I'm eighteen, but family is supposed to be forever. Unless you're in a family of treasure hunters.

I nod, watching a bird. It's a sandwich tern, white with a black crest on its head. It scans the water and plunges in, coming back up with a fish in its bill. Sometimes they drop their prey and come up empty, but they don't give up. They'll go up for a good view and dive right back in. Always trying again.

I turn to August. "How's that men's Bible study you're going to?"

"Really good. The guys are chill, and we're working through some tough parts of scripture. A lot is making sense for the first time."

I smile.

He bumps my arm. "You think you'll ever date again?"

I snap my face toward him. Nobody's mentioned dating to me since Tanner. I expect the wave of familiar pain to well in the depth of my stomach, and it does come, but not immediately. For some reason, I'm bothered by the delay. August waits patiently and I finally answer. "Maybe. I don't know. It'd take the right guy."

"Yeah. I just wondered since you suggested diving for fun today. It's good to see you getting back to your old self." Thankfully he's satisfied and switches the topic. "Anything in particular you want to find when we go down?"

"I brought the metal detector just in case."

August nods. "Of course. Always after a treasure. You're not just here for fun." His voice is clouded with a tinge of bitterness.

"Isn't everyone in this family?" I manage to suppress the snappiness in my voice, but I feel it deep inside, like an electrical shock flicking my nerves. *Abuelo* and the boys struck big. *Papá* and *mamá* are off on the Gulf to make more money. And me? I'm booted from the family business and am stuck cleaning dolphin poop for a living.

August looks at me and searches my face. "You need to laugh again."

"Then make me laugh."

August has always been the comedian of the family. It didn't matter if *abuela* was mad as a wet hen at us kids, August would get us out of trouble with his humor.

August smiles, and I see why Stacia is falling in love with him. "You think I'm a circus dog, performing on command?" He cracks his knuckles. "My best jokes have to happen organically. Besides," he sniffs, "I don't do jokes and card tricks. They're miracles."

"Miracles, right." I laugh. "Tell me more about Stacia."

He can't hide his goofy grin. *Menso*, sucker. "What do you want to know?"

"Have you told her you love her?"

August gets serious. "I think I love her. But I haven't told her."

"What are you waiting for?"

He swallows. "How do you know you're in love?"

I arch an eyebrow. "You're in love."

He smiles sheepishly. "Other than that floaty feeling, how do you know? This is so much different than what I ever had with Destiny." Ah, yes. Destiny who wasn't his destiny. No need to rehash that heartbreak. Right now he's asking me to share my personal experience.

I gulp. "I didn't realize it until I lost him. I was too focused on the treasure diving to see the real treasure." I pause, thinking about the words that just came out of my mouth, words that were so deep inside I didn't know they existed. Words that are too deep for me. I swallow. "Looking back, I know I was in love because at the time I would've done anything for him." I look at August. "Don't wait too long to tell her."

August watches me with his mouth in a small O. He shows his surprise for a beat and then cracks a grin. "Don't go all serious on me like that again."

I laugh and a second later *abuelo* and Axel break through the surface. Fifty seconds later August's alarm dings. The divers are safe and it's our turn. August and I suit up and I grab my metal detector. You never know where a piece of Spanish eight is buried in the sand. Like

August telling Stacia he loves her while he can, I don't want to miss my chance at a treasure. If it's right in front of me, I don't want to blindly swim past.

Abuelo and Axel brief us on what to expect and we go through all the safety checks. "Two hundred feet southeast is a small wreck, but you don't have enough time to check it out."

August nods in agreement, because he has Stacia and his men's Bible study and Ruby Sunset to resurface for. He's a sandwich tern that has patience to take to the sky between dives, the level headedness to get perspective before diving in. He wisely says, "We'll save that for another day." I tamp down a twinge of resentment in my chest.

When it's my turn, I sit on the edge of the boat, press my finned feet against the deck, and flip backward over the edge. I settle down, my eyes adjusting to the blue filter down here, listening to my regulator and keeping an eye on August. Dive buddies are supposed to stay close enough to help in an emergency, but with clear visibility like this, it's tempting to stray farther. With *abuelo*'s casual comment about a shipwreck so close, the sensible and reckless halves of my brain are battling. Two hundred feet is out of visibility, way too far to be ready to help in less than five seconds. But a shipwreck? If it's so close, why'd we bother at the reef? Why did I say I wanted to dive for fun, anyway?

Sometimes, if I stop to think about it, scuba diving is kind of scary. Choosing to go to an environment that would kill me in less than two minutes if I mess up. Going somewhere that requires me to wear a bunch of protective gear and carry the brightest flashlights known to man. Swimming into the depths where potentially dangerous animals with gills thrive. Yeah, it's kind of unnerving, so I don't stop to think about it.

Abuelo warns me that I should slow down and think more often. And *mamá* calls me every Monday, Wednesday, and Friday at 8:00

p.m. Not to catch up, but to check up. She knows where I like to be and she knows when sharks hunt, so she calls me at shark feeding time because she knows I'll be out of the water to answer, even if for no other reason than to prevent the embarrassment that I would endure if she has to call *abuelo*, or worse, my brothers, to check on me if I don't answer.

But it's only 2 o'clock on the weekend, so time is on my side and *abuelo* and my brothers are with me. They never let me leave their sight. Like I'm a problem child or something. August and I hold onto the anchor line as we descend. It's a shallow dive, so we won't need any deco stops if we're only down for forty minutes. I look at my dive computer.

August and I hover just above the coral reef and watch with amusement as the fish scatter. They're part of a whole other world that never even thinks about ours until our fins and masked faces invade. Carefree little fish, none of them fazed by their schoolmate who got snatched by the sandwich tern. They're just darting around, living for the moment in their isolated world.

August and I nod and begin perusing the reef, letting the colors and busyness flood our senses. Using my overpriced scuba-safe phone case, I take some pictures of the coral. I haven't uploaded anything to the dive app for months, but these pictures are turning out fantastic. When August is good and intent on a large piece of brain coral, I check my dive computer. Twenty minutes. Plenty of time to wander two hundred feet southeast at this depth. It's shallow enough that there's adequate sunlight. Two hundred feet isn't that far. I'll be able to find my way back to August. My accomplished *abuelo* and overachieving twin brothers would disagree that twenty minutes is plenty of time to start exploring two hundred feet away, but I don't want to pass up the chance.

With the compass on my dive computer as my guide and my metal detector in my left hand, I swim southeast. In a few minutes I see a dark shape resting on the seafloor. A shipwreck. It's not a modern vessel, but I can't tell if it's an old Spanish galleon. I swim closer, the familiar excitement in my stomach building. This ship is upright, as if it peacefully settled straight down to its grave. A treasure diver's rare jackpot. Spying an opening just under the deck, I swim over and assess it. Large enough for my shoulders and air tanks. I check the time. Fifteen minutes. I'll take the risk. I reach up and click on my headlamp, then squeeze into the narrow chamber in the old ship, tucking the metal detector close against my chest so it doesn't snag. Maybe if I find an artifact of value or historical interest, the archaeology society will give *abuelo* the grant again. And something tells me that this would have been a perfect spot for a rich captain to hide a nice piece of treasure. Or at least a favorite navigating tool.

I grab a narrow door frame and pull my body further into the dark. My light illuminates the pulse of bubbles from my regulator, a wooden wall full of barnacles, and a long narrow hallway. Nothing too spooky, so I swim forward. A few angelfish swim in front of my face. Through a gunport, a diluted ray of sunlight gives a weak glow of blue. I keep swimming, picturing the sweaty sailors running along the decks, firing the cannons, fighting to keep the vessel afloat. Did one of them hide a little something for me to find all these years later?

At the next gunport I stop to investigate a mound on the floor. It's covered in barnacles but is mostly round. A cannonball. I take a few pictures, playing with the sunlight trickling through the gunport. The pictures are the only evidence I'll take with me. It's definitely not worth my energy to haul it up right now. Besides, we're not *those* divers who wreck ship gravesites. I glance at my watch. Nine minutes left. I keep swimming.

A thump on my air tank startles me and I almost scream into the water. I whirl around and see a turtle coast past me. Who sneaks up on people like that? And why was I so unaware that I didn't know it was coming? I spin my body around and bump my face against the wall, knocking the regulator out of my mouth. Don't panic. It's happened before. I exhale through my mouth, stretch my right arm out, grab the regulator, and pop it back in my mouth. Except somewhere in the process, my hose gets hooked on something just far enough behind my body that I can't tell what's going on. I turn back around, and the regulator gets pulled out of my mouth again. What am I tangled in? I give a little yank to free my hose and just then my wrist computer alerts me that I need to start going up. Now. I turn to swim back toward the doorway. Except I'm still tangled. Not my best dive, that's for sure. And my wrist computer insists that I have to start going up.

Don't panic. Don't hold your breath. Those are the first diving rules *abuelo* taught me. This hallway is starting to feel too narrow and dark. A pair of angelfish swims past me, oblivious that I don't have gills. I reach behind me and try again to disentangle my hose without pulling the regulator from my mouth. It feels like a piece of chain or something. A little something left for me to find from some rich captain. I fiddle with the hose behind my back, focusing on steady breathing. Ahead of me a shadow approaches. August. When he makes it to me, I point to my back. He reaches over my head and works for a minute. He grabs my hand and pulls me out of the narrow hall, out of the ship, and into the open water. We swim northwest fast and find the boat's anchor rope and ascend.

With about two breaths left in my tank, we emerge. The fresh air feels amazing, but I keep my face down. I can't look at *abuelo* or my brothers. They know. They know that once again, I was impulsive and chose *tesoro*, treasure, over safety. I don't want to hear about it from them. August nudges me to climb into the boat first and I see *abuelo*'s face. Locked on mine and a mix of disappointment and fear. Exactly the opposite of what I intended.

One day I'll make him proud.

He holds up my reserve air tank, the pony tank. "Never leave this in the boat again." He's told me that before. Today I ditched it after the triple check because I planned to not need it. I made it up in time.

August tugs my short, sporty ponytail. "Ya' know, to some of us, you're worth more than a tissue donor."

2

—·—

"**G**ood Monday morning, Ruby." That would be my boss, Robin.

"What's your plan to tempt me to quit today?" My tone is dry, but we both know I'm joking. I've worked here since I was sixteen, two years and counting. The first month I was pretty sure Robin gave me all the nasty jobs just to see if I could really make it in the aquarist role. But either I passed the initiation or I just got used to scrubbing rocks and glass, because I do whatever Robin assigns me without batting an eye.

See, everybody thinks that I should apply for the apprentice aquarist program like my best friend Janie. She's already a junior aquarist and well on her way to earning a senior role. When she graduates, she won't owe student loans and she'll make a ton more money than I will, even though we'll be doing pretty much the same thing.

Everyone wonders why I don't enlist myself in the apprenticeship. *Here's* why: because I don't know if I really want to be an aquarist. Based on an aptitude test I took when I was sixteen, this is the best fit for me. *Mamá* wasn't exactly thrilled to see how high I scored for Ability to Work In Dangerous Situations, but *papá*'s an underwater welder, and *mamá* is a self-employed pilot, so what did she expect? That I would get a safe office job? No, thank you. I wish I could be a full-time wreck diver, but that's not exactly a paid position, at least until you find a big treasure. And working at my entry-level baby aquarist role makes me enough money to live now, to be free to dive in the ocean whenever I want.

Really, I'm mostly cool with all the aquarist duties. Well, swimming in the tank with that huge grouper makes me nervous, and flipping the sharks upside down for exams is a little intrusive. I love the dolphins, but I'm not a big fan of the whole captivity thing, because everybody knows that dolphins need to swim hundreds of miles a day to be healthy. And don't get me started on the annoying tourists. They're relentless with their stupid questions. I expected to siphon marine mammal poo by the ton, but I didn't expect to answer questions about it from forty-two people every week. But other than that, the aquarist thing should work for me.

No, diving in a tank is not like diving in the open ocean, tank props are a joke compared to a real shipwreck, and swimming with the captive animals isn't as adrenaline-inducing as when a wild shark or stingray approaches, but it's still cool. I love when the little kids light up when I wave to them from underwater or make bubble rings with my regulator. On the dry side of the glass, I can see they're squealing with delight, jumping up and down to see my tricks. It's easy to share my love for the ocean, so I guess the aquarist career is a good fit in that regard. I toss another handful of cold fish on the scale, watch the numbers register, and push them into Baby's food pail.

Baby. When I first started, I had mapped out a detailed plan for how to release Baby, one of the bottlenose dolphins, and her *mamá*. My plan was flawless, *à la Free Willy*, and would've gotten me locked up, no doubt. Transplanting her into a wild pod would be like throwing a long-haired, declawed, snooty cat into the jungle without its pureed food. So now, instead of plotting her escape, I just put a little extra love into weighing her feed. But every time I see a wild pod, I fantasize about secretly teaching Baby life skills and then sacrificing my own freedom to release her. Maybe the jail time would be worth it so I could eventually swim with her in the ocean and we could explore shipwrecks together. I smile at the thought.

Most people assume I'm reckless and have an adrenaline addict's death wish. That's not exactly how I see it. I'd love to live a long time and make all sorts of famous finds. Like Tanner and I planned. Tanner was my diving buddy, and someday we might have even gotten married, assuming I had enough time to mature into a responsible adult. Tanner was smart and responsible and adhered to rules like a Navy diver. We always had air reserves, tethers, dive flags *and* surface marker buoys, and we had to follow every stinkin' diving rule to a T. And look where it got him. Some *menso*, loser, was stupid enough to get high and drunk before riding a jet ski and plowed Tanner over. Tanner always told me to look on the bright side of things, so the only bright side of his pointless death was that his corneas and a bunch of other tissues made other people's dreams come true. He didn't deserve to die then and in that way, but to a few people out there, his death meant their quality of life. So the way I see it, you gotta live while you can, because when your number's up, it's up.

Tanner and I set our sights on discovering the location of *Dos Hermanos*, a Spanish galleon that's been missing since it mysteriously sank somewhere between the Bahamas and Florida back in the 1600s. Emphasis on somewhere. The ship was rumored to have almost three hundred tons of gold coins, with precious stones besides. That's like twenty billion dollars today. Never mind the two hundred cannons and six hundred men to protect it all. For a long time nobody else had *Dos Hermanos* on their radar, but last summer a couple divers mentioned the wreck in an interview that went viral, so now loads of divers have gotten excited to find one of the biggest underwater treasures. Among treasure divers, there's basically an unspoken race to find her.

But Tanner and I were excited about *Dos Hermanos* long before anybody else even thought of her, way before the viral video. And not just for the lore of saying that we found the treasure, but for the challenge and thrill. It'd be like the ultimate game of Hide-N-Seek. That's not to say that I wouldn't want a lifetime of glory in the diving world too, but what Tanner and I really loved about *Dos Hermanos* was the mystery behind her. Hurricane, maybe. Pirates, maybe. Ship design flaw or sailor error, maybe. All these questions surround *Dos Hermanos*, and the only thing people know for sure is that she was carrying one of the most valuable loads of all time. Tanner was determined to locate an original parchment of an ancient Vulgate – the Latin translation of the Holy Bible. I didn't see how a parchment could still be legible after soaking in seawater for four hundred years, but he never laughed at me for wanting to find an old ruby, so I didn't laugh at him either.

I wouldn't say Tanner and I dedicated our lives to finding her, but she did take over all of our spare time for a couple years. We weren't in a race, just a real-life game of deduction and reasoning. Our days of diving and our evenings of research were fun, and life was good. We'd study pictures of the ocean taken from space until our eyes ached, stare at the boat's sonar while we slowly hunted an area, and bought every book about galleons we could afford. We found some clues as to where *Dos Hermanos* might lay, and we learned a history professor's worth of knowledge. I think we were close to finding her. We always kept a list of locations that made the boat sonar beep wildly, and as we had time and gas money, we'd dive, find nothing overly interesting, and check the locations off the list. We had a few coordinates left to explore.

When I saw Tanner's head get smashed in by that stupid jet ski, it overhauled the way I view the whole life and death thing. Recently, I overheard *abuelo* tell his lady friend that I've become jaded. I think I'm just realistic about it, after watching what happened to Tanner. One second you can be at the top of your game, so close to your treasure, and the next you can be getting sliced apart into organ donations.

A sudden surge of energy swells in me and I throw a dead fish onto the scale and grit my teeth. I'm losing time. Fast. The other divers are closing in. I took off too much time from searching for *Dos Hermanos* after Tanner died. It's time for me to get back in the game. I need to find *Dos Hermanos*, because every day that ticks by is lost time. Because if I don't find her for Tanner and me, someone else will. And that someone will probably be more like a seagull than a harmless observer. Treasure diving is what my family does and what Tanner and I did, and I need to win this round of the game.

The beach is quiet right now, just the way I like it. The tourists have gone out to eat, so I jog to my favorite tide pool with my nature notebook in hand. My work schedule often interferes with low tide, so this is my once a week treat to myself. Nature journaling is one of the many parts of the aquarist gig that I'm drawn to. The Latin names, watching wildlife in its habitat, getting eye level with the creatures. I smile.

I flip open to the first blank page and start sketching a sea star. When I have the basic outline, I write, from memory:

*Kingdom: Animalia. Phylum: Echinodermata. Class:
Asteroidea.*

Then I grab my colored pencils from my bag and add the perfect
shading. I jot down some observations:

> *Tube feet respond to stimulus (gentle pressure with a
> small rock). Movements along rocks appear normal
> with steady speed. Bright colors and firm body shape
> indicate good health. All five limbs–*

"Ruby, I thought I'd find you here," a man's voice makes me jump
out of the tide pool. Yipes, it's Marco, the thorn in *abuelo*'s flesh. I slam
my notebook shut and clutch my bag. I don't trust Marco at all. Never
have. "How's your *abuelo* doing?"

"Good. I'll tell him you said hi." I take long, fast steps toward the
road, hoping Marco will take the hint. He grabs my arm. Ew. His dirty,
skinny fingers smell like dead fish and cigarettes, and his mustache is
thin and screams untrustworthy.

"Has Francisco applied for the grant yet?" Francisco is *abuelo*, and
Marco is talking about the nautical archaeology grant that sponsors
treasure hunting dives. Receiving the grant makes it possible to go
on a big dive. It's a big deal and there's a lot of competition among
dreamers. Marco doesn't care about *abuelo*, but he does care about
treasures. His gnarled knuckles are unnecessarily tight around my
upper arm. I have to keep my cool.

"The treasure diving grant? I assume he applied. I'll ask him for
you." I know for a fact that *abuelo* applied for the grant, and I'm pretty
sure that Marco knows that too. Once upon a time he and *abuelo*

were diving buddies. But that was before *abuelo* and the twins made their huge discovery. Then we all saw Marco's true colors, that he only wanted to ride in on *abuelo*'s coattails and be credited with the legendary find. I pull my arm free.

His dry lips curve into a sly smile, emphasizing his gray whiskers. "When you find *Dos Hermanos*, I'll be right behind you." Super creepy.

"*Dos Hermanos*?" Marco might be messing with me, but I'm from Florida. I grew up dodging tourists, avoiding eye contact with druggies, and staying clear of selfish divers. I know how to fake a poker face. "I haven't even thought about her since Tanner died."

One year, four months. Tanner was ticked when I blurted out to Marco what we were searching for back when we were like fifteen. I couldn't help it. The weasel of an old man was talking down to us like we were young fools. So I marched up to him and informed him that we were smart enough and skilled enough to find a wreck like *Dos Hermanos*. Tanner gave himself a face palm and then dragged me away from Marco, who grinned wickedly with his new bit of information. He got exactly what he wanted, and that's the way Marco is. He makes a snide comment just to get someone to spill the information he wants.

Like right now, he's holding a map, tempting me. "You don't have to search alone. I have some information about her location." His dark eyes bore into my face, daring me to call him out on his selfish motives. "Let's join forces, Ruby." On top of his primeval motive, he wears a salesman smile.

"I'll think about it. I gotta take this call." For the first time ever, I'm glad my *mamá* is calling me right on schedule. I answer my phone and hurry away from Marco, looking over my shoulder every four steps. It's a short walk home, and I lock the sliding door on the patio as soon as I'm in. I duck behind our potted plants and scan the yard for any sign of Marco. Nothing. I run through the house and lock the other doors, too.

Abuelo appears just as I'm shoving my weight into the front door, which is swelled from humidity. I force the deadbolt down. *Abuelo* lowers his salt-and-pepper eyebrows. "You okay, Ruby?"

I point to my phone and force nonchalance. "Just talking to *mamá*!"

He doesn't believe me that nothing's wrong, I can tell, but he nods and says, "Tell her *te quiero*."

I nod and flop onto the wicker sofa to proceed with our conversation, which I don't expect to go very deep, as usual. "*Abuelo* says he loves you." *Abuelo*'s weathered face gives me that deliberate unimpressed look. We both know that I was supposed to say "I love you," rather than "*abuelo* loves you." I love my *mamá*, and she loves me, in our own sort of way. Last year, just a few weeks after Tanner died, *mamá* and *papá* decided to move to the Gulf so *papá* could take an even higher-paying underwater welding job. As if he didn't make enough running Ruby Sunset and doing underwater welding here. Whatever. I'm named after a treasure, so obviously money and precious metals and stones are a big deal to my parents. *Papá* probably just wants to make enough so he can retire early and have more time to treasure dive with *abuelo* and the twins. Weird priorities, I know. But I get it. I really do. Even if they picked a horrible time to ditch me for more money.

I could've gone with them if I'd really wanted. But my life is here with *abuelo* and the diving shop and my job at the aquarium. If I had left here, it would've been the end of *Dos Hermanos*, and many times, the hope of eventually finding *Dos Hermanos* has been my reason for getting out of bed, for taking on another day. Like the sandwich tern diving for the fish again, trusting that the treasure is down there.

I'll be honest, I'm pretty spooked by Marco right now. Not only is he both smart and selfish enough to beat me to *Dos Hermanos*, he's shrewd enough to use somebody to get more information. And *abuelo* is way too smart to give out any intel, but that doesn't mean Marco will leave us alone.

I've got two hours before my shift at the aquarium, so I walk down to Ruby Sunset. I don't know who was named first, me or the dive shop, but *papá* and *mamá* started it around the time I was born. When *papá* canceled his welding contracts here and took the underwater job on the rig last year, they passed the business to August and Axel. Nobody even asked if I wanted to be part of the family business. It's probably because they all think I'm impulsive and would run down the business in a month, but it still stings to be left out. I mean, we're family, not politicians. *Papá* and *mamá* had always had a job for me at the shop. When August and Axel took over, they said they might occasionally hire me as a contract worker when things got busy, but that I should keep my aquarium job and make long-term plans outside of Ruby Sunset.

I sigh, trying to blow out the same pang of frustration I feel every time my thoughts wander back to the scenes in my life that can be symbolized by tripping over metal pails that bruise my shins. I step onto the parking lot and instantly recognize a brand new car. Marco is here. I walk in like I own the place, because even if I don't, I grew up here, and stride to the counter. August and Axel are facing Marco, who only acknowledges me with his wicked smile.

"I've got the coordinates. Forty-thousand and you'll have them, too." Marco extends his right hand. But he's full of it, because nobody would sell the GPS coordinates to a huge find, even for forty-thousand. Partly because even though it worked for Mel Fisher to have exclusive dive rights, that's pretty much impossible now. And partly because when you find a big wreck, you want your name linked with it, not the name of someone who bought your effort from you.

"What's the offer?" I ask in my sweet, youngest sibling voice. Sometimes it still works, though its effectiveness drops more with each birthday.

All three men turn to me. The twins both have their arms crossed on their muscular chests. August tips his head toward Marco. "He says he found *Dos Hermanos*." August says this gently, because he knows what that ship means to me.

I feign surprise and address Marco with my best confused face. "So last night, when you invited me to join forces, you already knew where she was?"

Marco gives his salesman smile. "I had a busy night. Let's summarize to say now I know with certainty."

I don't believe him, but I'll go along with his tactic. "Lucky! Why would you sell us the coordinates?" Because that would be really stupid.

Marco looks hurt, but we all know he's acting. "Ruby, I'm surprised you have to ask. Francisco and I were like brothers. His grandkids are like my own grandkids. When one of us wins, we win together." If Marco has any grandkids, nobody knows because his wife left decades ago because she was sick of being bullied. Rumor has it she and the kids snuck their way back to her parents and they all moved into the woods together. This guy is not to be trusted.

"It's nice of you to offer, but we can't afford forty-thousand, and you know how our family feels about loans," Axel says.

Marco turns back to my brothers. "Or are you saying you don't need the coordinates? You already know where she lies?" A-ha. This is the information Marco is seeking.

August puts his hands on the counter and leans forward. "He's saying we're not interested in buying the coordinates. We find wrecks ourselves, no purchase necessary." True. And it's obvious Marco is trying to use me to get to *Dos Hermanos,* because August and Axel have never been interested in finding her.

"Have you found *Dos Hermanos,* too?" Marco asks in a low, gravelly voice. His eyes are tinged black with greed. I want to call his bluff. My heart hammers because I so badly hope he's lying. If someone as evil as Marco finds her, she'll be raided like the Egyptian pyramids before any country's jurisdiction has time to protect her. But we can't let him know he's under our skin.

Axel points to the door. "Here comes *abuelo,* and we don't want him to catch us wasting time during business hours. Marco, make your purchases. August, get back to hanging the new wetsuits."

"*Abuelo,* do you think I'll ever find *Dos Hermanos*?" I ask as he turns off the evening news. He's all comfy in his recliner with his mug of coffee. He's one of those tough old guys who could drink caffeinated coffee five minutes before bed and sleep well.

"Are you looking for her again?" He includes the word *again* at the end of his question since I haven't technically searched since Tanner died. *Abuelo* takes a sip, eyes studying me over the rim of his mug. Like my brothers, *abuelo* has never shown much interest in *Dos Hermanos*. He's more into the history of a wreck than its monetary value. But there's lots of history with *Dos Hermanos*, too, like the mystery of her sinking and the Bible parchments. Some scholars have speculated that she might have had parchments as valuable as the Dead Sea Scrolls. But the rumored amount of treasure gets all the hype, and *abuelo* is too smart to follow hype.

I shrug my shoulders and then look him in the eyes. "Tanner and I still had four spots to search when Jet Ski Murderer hit him." If only I'd known that those sunny days in his parents' big boat were some of the best times. "We had to have been close. I wouldn't be surprised if one of those spots is *Dos Hermanos.*"

Abuelo sets down his mug on the glass-topped wicker side table. "Do you still have the coordinates of those spots?"

I nod.

"Do you want to find her now?" Now, meaning alone, without Tanner.

"More than I want someone else to find her." I don't want him worrying about Marco trying to manipulate me, and it's true that I don't want anybody else to find her.

"They're looking for her, alright." *Abuelo* picks up his mug again and takes another sip.

"Lots of people?" I ask.

"Enough people. But that doesn't mean I think you should join the race." He lowers his mug and eyes me. "Too many seagulls out there." *Abuelo* refers to selfish, dirty-playing treasure divers as seagulls. He thinks I'm not strong or smart enough to stay safe with them eyeing the same prize.

"Tanner and I started searching before the race began," I remind *abuelo*. "I'm not in the race. I just want to find her. It's personal, ya' know. We wanted to find her back before anybody else even knew her name."

"And that's why I worry about your safety. You care and you have more information than most. So the gulls will see you as a business expense to get what they want."

A business expense? I shudder. "So who's my competition?" *Abuelo* is highly respected. Everyone trusts and likes him, so he acquires lots of information. Even though he isn't personally invested in *Dos Hermanos*, he'll know who is after her.

Abuelo sticks out his chin like he's ready to make a point that I better not miss. "Ruby, the dirty seagull treasure hunters are your competition. They have too much money and not enough conscience, so that makes the competition dangerous."

I narrow my eyes. "Besides the seagulls, who else is searching for *Dos Hermanos*?"

Abuelo tucks his chin in and takes another sip. Swallows. The old clock in the corner ticks. His voice drops. "The only others I know of wouldn't hurt you."

I stare at him for a long minute, considering his odd answer. *Abuelo* mostly focuses on his coffee now and only glances at me every few seconds.

The truth dawns on me. I can't believe it. My jaw drops, but for a moment I stutter before blurting out, "*You're* searching? Since when do you care about *Dos Hermanos*? You know what that wreck means to me!"

Abuelo's jaw is tight and he sets his empty mug back on the wicker side table. "I wasn't particularly interested until Marco started poking around, prying for your and Tanner's research. I'd rather find her first than have you caught between that wreck and him."

"You'd steal *Dos Hermanos* right out from under me?" My voice comes out as a hiss, like an angry possum. "Because you think I can't handle Marco? Why wouldn't you at least ask me to join you, like Marco did? At least he treats me like I'm capable of finding her." I shake my head on my way to my bedroom door and call back, "Maybe I should've moved to the Gulf with my parents. I guess everybody in this family just wants to strike it big." I resist my inner middle schooler urge to slam the door and instead, I crumple onto my bed.

How could *abuelo* do this to me? And the twins must be in on it. August wasn't stretching the truth when he told Marco that they find wrecks themselves. *Abuelo* and the boys already made a sick discovery when they found *El Enrique*. The museums and news stations were like kids jacked up on caffeine. For two years, I was pretty much the phone answering service, doing all the PR while the three famous treasure hunters gave seminars at maritime museums and talked about *El Enrique*. Oh, and let's not forget that I worked a ton of extra hours to keep Ruby Sunset going, all while I was still a student. And what thanks do I get? Fired from my own store and now they're trying to steal *Dos Hermanos* from Tanner and me.

I punch my pillow fifty-three times and clench my jaw so hard my teeth get sore. Why does nobody take me seriously? Other than, ironically, Marco, who at least treats me like competition.

3

— · —

I 'm laying awake, feeling deflated. If Tanner was still alive, he'd answer the phone, even though it's 11:49 p.m. He'd probably say he'd pray for me and tell me to read a Psalm that he recently studied and thinks will be helpful in my situation. If *mamá* and *papá* were still here, *mamá* would at least listen to me vent.

Tanner and I dedicated three years to finding *Dos Hermanos*. *Abuelo* and my brothers know that. They saw my heart shatter with Tanner's life. They know what this wreck means to me. Yet they don't bat an eye at swooping in and taking her from me? *Abuelo* calls other divers gulls; what a joke. I'm sick to my stomach thinking about it. This is going to be a serious wedge in our tight family.

Like many Hispanic families, we've kept several generations together under one roof. When the twins and I were little, it worked well because between two parents and two grandparents, and some *tías* and *tíos*, aunts and uncles, at different times, someone was always available to watch the kids. With a family business, that was necessary. All the family time has made us pretty close. *Papá* never allowed the boys to fight, and he insisted they treat me well. *Abuelo* is a strong patriarch, *abuelo* in every sense of the word.

And we've always been there for each other. When *abuela* died, *abuelo* had constant support just like I constantly had a family member to help raise me. When *abuelo* and the twins found *El Enrique*, they had the ongoing support of their family who loved them before they were rich and famous. Now, the twins both have girlfriends and a circle of their guy friends, so they're busy with their social lives and Ruby Sunset, but they still sleep here and eat here most of the time, because it's home and *familia*, family, is forever. Or so we were taught.

Mamá and *papá*'s decision to move to the Gulf came as a shock to everyone. We'd always been together, and nobody expected they wanted to leave. *Papá* grew up on the Gulf side, but his parents died when he was a teenager. We'd visit our cousins on his side of the family a few times a year, but home was here for all of us. When *El Enrique* became part of our life, *papá* got a little weird, especially as time went on. Comparison syndrome, maybe, and not wanting his boys to have done something bigger than he'd done – at least that's my theory. The next thing I knew, he found a higher paying job on the Gulf and said he and *mamá* would be back in five years.

I'm glad *abuelo* said I was always welcome to keep living here with him. Well, until earlier tonight, when I found out he would take the treasure I've searched so long for. Why wouldn't he just ask me to work with him? Why go behind my back to beat me to her?

I puff out my cheeks, blow my bangs off my forehead, and pull up the *manta*, the quilt, *abuela* made for me when I was little. Rolling over, I rub my eyes, and look at the clock. I hadn't realized that I dozed off, but after a groggy moment, my ears tune into a voice. *Abuelo*'s voice. From my bed, I pull back my curtain an inch and see him outside under the street light, with an arm bent, apparently holding a phone to his ear. I check my clock. 4:23. Who is he talking to, practically still in the middle of the night?

I let the thin curtain drop but press the side of my face to the window. He's talking in Spanish, fast and hushed, and unmistakably angry. It's hard to understand him through the window, but I do pick up on a hurried command to meet at the dock and be ready to dive. There's an hour and a half before daylight. Nobody dives this early, and the only divers who meet at the dock this long before dawn are paranoid about somebody figuring out their plan.

I hear the entryway door open and close lightly and then some quiet rustling in the kitchen followed by footsteps up and down the hall. It sounds like *abuelo* is getting ready to leave the house, and if he's meeting someone about *Dos Hermanos*, I'm inviting myself.

Using my phone for light, I tiptoe around my room and get dressed. I pull my hair into a ponytail, slip my sunglasses on top of my head in preparation for a sunny day, and wait until I hear the bathroom light turn on. The bathroom door closes, which means I have two minutes to get ahead of *abuelo*.

I step out of my room, close the door behind me, and jog down the hall. On my way to *abuelo*'s office, I poke my head into the twins' rooms and find them empty. Go figure. They're all against me. The office door is open, and without turning on the light, I pull open the top left drawer of the desk. In the dark, my hand finds *abuelo*'s dive log, which I slip under my T-shirt to conceal on my way through the house. In the kitchen, I grab a water bottle and a banana, pick up my shoes, and let myself out the door.

Under the cover of 4:33 a.m. darkness, I put on my shoes and briskly walk to the marina. Some noisy fishermen are loading up, and I don't want to wind up in a conversation with them, so I hunker down behind some palm trees and eat my banana. I clutch *abuelo*'s dive log and listen to the fishermen banter back and forth about who packed what and where is this and where is that. Most unorganized people I've ever seen. They're taking forever, messing up my chance. My only chance. Finally the motley crew of fishermen departs and I'm free to go.

I hustle down the dock toward *abuelo*'s boat. And stop in my tracks.

There are people by *abuelo*'s boat. My knees feel weak. They'll beat me to *Dos Hermanos*. I should've risked being seen by the fishermen. Suddenly I hear my name. I slip beside another boat, close enough to hear but hidden from their sight.

"Ruby doesn't know. Leave her out of it." August's voice, firm and defensive. As if I haven't already been left out.

"No problem." That's Marco talking now. "She's so ornery, I'm happy to leave her out of it and only work with you."

Ornery? That does it. I'm ready to give Marco and my family members a piece of my mind. I step forward in the dim daybreak light, into Axel's line of vision. Axel's expression says he's surprised and terrified to see me. As fast as lightning and as discreet as an alligator, he flicks his wrist, motioning me back. Slowly, I work my way backward on the dock. I hide myself behind the boat, a large yacht whose owner won't even wake up for four more hours.

Peeking around the yacht, I watch Marco hold a handgun up as my brothers step onto *abuelo*'s boat. One old guy is subduing both of my young, fit brothers? No way. Marco must have a couple machine gun-clad accomplices somewhere close. *Abuelo* is still standing on the dock. Marco turns to him and gestures to somebody, or more than one somebody, who is out of my line of vision. "No time like the present, Francisco. Show me where she is." He pushes the gun into *abuelo*'s back and shoves him onto the boat. I consider running out of my hiding spot, but Axel looks at me through the captain's window. His serious eyes bore into mine. He points at me, then points at his eyes, then holds his palms open, like a sign for a book. Read something. Read...a book. The dive log? What else would it be but *abuelo*'s dive log? He probably wrote down the coordinates. Which makes me mad all over again, and I'd much rather investigate the four locations Tanner and I had next on our list, but this is an emergency now that Marco and his evil friends are turning to crime.

If it weren't for the gun and whoever Marco gestured to, I would run over and jump on *abuelo*'s boat. But I don't want to get shot. And since I don't want my family to get shot either, I have to figure out where Marco is taking them. Our family has two more boats at the marina, and I know how to drive them both, but their keys are locked inside the dive shop. There's no way I can get the keys fast enough to follow them now, with this boat's engine firing up. They'll back out in less than a minute.

In five more seconds, the boat backs out of the slip, and in two minutes, she's a dot on the horizon. I briefly consider calling 9-1-1, but I need to know where they're going before I try to explain to a dispatcher. I guess if I'd really been thinking, I would've called 9-1-1 as soon as I saw Marco holding a gun. But I've never had practice at deciding when to call the police. The day Tanner got hit, it was a nearby fisherman who made the initial call.

I kick the boards of the dock, stubbing my toe through my shoe. Grumbling, I clutch *abuelo*'s log and remember Axel's silent instruction. Read *abuelo*'s dive log. My *abuelo* does not keep a diary; it's his dive log. But as sure as the sun rises in the east, I can count on his dive log to get to the heart of whatever is on his mind. As far back as I can remember, *abuelo* would write in his dive log every evening after a dive. When I was little and wanted him to read it to me, he'd smile, and sometimes those stories were better than the classic fairy tales. And it wasn't just the exciting things he saw, but it was also the other things he wrote about. How much fun a dive was, or how a pod of dolphins would greet him time after time, or the way he'd ruminate the stressors of a day and come up refreshed. It felt like hearing a custom adventure story, and the happy ending was me sitting on *abuelo*'s lap with fresh orange juice squeezed by *abuela*.

Glad that I thought of grabbing the dive log from the office so I won't have to waste time by going home, I sit down on the dock and flip it open. Using the flashlight on my phone, I pick a page to study.

At first glance it appears like a list of dates and GPS coordinates with minor notations about currents and wind speed, depth and wildlife. I read a page dated two months ago.

Location of dive: Ivory Coral Reef

Depth: 284 feet

Observations: Some healthy, prolific reef. The rare Ivory Tree Coral is abundant here, some of them 60-70 feet tall. Must anchor away from reef and swim in. Dolphins, tuna, grouper, angelfish, and hogfish doing well. Obvious signs that shrimp trawlers have damaged areas of the coral. Afraid this is what will happen from the wreck divers applying for the grant. Too much interest in a too-fragile ecosystem.

Hmm. *Abuelo* has often gotten defensive about the ocean and expressed frustration that divers need to be careful. Especially treasure divers. He's never wanted a couple bad ones to give the whole community a bad rap.

Whether to turn the page is a small moral dilemma. I need to find something giving me direction, but I desperately don't want to see the coordinates of *Dos Hermanos*. Eighty-five percent of the fun is in the search. Seeing her coordinates will be like giving up in *Clue* two minutes before the end, or like reading ninety percent of a riveting mystery and then skipping to the last page. The answer without the effort will suck the joy out of the discovery. But coercive Marco is threatening to suck life, so I have to keep studying the dive log.

Another entry, dated four weeks ago.

Location of dive: planned to go to Pelican Reef

Depth: estimated at 183 feet, but wasn't able to get there to confirm

Observations: Divers have combed through many of the Spanish shipwrecks already. They dive, take, retreat. Not me. I dive, study, keep quiet. I had a close call today, but I've seen it coming. While I was loading my boat at the marina, a gull swooped low enough that I heard the wind on its wings. Greedy thing thought I'd toss food scraps like the tourists do. The bird got my adrenaline going and I thought today would be the day. The tide, the salty breeze, the steady waves – it's a good life. I've been searching for an unknown vessel to explore. Some-

thing fun to get my mind off the grant. Not for the gold, not for the glory. I only want to go down, check it out, go home, and think long and hard about what to do with what's there. If it's records of people, I'll get in touch with that genealogy society again. If it's weapons, I'll consider calling the Smithsonian. They really liked the last find and I still get letters from classrooms thanking me for getting the display of swords and cannonballs. If gold's down there, well, I'll probably not say a word. Best to leave these underwater fortunes alone. Like the gulls, people will flock in to take. That's when things get ugly.

And man, oh man, did they ever get ugly today. Footsteps on the dock interrupted my preparations, but for once it wasn't tourists wanting a coastline tour. Marco was there. Marco with a map of the ocean floor, a pair of handcuffs on his belt, and his revolver on his hip. He's threatening me, saying the only way to keep my family safe is to give him all Ruby's information about Dos Hermanos.

My hands shake. Marco threatened *abuelo* a month ago? And why would he go to *abuelo* first? *Abuelo*'s a hundred times stronger and smarter than I am. It would've been way easier for Marco to apprehend me and get the information he wants. I flip to the next page, dated three weeks ago.

Location of dive: Dos Hermanos, *possibly. Large wreck located 4.2 seconds north-northeast of* El Enrique

Depth: 92 feet

Observations: Need confirmation that this wreck is Dos Hermanos, *but location and condition are consistent with the few historical notes available. Ruby will not understand why I have to find her first. I hate that I'm now a seagull, but at least I didn't steal her and Tanner's research. I pray she can forgive me in time. Will return with August and Axel to search for ship identifying clues.*

My eyes and throat burn with angry tears. Reading this makes me feel as betrayed as if *abuelo* grabbed my neck and kicked me out of the house. I'd rather be abandoned in the Everglades than have him and my brothers find *Dos Hermanos* behind my back. Why didn't he just ask me? I would've loved to find *Dos Hermanos* with *abuelo* and my brothers. It wouldn't be nearly the same as finding her with Tanner, but it'd be better than finding her alone. It'd be better than my own family stealing her from me. If they had invited me, I probably would've shown them the coordinates Tanner and I had. We could've explored together. Why did *abuelo* take on the challenge of finding her without me? He and the twins are so sneaky I hadn't noticed them acting weird at all until last week. Clearly I'm a fool. This knowledge makes me want to crawl back under *abuela*'s *manta*, quilt, and never come out. I've been played, big time. Treated like I'm no competition. Treated like my efforts don't matter. Treated like I'm not good enough to be on their team. I gulp and clench my fists.

But as upset as I am, I can't give in to my emotions now. Locking myself in my room and sobbing won't prevent Marco from harming my people, even if my people are backstabbers. No, I have to look past my emotions right now and beat Marco at his own wicked game. I have to save my *familia*.

And step one to saving them is to find the coordinates for *El Enrique*.

The flashback is clear in my memory.

"Did you get to help find *El Enrique*?" Tanner asked me. It's still a frequently asked question.

"Do I look rich and famous to you?" I'd known Tanner for years, but we'd never talked much, and trying to use me for coordinates was not the way to win me over.

"It seems like your *familia* does everything together. I thought maybe you helped. I only wanted to ask-"

But I cut him off. "You wanted to ask where she is so you can check it out too."

He frowned. "No. I was going to ask what it felt like to be one of the first people to see the ship since she went down."

"Oh. Sorry." I shrugged. "Well I didn't do that with my family."

Tanner nodded. We didn't talk any more that whole day. We were on a youth trip to the Everglades, and technically Tanner and I were counselors-in-training, which really only means we were older than the kids but younger than the leaders. We were the awkward in-be-tweens, but we worked through all the awkwardness during the thunderstorm the next day. One of the leaders, Audrey, got sick. Really bad heat exhaustion, to the point that she looked half-dead. The other leader, Jacob, was trying to take care of her. In the emergency, he told Tanner and me to watch the six kids on the trip while he took Audrey to the ranger station. It seemed like it would be easy enough, and we thought they'd be back in a couple of hours with Audrey back to her bubbly self. Tanner led us through the prayer and Bible study, and then we took the kayaks out. Everybody was getting along, and when we first saw the black clouds and lightning on the horizon, we thought it was exciting; some action to break up the long, hot day. But the huge, black clouds came our way and the booming thunder rattled our nerves. The wind reminded me of a hurricane, and our camp never felt so far away.

We paddled with all our might, all eight kayaks fighting the wind, to get back to our camp. When we made it back, exhausted but full of adrenaline, we all huddled together in one crowded tent on the campsite, which was nothing more than a dock perched a few feet above the alligator-infested water. At noon the sky was thick and black, and when lightning struck close, it lit up the inside of the tent, and every petrified face showed in the spotlight. The thunder made the whole dock vibrate. I honestly thought we were dead, especially when I heard the howling wind of a water spout.

"*Deus, salva nos,*" I whispered over and over into my knees. Latin for "God, save us." And as I was reciting my plea, I heard Tanner say something altogether different, though I recognized it as Latin. Yes, Latin, the language that some people claim is dead. But super smart people study Latin because it's supposed to be like burpees for the brain. For me, studying Latin has always felt like solving a puzzle, and

I graduated early, so there. Call it a dead language if you want, but I like it, and that day I learned that Tanner did too.

Just then I heard Tanner say, *"Per ardua ad astra." Per*, by or through. *Ardua*, arduous. *Ad*, to. *Astra*, star. Through arduous...arduous?...maybe adversity. Through adversity to the stars. Really? He thought we'd go through the storm and emerge like stars? I looked at his face in disbelief. He smiled. "I added on to your prayer. After God saves us, He'll strengthen us. We'll be as bright as stars."

"We're already as bright as stars with the lightning." Sure, his prayer sounded nice, but at that moment, I didn't have the energy to think about what he expected of God. I just wanted everybody to make it out alive. It wasn't until we did survive the storm, and all six kids and their parents hugged us, that I thought again about what Tanner had firmly believed during the dark of the storm. He was right.

I wasn't the only one who liked Latin phrases, but Tanner didn't ask me about *El Enrique* again for a very long time. He wasn't even trying to win me over with shipwreck talk, but he won me over with Latin and his smiling eyes.

Like most people born in this century, I consult the internet to see if by chance, *El Enrique*'s coordinates are posted. It's not that I trust the internet more than *abuelo*'s notes (fat chance of that), but if they are online, it'll be so much quicker than sifting through his dive logs. Lots of wrecks' coordinates are widely known. *El Enrique*'s location was largely disputed for years before she was found so it's easy to find where people predicted she might be, but much harder to determine where she actually lies.

Depending on where it is and who found it, a ship's resting location can be kept relatively quiet, at least for a while. The lucky finders of a wreck don't own the ship or even get exclusive rights to dive there, but they will become legends in the treasure diving world. That's how it is with *El Enrique*. Anybody *could* dive there, but the coordinates aren't broadcasted, and there's a deep respect for the divers who found her. She's a bit too deep for average tourist divers, and crazy treasure divers like me are too busy searching for undiscovered wrecks to prioritize *El Enrique*.

Abuelo and the twins, on behalf of Ruby Sunset, fought Spain and Florida to let them keep the rights. Much like Mel Fisher has with *Atocha*, they wanted the dive shop to have exclusive rights to dive at *El Enrique*. It would've been a motherlode for our guided tours' end of the business. They lost. Nobody was surprised that they weren't awarded special dive rights for their effort, but the twins were so hopeful that only divers on a tour guided by Ruby Sunset would be allowed there. Tons of the guided tours they take out are to see *El Enrique*, but since they don't have exclusive rights, they can't charge as much as say, the EpiPen company can charge for their medicine.

More than the money from tours though, they wanted some level of legal protection to guard her from the "finders keepers" practice of the ocean's Wild West days after World War II. Some legitimate threat that a seagull could get in trouble. Since that didn't happen, they rely on the honor system that other divers will respect *El Enrique* as a grave and historical site. The law does protect *El Enrique* from scavengers, so it filters out the cowardly seagulls, but the dirty ones still exist. The greater diving community knows better than to fish around, and most divers are respectful, so some of these highly-sought after coordinates are kept relatively quiet, to keep the worst of the seagulls at bay.

So, no surprise, I don't see *El Enrique*'s coordinates on the first page of search results. I don't waste too much time scrolling on my phone though. By now it's getting close to light out, so I tuck *abuelo*'s dive log under my elbow, stuff my phone in the waistband of my shorts, and jog to Ruby Sunset. Thankfully the twins insisted on installing an electronic lock to the store's main entrance, and I know the keycode to enter. Locking the door behind me and using the light on my phone, I locate a *linterna*, flashlight, under the counter. I plug in my phone to charge and scribble a note that says, "Out Sick" to hang on the window next to the Closed sign. I flip open the notebook-sized schedule to see what my brothers will miss today. Ugh, they have three tours booked for today. That'll be a loss for the business. If I can't save the day soon, I'll text Tanner's *papá*, the owner of The Dive Shop, and offer our day's business to him. Hate to do it, but the customers' vacations shouldn't be interrupted. Just like at the aquarium, happy customers are the goal at Ruby Sunset. And Marco had a gun, so for all I know, Ruby Sunset might not even have owners anymore.

That thought sends my heartrate into overdrive. I close my eyes for a second and take a few deep breaths. Find *El Enrique*.

Considering the fact that a huge source of Ruby Sunset's income is giving paid tours of the famous wreck, there should be some record of her coordinates here. If so, that would be quicker than going home to thumb through all *abuelo*'s dive logs. I puff out my cheeks, trying to think where my brothers would keep her coordinates. Customers are asked to not track the location on their phones. I'm sure many of them do anyway, but I can't imagine they're scratching the coordinates into the bathroom wall paint for me to find. By now, *abuelo*, August, and Axel would have the coordinates memorized, so the information wouldn't need to be somewhere they'd see often.

My first thought is the cash register, but since that would be a robber's first stop in the store, I doubt the coordinates are there. Besides, the till, the part of the register with the money, is in the safe, so I'll check the safe. There are actually two safes in the shop, one where customers can keep their valuables during their dive and the one that holds the money and I'm not sure what else. The customers' safe is unlocked and wide open right now, as it usually is when the shop is closed and no tours are out. The cash safe is under the counter, between the phone and cash register. *Abuelo* and the twins had it installed around the time they found *El Enrique*. Before then, they just kept cash in a zippered pouch in the bottom drawer of *abuelo*'s desk in the locked office. After *El Enrique*, they got sort of famous, business skyrocketed, and they started to get a little suspicious of people.

The day after the safe was installed, I remember both twins pulling me aside separately and letting me in on the confidential information. I can still picture Axel's face, more serious than usual, when he locked the door behind the last customer and stood me in front of the safe. "Ruby, I'm telling you this in case there's ever an emergency. And I'm talking like a *big* emergency. You gotta know the code to get into our new safe. Promise me you'll remember these numbers. Don't ever tell a soul. Can I trust you?"

"Do you seriously have to ask? I'm your sister." I didn't see what the big deal was. If there was ever a big emergency and I was the only one left to get into the safe, couldn't I just call a locksmith?

"Just promise me."

"I promise."

"Promise to....?" Axel said.

"I promise to remember the numbers and not tell anyone how to get into the safe."

"Good. Okay, you gotta go clockwise, counterclockwise, clockwise, counterclockwise. The numbers are 26, 57, 78, 89. Say it back to me now."

I did and he seemed satisfied and then he pretty much went back to normal Axel, overly focused on work and working out. Even August, who can turn punches into punchlines, acted like he was conspiring with me from inside the Pentagon. He held my shoulders and wasn't making me laugh. "This is the most serious thing I'll ever tell you."

"Was I adopted?" I was joking, because our strong family resemblance leaves little room for DNA variance.

"This is serious. 26. 57. 78. 89. Don't ever use it until you absolutely have to," August said. His heavy tone put me on edge.

"Like if a hurricane wrecks the whole coast and looters are coming to burn down Ruby Sunset? Then I should open the safe?"

August sighed, pulled off his hat, and scratched his head. "Probably then. Just make sure you remember it. And keep it completely confidential." He jammed his hat back on his head, backwards as always.

"I'm not going to tell anyone. How stupid do you think I am?"

"Not stupid, just reminding you to be careful." Then he furrowed his eyebrows to imitate Marco, which he does hysterically well, and said, "You know I think of you three as my own grandkids. Now that Francisco is successful, I'll stalk all of you to get what I want."

I laughed and elbowed his side, but I haven't forgotten. *This* is an emergency. So rather than calling a locksmith, I kneel down, twist the combination dial clockwise, twenty-six, counterclockwise, fifty-seven, clockwise, seventy-eight, counterclockwise, eighty-nine. There's a click and I'm in. It's not a huge safe, maybe big enough to hold two small grocery bags. I lift the cash box and set it in my lap to inspect. I finger through the organized bills, jiggle the coins around, look at the bottom and sides of the cash box, finding absolutely nothing about *El*

Enrique or any ship. I set the cash box on the counter and lean into the safe, illuminating the inside with the flashlight. No dive logs, no envelopes with my name on them, no official documents telling me what to do when my family gets kidnapped. There's *abuelo*'s old wedding ring that he stopped wearing about five years after *abuela* died, my brothers' and my birth certificates (confirming I wasn't adopted), a stack of paperwork about this year's grant (*abuelo* got it), all of our scuba certifications and the shop's insurance policies, a spare key with a sticker labeled "desk", and a few pieces of Spanish eight, which I'd guess are probably from *El Enrique*. Discouraged, I put everything back and close the safe, trying not to worry. A lot of good memorizing the safe's code did.

How far away are they by now? Is Marco forcing them into telling him where *Dos Hermanos* is? Has he shot them all? I have to catch up to him. *Keep searching, Ruby.* There's an open space under the counter next to the safe. Shining the flashlight up, I scan the whole underside of the counter. Nothing more than a couple cobwebs.

The office is in the back corner of the shop. The key is wedged between the wall and the trim above the door, and my fingers quickly locate it. I unlock the door and let myself in. It was *abuelo*'s *papá*'s office, then *abuelo*'s, and now *abuelo* shares it with the twins. The old desk is an antique and probably weighs as much as a male bottlenose dolphin. Built to last. Sturdy enough to have locking drawers. A perfect hiding spot. The desk key we always use is taped to the top of one of the blades on the ceiling fan. I climb on the desk, reach the fan, and feel the tops of the blades until I locate the key.

Nervously, I glance at the clock on the wall. Only forty minutes have passed since Marco kidnapped my family, but it feels like it's been hours. I step down from the desk, unlock the drawers, and start hunting. The biggest drawer is stuffed full of bulging file folders all labeled as tax paperwork for the last several years. The next drawer up has manuals and warranty paperwork for diving equipment and our three vessels. Sure all this stuff is important, but important enough to keep in a locked desk in a locked office? There has to be something if I keep looking.

The next drawer up has *abuelo*'s old Bible. The cover is cracked, like it's been around almost as long as the desk. It isn't the Bible *abuelo* studies daily at home, and I barely have any memories of this Bible. As if I'm picking up an injured baby turtle, I delicately place the Bible on the desk in front of me and roll the chair in close. The inside cover has a long list of my family's ancestors with a list of dates. Interesting, but not in an emergency. I keep flipping. I start slowly, turning a page, scanning it for any unusual marks or slips of paper, but there's nothing out of the ordinary. No folded corners or highlighted numbers. By the time I reach the middle of Genesis, I'm holding the Bible by its spine and zipping through the pages with my thumb. I do it again, but still nothing.

Replacing the Bible, I look at the next drawer. A stack of blank gift certificates and some miscellaneous business cards. The top center drawer is full of old GPS units, diving watches, tape and paper clips, and one of those big, old, clunky calculators that prints out a receipt. I take a breath before opening the last drawer. Surely it must be in here, right? Why keep all this stuff locked up?

The last drawer is empty except for two things. The first is *abuelo* and *abuela*'s wedding picture. Black and white, a little blurry, with a boat in the background. No doubt the sailor who married them took the picture. Their bright smiles make me think of Tanner and shattered dreams, so I turn my attention to the other item, a folded piece of printer paper. It says, in *abuelo*'s handwriting, "26. 57. 78. 89." The code to the safe. Well a lot of good that does me. I shove the drawer shut, lock the desk, tape the key to the top of a ceiling fan blade, and shine my flashlight around the rest of the office, including the underside of the desk. Absolutely nothing. I'm on my own.

Okay, not exactly on my own. There's God. *You always have God, Ruby*, I hear *abuelo*'s voice in my mind. But I haven't paid God much attention the last few years, so I would feel presumptuous to cry out to Him now. I've heard enough stories at church to know that I'm as bad as the flaky Israelites who were so quick to forget how God saved them and only thought of God when they complained to Him about everything. I don't want to be a complainer. I'd rather get my life in order and then be able to thank God. Since I've barely read my Bible or prayed, I don't think I'm worthy to complain to Him or beg for help. *He's just waiting for you to ask*, I remember *abuelo* telling me.

I let out a huffy breath and lean my forehead against the wall. I don't let myself cry or punch the wall, but I do mumble a prayer, apologizing for being a lousy Christian and asking God to please keep my family safe and to help me find them.

4

"**M**ija, is everything okay? Baby girl, is everything okay?"

It's no surprise that my *mamá* answers the phone this way, because I rarely call her. There's no need since she calls me three times a week, and I don't have much to talk about with her. *Abuelo* has always been my main listener, and even more so since Tanner died. Since my parents moved away, it's weird talking to them. Not weird like I don't trust them, just weird like I don't feel as close to them anymore. Weird, like now that I'm legally an adult, they're free to go chase their dreams and obviously I'm not one of them. It's distant, that's what it is.

"Hi, *mamá*. What are you doing?"

"Getting ready to take off. I have three passengers on my plane right now. Maintenance workers for the oil rigs." She sounds rushed but in a good mood, like she's excited for the day. Like she slept well and doesn't know that her *papá* and sons were taken hostage.

"Do you think you'll have time to fly over to the Atlantic side today?" I don't want to freak her out by dumping the whole story on her, but she could search from the sky if she came over.

"To see you? I thought it was Tuesday of next week that we planned for me to visit."

"Something came up." I have to be vague or she'll totally freak.

"Ruby, what's going on?" I have her attention now. I still have to tread carefully though. She has passengers on board. I'd be kind of heartless to get into the nitty-gritty now.

"*Mamá*, I have a super serious reason for asking you this. Do you know where *El Enrique* is? Or *Dos Hermanos*?"

There's a long, strained minute of silence and then I hear her splutter. "Did you really call me on a busy work morning to ask me to find a shipwreck for you?" She sighs and mumbles something in Spanish, fast enough that I can't fully pick up everything because of her hushed frustration. Then she speaks to me again. "I'm sorry. It drives me crazy that you inherited the treasure hunting obsession, too. I worry about you. And no, I don't know where those two wrecks are, and no, I don't have time to help you look for sunken ships today." I hear voices over the radio in the background. "Honey, if that's all, I have to go. I'll call you tomorrow at 8:00 p.m. I love you." The line goes dead. I sigh.

I don't even know what to do next. Without those coordinates, it would be hopeless trying to track down Marco in the ocean. It would be like looking for an asteroid in space, or one baby tuna in a commercial net. I should call the cops, but I thrive on half-baked plans and don't know what to say to the police. Would they even take me seriously if I called and said, "Marco took my family somewhere, but I can't tell you where, so good luck!"? Probably not. So I need to narrow down the scope before I call the cops.

Defeated, I lock the office and hide the key in the door trim. Grabbing my phone, I replace the flashlight, taking a picture of today's schedule before letting myself out of the shop. I'll call Tanner's *papá* and give him our customers for today. Then I'll go home and start perusing *abuelo*'s dive logs to find *El Enrique*.

I'm leaning my weight into the heavy door of Ruby Sunset, double checking that the deadbolt is secure after the electronic lock makes its little whirring sound. My scribbled sign that the shop is closed today is readable through the tinted glass, and since I kept the main lights off, only a few security lights are lit. The store should be secure. When I find out where to look for my family, I'll be back for the boat keys and air tanks. I take one last look at the glass door and windows and almost scream out loud at the reflection. Someone is right behind me. I whirl around and find Marco standing about five feet away from me, leaning his hip against his hot sports car, looking like a shark eyeing the seal in those nature shows. Except unlike a submissive seal, I'm not going to be easy prey. I'll be the dolphin, preparing to outsmart the shark. I muster my most confident stance and expression and match Marco's unwavering eye contact.

"Where are they?" I demand.

His lip curls up into his wicked smile. "They're working for me. No need to worry."

I hold my fists at my side even though I'd like to shove him into his pristine car. I clutch *abuelo*'s dive log so hard my fingers hurt. "Where did you take them, and how did you get back here if they're not with you?"

Marco furrows his eyebrows and cocks his head. "Ruby, surely you know where they are." Is he still trying to trick me into blurting out secret coordinates that I don't have?

"I'm calling the cops." I pull out my phone.

"And what will you tell them? That your beloved *abuelo* and brothers worked behind your back to find the ship of your dreams? That they've been lying to you? That they-"

"No, I'll report that you abducted them at gunpoint! I'll report them missing. I'll-"

Marco pastes a patronizing look on his face. He has the gall to play on my emotions? "They're not missing. You know the stakes are high to find *Dos Hermanos*. You said you're not competing, but surprise! Your *familia* is." He pulls a cigarette from his chest pocket.

"Don't light that in this parking lot."

He glares at me but replaces the cigarette. "They've been working with me for a couple months now. Want me to take you to them? You can tell them how selfish they are to steal the wreck from you." Yup, he does have the gall.

I don't want to let him play on my emotions, so I skip the thoughtful stuff that he assumed would disarm me. "Why did you come back? If you're forcing them to give you coordinates, shouldn't you be there with them?"

His response is that evil grin.

"You left them in the ocean and brought the boat back here?" I shake my head in disbelief. I dial 9-1-1 and hit the call button. I start running down to the dock. A dispatcher answers and asks me the address of the emergency. I take a breath. "Hi, an armed man abducted my grandpa and brothers." I'm almost to the dock, and the dive log is clamped between my elbow and my ribs. Marco follows, but he's old enough that I'm easily outrunning him, even with my awkward gait from clutching the dive log and the phone to my ear. "Probably somewhere between Palm Beach, Florida and Grand Bahama." I'm breathing heavily now as I leap onto the dock and run toward *abuelo*'s boat, *Abuela*, the same one Marco abducted them with. "No, I can't be more specific. That's all I know so far, unless you're able to find where the shipwreck *El Enrique* is. Or *Dos Hermanos*. If we can find those wrecks, we can find my family." I jump onto the boat, but of course, Marco took the key out of *Abuela*'s ignition. Without the key, I can't do anything. Marco is only steps behind me now. "Please, I need help immediately! I'm at-"

My phone flies out of my hand and splashes into the seawater. I whirl around and Marco faces me, a triumphant look on his face and his fist at his side. He successfully knocked the phone out of my hand without touching me. Way to protect himself in a future court case. Even if the phone wasn't sinking like an anchor, I don't dare dive into the water right now or Marco will gain the upper edge. Plus, he'd get the dive log. In desperation, I peer around the dock, which is eerily empty of people. Without a second thought, I turn toward Tanner's family's business and run with all my might.

It's only three blocks from Ruby Sunset, which is like a hundred steps from the dock. I run forward and take a second to look over my shoulder. Marco is backing *Abuela* out of the slip. Opportunist. What was his motivation to come to shore, only to leave again? I assume he left my family in the water to scare them into telling him the coordinates. By coming back to taunt me, he probably just wanted to slam a wedge of distrust within my family.

In two minutes I'm at Tanner's family's dive shop, The Dive Shop. Boring name, I know. Which is part of why I grew up hating our competition. But it turns out that when tourists have the choice between The Dive Shop and Ruby Sunset, they assume Ruby Sunset has something to do with hormonal sailors, so seven out of ten tourists will claim The Dive Shop as *the* company to dive with. We were the last resort, everybody-else-is-booked-tight phone call. Made me so mad, and I wanted to show The Dive Shop what we were made of. That we weren't desperate for business. That our tours were fully booked too, even if it was at the last minute. For years when snooty celebrities called us, I'd refer them to The Dive Shop because I didn't want to deal with their mood swings and manicures. *Abuelo* eventually caught on to me. A few times he saw me answer the phone and take it into the office, only to come out a few minutes later and say the person wasn't interested in a dive today, so he got suspicious. Once, after a particularly flabbergasting conversation with Hollywood superstar Lylah Tucker's agent, I stormed out of the office and found *abuelo* with his ear pressed against the wall. He sat me down and lectured me for a long time. He explained competition is a good thing for businesses, customers, and the economy, and that we need to support the competition rather than tear each other down. That it was in poor taste to give all the awful customers to The Dive Shop and besides that, we need every customer we can get, even the annoying ones, as long as they can pay. That was before Tanner and I were friends, and I can only hope that his parents have forgiven me for all the times I told an aggravating person that they'd be happier with the service at The Dive Shop. If even half of them called Tanner's family, they've had some miserable customers, all thanks to me.

I run to the door of The Dive Shop and find it locked. The Open sign is still off, even though it must be after 7:00. Len, Tanner's *papá*, always comes early to start his work day. I press my face against the window. It looks like a light in the back storage room is on, so I run around to the back of the building and climb on top of the dumpster so I can look through the sky-high first-story window. It takes my eyes a minute to adjust, and it takes my mind a minute to process what I'm looking at. Len, at least I think it's Len, is tied to a chair that is lying on its side. Why would Marco be after Len, too? If he thought Len knew the coordinates, why isn't he in the middle of the ocean with my family?

Wait a minute. My family is in the ocean, and Len and I, who might know the coordinates, are on land. I blink. Okay, so that's how he's going to play. It'll take me a while to get ahead of Marco's plan, but right now I've got to help Len. Did he get knocked out when the chair fell?

I rap my knuckles on the window and see Len try to turn his head around. Good. At least he's not dead. I see him use his feet to try to twist the chair on the tile floor. How can I get in with the doors locked? Len heaves his body, inching the chair around. After an uncomfortable looking struggle that resembles a wrestling match with a shark, Len can see me through the window. His eyes light up, but there's a gag in his mouth. I make a fog on the window with my breath and write, backwards as clearly as I can, HOW DO I GET IN?

Len points his head toward the ceiling. I look up, confused, and when I look back to him, he's nodding emphatically. The ceiling? There must be roof access. I hop off the dumpster and walk around the building, looking for an easy way up. Nothing. No conveniently placed ladders propped against the building, and the storage shed at the edge of his parking lot is shut with a padlock. The building is only one-story, so the dumpster will have to be my ticket to success. I get back on the dumpster and can almost reach the gutter. I sigh, expecting torn up hands, bashed knees, and possibly a concussion if this doesn't work. But it has to work. Marco is an evil force, and my family and Len need help, stat.

Stat. Tanner and I always said stat when we meant ASAP. Most people think it's a medical show thing, but it was a Latin thing first. *Statim.* If only Tanner was here now to help me onto the roof. I stretch my arms up and gently toss the dive log on the roof, then shake my arms and wrists and do a couple torso twists, calculating that I'll have one chance for a good jump before the plastic dumpster lid caves in. Let's hope my core strengthening will pay off.

Now or never. I bend my knees, jump up, and wrap my fingers around the gutter. Swinging my legs sideways like a pendulum to build momentum, I hook my right knee onto the gutter, utter a short thanksgiving for my weekly Pilates class, and pull and roll my way onto the roof. There's a bruise on my left leg, and one small tear in my right hand spots with blood, but it's not bad enough to keep me out of the water for more than a day. Phew. I grab the dive log and tentatively make my way across the roof. I've never been on a roof and I don't want to walk off the edge. About twenty feet to my right is a recession, and when I get to it I see a hatch. Without a lock. Score. The lever on the hatch requires some wiggling, but when I loosen the lever, the hatch itself opens easily. I lift it up and it stays open thanks to a skinny metal arm in the corner. Below me, a ladder leads into the back storage room. "I'm almost there!" I call to Len. He tries to mumble something through his gag, and I sure hope he's not trying to warn me that Marco has some evil accomplice in the corner ready to take me down.

I tuck the dive log into the waistband of my shorts, hesitate on the top rung, and give the room a quick scan. Len looks happy to see me, so hopefully that's an indicator that there's nobody else in here. I hop down from the ladder and run to him. First I untie the gag, which is only a bandana. He swallows a few times and says, "*Gracias.*" I try to upright his chair, but when I get his upper body to my shin-height, I realize he's too heavy for me and the floor is too slippery. I'll wind up dropping him, so I lower him back down and untie the ropes securing his ankles together and his chest to the chair back. His wrists are tied to the armrests, and the knots are so tight that his hands are a deathly shade of white. Working the knots hurts because of the cut on my palm, but finally I get him all untied. He rolls his wrists around and sits on his knees for a few seconds before standing. As he rises to his full height, I can see a swollen bump on the side of his head, probably from when the chair tipped over. The gag left red marks on the sides of his face, but I think he'll be okay. Sore, but okay.

"You're the last person I would've thought I'd see," he says.

"I didn't know who else to go to for help. Marco has reached a new low. We need to stop him."

"Marco?" Len stares at me.

"You know, *abuelo*'s sketchy ex-friend Marco Gonzalez? The one who always stalks treasure divers," I say.

"Yeah, yeah, I know Marco. And I know he's sketchy. But it wasn't Marco who tied me up."

Huh?

"It was your brother."

"My brother?" My jaw drops. "My brother tied you up?"

"Yeah. So why are you here?" Len asks.

"Which brother?" I'm trying to wrap my mind around this. Are my brothers working *with* Marco, like he said? But if they're with him, then why did they get marched onto *abuelo*'s boat at gunpoint? Unless that was a show to confuse me.

"It was hard to see, but I think it was the serious one," Len says. As opposed to the funny one, August.

"Axel."

"I think so. He's the one that's clean-shaven?"

"Yup. Axel. You're telling me he walked in here and tied you up?" My gut wrenches, hoping that my own family isn't really against Len. Against me.

Len nods. "I was getting ready for the day. I'd unlocked the door and was counting the money in the cash register like I do every morning. Door opened and I heard footsteps. Looked up and saw your brother. I told him good morning and asked what he was looking for. He came right up to the counter, jumped over it and grabbed my wrists. Didn't say a thing, just yanked me around in front of him. I pulled and tried to get away, but he kneed me in the back, tripped me, and pinned me down. I heard the door open again and someone else came in. Didn't see who, but the two gagged me and forced me into the chair. They locked me in here and left. I couldn't see who the second guy was." Len shakes his head, trying to process what happened. "I don't know what's going on, but I'm calling the cops." Len walks out of the back storage room and towards the main part of the shop. This isn't right. Len and his wife Tara were like, are still like, second parents to me. We're supposed to be on the same side.

"Hold on just a second. Please." I step in front of him. Something about this equation isn't adding up, and I want to talk to Len for a minute without the cops. "Before we call the cops, let me tell you what I saw, because I think there's more going on here." Len agrees to hear my story. "I watched Marco march my brothers onto *abuelo*'s boat at gunpoint about 5:30 this morning. He took off fast, and all I could think is that he's forcing them to tell him coordinates. I went to Ruby Sunset to look for coordinates for wrecks that Marco might want to find, but I didn't find anything. When I was locking up to leave, suddenly Marco was there, telling me that my family stabbed my back and is at *Dos Hermanos*. I didn't believe him, so I ran to the dock and called 9-1-1, but he knocked my phone into the water and drove *abuelo*'s boat back out to sea."

Shock overtakes Len's face as he processes this.

"I didn't know what to do next, so I came here. First I thought you and I could find the wrecks and my family, who is probably out there soaking in sea lice while Marco wags a gun over their heads until they tell him some coordinates." I shake my head. "But then you told me that Axel and somebody else tied you up." I let out a confused sigh. "So what's the connection?"

Len considers this, rubs his sore wrists, and says, "Obviously the main connection between you and me is Tanner." His eyes flick over to the photos on his bulletin board and he nods. "And everybody knows that you and Tanner were closer than anybody to *Dos Hermanos*."

I nod. "So why didn't Marco take you and me hostage? Why *abuelo* and the twins? If Marco wanted the coordinates, he should've taken *us*."

Len locks worried eyes with me. "Maybe he'll be back," Len says. I shudder.

I don't want to think about Marco coming back. We have to outsmart him. I drum my fingertips on the counter, thinking. There has to be a reason he took them rather than us. "You're on the up and up with the nautical grants and stuff. Do my brothers and *abuelo* have a chance at finding *Dos Hermanos*?"

Len shrugs and looks away, pretending to massage his sore wrists again.

"Tell me," I demand.

He looks back at me and whispers, "There's some serious competition for her these days. And yes, your family has shown interest."

My eyes close as I let out a breath. "They've never said a word to me about wanting to find her."

Len hesitates, then says, "I'm sorry, Ruby. Given more time, I know you and Tanner would've found her."

I nod, but I realize he's changing the subject. "Why didn't my family ask me?"

Len thinks. "Maybe they'd rather find her before some greedy grasshopper does."

Possibly, but why go behind my back? "What else, Len?"

Len looks oblivious. "What?"

He knows more than he's letting on. "If there's serious competition, why is Marco only after my family? You're telling me they're the *most* serious competition?"

He nods, but at least has the heart to give me a sympathetic expression. "But now-" he trails off.

"Now they're working *with* Marco instead of against him." It tears me up to say the words out loud. Tears, like when guys in the Old Testament would tear their clothes, not tears like crying. I feel like punching something, but I have to think reasonably. "Maybe Marco forced them to tie you up," I say hopefully.

"If Axel didn't want to tie me up, he could've been gentler about it." Len rubs his bruised face and carefully fingers the back of his head. I swallow bile. My own brother is a criminal.

Len steps to the counter and reaches for the phone. He dials, waits, then explains that he got tied up by a couple of thugs. "Yeah, send an officer over. Thanks."

"That was quick," I say, watching two squad cars park outside the shop.

"They're here already?" He tells the dispatcher that the cops are pulling up, so he sets down the phone. "Must be a quiet morning."

"Until now," I say, wondering how the dispatcher had time to pass the memo onto the cops. And for them to arrive in less than a minute.

Two police officers, both muscular guys, stride into the shop, hands on their holsters. The first cop briskly walks through the few short aisles displaying diving gear and stops at the counter facing Len and me.

The other cop is tall, probably about the same age as my brothers, and with similar coloring and features. *Boricuo*, Puerto Rican, if I had to guess. He takes worried glances around the shop. When his eyes land on Len, he says, "Len, are you okay?" So Len is friends with cops now?

"Better now that you're here," Len says.

The tall cop grabs Len's shoulder and then gives him a once-over. Where do they know each other from?

The first cop is short but built like an ox, and looks about the age of my *papá*. Through the large windows out front, I see another cop car park, and this officer starts walking around the building, like he's searching for bombs or criminals. Something is up. Somebody else called the police before Len did.

"I'm Officer Tomes," the short cop tells Len. I look back to the two cops in front of us. "We received a request for a welfare check. Is everything alright here?"

"No, I called 9-1-1 and asked for an officer." Len says, confusion in his voice. "Two people tied me up and gagged me this morning. Ruby here untied me about ten minutes ago. Who called for a welfare check?"

Another cop pulls up. Marco sent them, I'm sure. A diversion, of course. I can't let them suck me into hours of questioning. I have to get to my family.

"Ruby, that's you?" Officer Tomes asks me.

"Yes, sir. I came to The Dive Shop this morning and found Len tied to a chair. I untied him and he called 9-1-1."

"Miss Ruby, what's your last name? And what time did you find Len?"

Just great. I see a bajillion questions in the officer's eyes as he holds a notepad and poised pen. I'll be honest and try to get out of this as quickly as possible. *God, please be with my family.* "Salazar. Probably around 7:30, maybe twenty minutes ago."

Officer Tomes checks his watch and nods. "8:02 now." He turns to Len. "What time do you normally open the shop?"

"I'm always here at 6:00. Shop opens at 7:00. I hadn't opened for the day, but the door was unlocked while I was counting my cash register. Heard the door open." I listen to every detail as Len recounts the story to the officers. I feel the eyes of both of the cops shift between watching Len's face and mine. Like they're daring us to be inconsistent in our stories.

Officer Tomes turns to me. "Miss Salazar, when you arrived, was the door unlocked?"

I shake my head. Clearly Axel and the other thug, possibly August, locked Len in on their way out. "I saw a light on so I walked around the shop until I saw Len in the back storage room."

"How did you know it was the back storage room? You've been in the building before?" Officer Tomes interrupts.

"Yes. Len's son and I were friends."

"You were friends? Not anymore?"

A little brash this morning, huh? "His son is dead," I fire back. "So yes, we were friends and I used to spend quite a bit of time here. So yes, I'm familiar with the layout of the shop."

Officer Tomes blinks. Good. He has a sliver of a heart. "I see. How did you get inside this morning?"

"Len saw me through the window and kind of pointed his head toward the ceiling, as best he could considering he was tied to a chair that was lying on its side. I guessed he was pointing to the roof access. So I climbed from the dumpster to the roof, used the roof access hatch, and entered the building."

"You climbed onto the roof?" Officer Tomes asks, that same skeptical tone lacing his words as he eyes me gripping the dive log.

I'd like to give him an equal amount of sass back, but I know that won't speed up this unpleasant process. "Yes, sir, I climbed."

"Was that hard?" He wants proof. Proof that I'm not a criminal. I hold up my cut hand, then lift up my knee and show him the swelling.

"Other than cutting my hand and smacking my knee on the gutter, it wasn't as hard as I expected." The officers evaluate my injuries and apparently choose to believe me.

"Upon entering the building, did you see anybody besides Len?" Officer Tomes asks.

"No, sir."

"And did you go directly to him, without calling for help first?"

"I looked around, didn't see anybody lurking in the corner, and went to him. I ungagged him and untied him. We talked for a minute and then he called 9-1-1."

"You placed a call to emergency services? What time?"

I look at Len. "8:00," he says. "Seconds before you pulled up."

He nods toward the door and we all see another police car park in front of the building. Probably the one we actually called for.

"At 7:45 we received a request for a welfare check. What do you say about that?" Officer Tomes challenges. Thanks a lot, Marco. Making *us* look like the sketchy ones. I'd like to ask him what he has to say about the call I placed earlier asking for help finding my family. Surely there should be *helicópteros*, choppers, circling Grand Bahama by now. What did Marco tell dispatch to direct all the attention here?

I need to slip out before this goes on too long. Len can answer the cycle of endless questions, but somebody has to get to my family. It looks like Marco has all the officers in the county gathering here to slow us down. To incriminate us. *Qué canalla.* What a scoundrel.

Both officers study Len's injuries and follow him to the storage room. Here's my chance. I take a few steps backward, tuck the dive log back into my waistband, and turn toward the door. The tall cop, the one who looks just a few years older than me, intercepts my beeline for the door. He pretends to just happen to notice me going to the door and opens it. A gentleman. I nod my thanks to him but I sense that the short, strong Officer Tomes sent him to question me more. I let out a frustrated sigh and look up. Just great. So close to making a break and now the questioning will start back at the beginning again.

"Miss," the tall cop addresses me, "are you in a hurry?"

You're innocent. Nothing to hide. Just tell him what's up. I stop just outside the door. "I thought if you guys were done with the questions, I'd get some fresh air."

"We're not done with the questions. We need to make sure you're safe before you leave here." His response is firm, but not rude.

I look around his shoulder and see a barrage of police officers around the building. "With all of you here, it should be the safest place in town."

He doesn't crack a smile, but I do see an amused glint in his wide eyes. "I'll go with you to get fresh air while Officer Tomes speaks with Len."

I don't let myself roll my eyes at the tall, cute cop, but another frustrated sigh slips out. "What's your name?"

"I'm Officer Cruz." He extends his hand.

I shake it. "Ruby, as in Ruby Sunset."

He squints, obviously unfamiliar with our family's dive shop. "Can you tell me more about what happened?"

"Like what?" It's not like we didn't already cover all the details, but maybe if I can keep him talking, he'll walk with me to the marina and I can at least keep moving in the right direction. I start walking.

"What were you doing before you went to The Dive Shop this morning?"

Realizing he could be the answer to my unspoken prayer, I impulsively decide to tell him everything. I need a cop's help, and here he is, ready to get to the root of Len's predicament. A breath rushes out of me and I blurt out, "Good, you can help me."

He stops walking, turns his face to me, and raises his eyebrows a notch. With a little trepidation in his voice, he asks, "What do you need help with?"

"I called 9-1-1 earlier, maybe about 7:00 this morning, but Marco knocked my phone into the water. That's why I ran to Len for help, but obviously he needed help, too. Marco forced my brothers and my *abuelo* onto my *abuelo*'s boat with a gun. We need to find them. Can you help?"

Officer Cruz's eyes widen. Studying my face, he adjusts his shirt collar on the back of his neck. "You're telling me there's a whole backstory as to why Len got tied up? Let's get to work."

5

— · —

This is how I find myself giving over the coordinates to Officer Cruz and a conceited Maritime Enforcement Specialist named Reg. According to Officer Cruz, Reg's department is like Coast Guard meets Maritime Law Enforcement.

I spilled the whole story, beginning at 4:23 this morning, which held Officer Cruz's attention rapturously. He took notes, nodding and listening as I spoke. He asked some questions, like how long I've known Marco, but he didn't interrupt me like Officer Tomes. He didn't know a thing about the nautical archaeology association, and he said since the coercion was taking place at sea, we had to call in the maritime officers. I asked if they're nice and he said they're good at their job. I took that to mean that customer service isn't their strength.

While the maritime patrol finished up with an illegal fishing outfit (no doubt the disorganized guys I overheard this morning), Officer Cruz came with me to my house to get the four coordinates. He stood at the threshold of my bedroom and I told him that the information was sacred. I explained I'd be the only one to look at the numbers and that I expected all the cops to turn off any GPS tracking devices as we approached the coordinates. He laughed. I said I was serious. He cleared his throat and tried to defuse the situation. "Miss Salazar, I don't know anything about treasure diving, but if you know where Marco may have taken your family and you don't share that information with law enforcement, your family could get hurt, and you could get in trouble for withholding information."

I flared my nostrils at him and crossed my arms. Heartless. How could he expect me to fork over the biggest treasure site since King Tut's tomb like it's the address to the closest Exxon Mobil?

He sensed my moral dilemma and offered a nice smile. A cute smile, which I tried desperately to ignore. "If it's any consolation, I won't be diving for your treasure." Your treasure. He called it *my* treasure. Finally, someone willing to acknowledge the work Tanner and I dedicated to *Dos Hermanos*.

I swallowed. "Will you announce it on your police scanner for all the nosy people to hear?"

"Details of the investigation will not be broadcast."

"What about the media after you've caught Marco?" I could already see the headlines declaring an arrest and triple homicide at the location of the world's biggest treasure site, GPS coordinates displayed for all to see.

He angled his head and said, "What about the media after you were going to find this sunken ship? If any of your coordinates are right, wouldn't that make you the person who found it?"

"Not if your marine specialist friends dive there first. Not if Marco is already forcing my brothers and *abuelo* down to claim it." I shook my head, thinking that this guy really doesn't understand treasure diving.

Officer Cruz looked a little exasperated at this. "What difference does it make who gets there first if people's lives are at stake? And if your brother really did tie up Len, he'll be arrested. Then you can swim down and get your treasure." He finished by letting out a huff, like he couldn't care less about the challenge and the strategy. And to think

I could just hold my breath, swim down, and grab a sack of treasure. *Bobo.* Nincompoop.

I crossed my arms. "It's about more than gold, you know. It's about Latin Vulgates and ancient rubies and solving an old mystery with your best friend. It's about finding the world's biggest treasure and knowing that your hard work paid off. And not for fame, but for the satisfaction of dedication and hard work. And yes, having enough money to keep diving every day in the ocean I love would be a big bonus, but it isn't just for the gold."

Officer Cruz sighed, like I was the *bobo.* "I will be as discreet as I can with the coordinates. If you're being honest when you say that Marco threatened your family with a gun, I would think you would want me to find them as soon as possible." He looks at his watch. "And if you last saw them about 5:45 or 6:00, and it's nearly 9:00 now..."

I slumped my shoulders and opened my top desk drawer. The whole time Tanner and I searched, we kept the flash drive in the glove box on his family's boat, *The Dive Boat*. Len's never going to win an award for inventive business or boat names, but the explanatory names don't leave any room for misunderstandings.

After Tanner died, his parents gave the flash drive to me and I've kept it hidden here at home since. Not even *abuelo* or the twins know. In the back of the desk drawer is a power strip, or what looks like a power strip. It's actually a safe.

I popped it open and grabbed the flash drive out, pushed the drawer shut, and opened my laptop. The computer loaded and I nodded to Officer Cruz. He stepped toward me while I put in the flash drive, hastily entered the password, and watched the folders appear on the screen. Information I hadn't looked at since the day Tanner died. Folder names like Possible Coordinates, Coordinates Searched, and Coordinates to be Searched. We had some other stuff too, like Our

Diving Playlist and Scavenger Hunt, the folder where we recorded stuff we dreamed of finding, like the Vulgate and the ruby, or crazy stuff we accidentally found, like a license plate from South Africa and a keychain from Wall Drug, South Dakota.

For a moment, my eyes lingered on the document titled To Do. I knew what was in that folder. All the things we dreamed of doing together.

1. Swim with whale sharks.

2. Go hang gliding.

3. Get married.

When Tanner typed that one, I couldn't wipe the grin off my face. When he added in parentheses, "If Ruby doesn't kill me first," I punched his arm. He laughed but didn't backspace. I was still grinning.

But with Officer Cruz in the corner, I swallowed, then clicked Coordinates to be Searched and the now short spreadsheet opened. It started as the longest list, and little by little, most of the coordinates were transferred to Coordinates Searched. I bit my tongue to keep from telling Officer Cruz to look away, because I knew he was trying to help. He stepped to my desk and knelt down to look at the laptop at eye level. "These are the GPS coordinates we need to go to?"

I nodded. "We narrowed down the location to one of these four spots. The boat sonar detected something at all of these, but we didn't dive them yet, so we don't know what's there. Could be *Dos Hermanos*. Or prominent features on the seabed or even huge schools of fish that were swimming through and excited the sonar." I shrugged. "It's news to me, but apparently my family has honed in on her location. If any of these coordinates are right, and if Marco forced them to tell him where to dive, we need to start at these locations."

Officer Cruz's eyes widened in confusion, like he was taking in a lot of foreign material and would be quizzed shortly. He let out a breath. "How deep are these?"

I turned back to the screen. "Um, looks like we have a predicted depth for this first coordinate of 175 feet. The next one is possibly 310 feet. The other two we couldn't get a consistent sonar reading, but we thought somewhere between 75 and 200 feet deep."

Officer Cruz looked at me like I'm the professor of the foreign subject and he's cramming for the exam. Then he smiled. "When this is all settled and everyone is safe, I want to hear how you and Len's son got all this information. It's like the ultimate scavenger hunt."

I nodded. He was starting to get it.

"Whereabouts are these?"

"They're all between here and Grand Bahama." I pointed to the map above my desk. Looking from the laptop screen to the map, I ballparked where twenty-six degrees north and seventy-eight degrees west are.

"That far? We'll need a plane, too." Just then his handheld radio came to life, alerting us that the marine team was assembled and ready to meet us at the dock. With reverence and attention to detail, I copied down the coordinates on a fresh piece of notebook paper.

Coordinates to be Searched:

    1. 26.78, -78.43

    2. 26.67, -78.88

    3. 26.62, -78.95

    4. 26.57, -78.89

As I copied, I wondered if any of these are 4.2 seconds north-northeast of *El Enrique*. I bit the inside of my cheek, looking for any constructive outlet for my anger.

I securely stashed the flash drive, put the notebook and *abuelo*'s dive log in my small waterproof bag, and stood. "I guess we're ready to meet your maritime cop friends." He didn't say a word as we walked out of the house and I locked the door behind us.

I hoped the neighbors weren't watching as Officer Cruz held the passenger door open for me and I climbed in. At least I scored riding shotgun rather than in the back. On the two minute drive to the marina he asked me how long I had been diving. I told him I couldn't actually remember learning, and he looked impressed. "I've had a little training so far. Not enough that they'll let me help with this search today, but maybe someday."

Officer Cruz parked the squad car behind Ruby Sunset and we walked onto the dock where the Maritime Enforcement Specialist boat was waiting.

Two officers jumped off the boat and Officer Cruz introduced me. "This is Ruby Salazar. She has a list of GPS coordinates where our suspects may be." I shuddered when I heard him say "suspects," plural, because I never thought my brother would be awaiting handcuffs.

"Good. Thanks, Miss. We'll take it from here," one of the maritime cops said.

Take it from here? "Um, hello, I have the coordinates. I'm coming with you."

The maritime officer smirked. "I know you're eager to help, but I need to ask civilians to keep their distance from investigations. Give us the list of coordinates and try to relax today."

Try to relax? Was this guy *loco*, nuts? I stepped forward, ready to give him a piece of my mind. Officer Cruz put a hand on my shoulder and spoke up before I landed myself in jail. "Miss Salazar is very serious about her work for this shipwreck."

"They all are. Treasure divers," the annoying maritime officer said with a scornful shake of his head.

Officer Cruz tightened his jaw. My fingernails dug into my palm as my fist did the same. Thankfully the other maritime cop spoke up. "Lay off, Reg. Her family just got abducted."

The reprimand appeared to take Reg, the annoying one, down a peg. He softened a little and actually looked at me. "My job is to find your family and the suspects. The sooner we do that, the sooner everyone will be safe. Do you have ideas where we should search?" I think it was hard for him to only sound a little patronizing.

I reached into my waterproof bag and grabbed the notebook, carefully tore out the sheet and folded it in thirds. Not appreciating Reg, I handed it to Officer Cruz, because he called it my treasure and showed interest in the ultimate scavenger hunt. "As soon as this investigation is over, please either destroy this or return it to me."

Reg gave a heartless laugh, but Officer Cruz's eyebrows crinkled and he said he'd do his best but that a judge may need to see it first.

"We'll let you know what we find out," Reg said, without even making eye contact with me. He handed me a business card. "Call me if you get any leads." The other maritime cop invited Officer Cruz to join them on the boat. Naturally, I followed. Well, I tried. Reg stuck out his arm. "No civilians."

My jaw dropped and I glared at Officer Cruz. He had sweet-talked me into copying down the coordinates, coming with him, and giving the coordinates to rude Reg. Now he'd let Reg push me out of this? "I'm the backbone of this investigation. Without me, you'd have no place to start looking."

"Without us, you'll have no answers to the investigation," Reg snarled, like a bull shark circling a bleeding fish. I already didn't like Reg and his condescending tone.

I glared at him. "Fine. Do it without me. But at least let me copy down the coordinates for myself. Pen, please," I said to Officer Cruz. He ignored Reg's warning look and handed me a pen and the notebook paper. Quickly, I copied the numbers with care into my notebook. Then, boring my eyes into Officer Cruz's, I fumed, "Thank you." I really wanted to stick out my tongue at Reg, but Officer Cruz's serious expression scared me out of it.

And the boat flew out of the harbor and into the open sea, leaving me alone.

So now I'm pacing back and forth on the dock, wondering what level of low I've reached to hate myself for giving up coordinates when my *familia*'s lives are in danger. Why did I hesitate to give the maritime officers the coordinates? Marco has a gun and probably at least a couple cronies with no morals. And my brother tied up Len. I clench my fists and blow a fast breath, making my bangs flutter away from my face.

At this point, my motivation for treasure diving shouldn't matter. I need to help. And since the arrogant cops are refusing my assistance, I'll have to search alone. *Siempre tienes a Dios, you always have God,* *abuelo*'s voice rings in my memory again. I can't deny that. And I wouldn't want to deny it, either. Lots of my Mexican friends' families say *Primero Dios,* put God first. I heard it a lot from them and my own family growing up, but *abuelo* had to come up with this custom blessing and reminder for when I really got into deep water. *Siempre tienes a Dios*, you always have God. Hopefully God would be as patient with me as *abuelo* has always been.

Even if I have been a fair-weather Christian and totally need to stop straddling the fence between my selfish life and the life of a Christian. But right now, the clock is ticking. Above me, a small plane flies east, probably the plane that Officer Cruz predicted they'd need. They'll beat me to my family and *Dos Hermanos*. But I can still try, because there are four locations, and there's always the chance that the treasure is somewhere else. And who knows how long Marco will threaten them before they actually spill and get to the dive site.

Where to start? I look at the coordinates in my notebook and read them, trying to remember any detail I can. 26.78, -78.43. 26.67, -78.88. 26.62, -78.95. 26.57, -78.89.

The first one excited us because it wouldn't be ridiculously deep. Less depth means fewer deco stops which means more dive time. When the sonar went crazy with the coordinates of the second on the list, Tanner and I had been singing "Country Roads" at the tops of our lungs. Neither of us had been to West Virginia, but he didn't criticize my off-key voice and I didn't laugh at his air guitar, so we sang out. Then the sonar alerted us that something was under us, so we scribbled down the coordinates like we'd hit the jackpot.

I smile at the memory.

I can't remember much about the third or fourth locations. It takes a few hours by boat from our marina to Freeport, Grand Bahama, so there was plenty of downtime between sonar beepings. Back then we thought we had plenty of time. Enough time to think that the mundane, slow time wasn't important. Enough time to think we had all the time in the world to explore together.

I stare at the list in my hands again, saying the coordinates out loud. "26.78, -78.43. 26.67, -78.88. 26.62, -78.95. 26.57, -78.89."

Huh. The last one. 26.57, -78.89. It seems familiar. But I'm certain Tanner and I hadn't dived there. We would've moved it from Coordinates to Be Searched to Coordinates Searched. I say it out loud again, this time without saying degrees, west, or north. Just the numbers. 26. 57. 78. 89. Just like that, I hear Axel's voice in my memory and see his serious face. *"Ruby, I'm telling you this in case there's ever an emergency. And I'm talking like a big emergency. You gotta know the code to get into our new safe. Promise me you'll remember these numbers."*

I almost drop the piece of paper. The numbers don't matter to get into the safe. The numbers matter because they're the coordinates. That's why I had to promise to remember them. It never was about what was in the safe. The code is coordinates! But to what? *Dos Hermanos*? Or *El Enrique*? Or 4.2 seconds north-northeast of *El Enrique*? Or maybe it's another wreck altogether. Either way, it must be of top importance since they made these numbers the safe's code and made me memorize them. Which means that unless they can outsmart and fight off Marco, it's where I need to get to. Stat.

6

— • —

The aquarium owns an amphibious aircraft. Picture a big two-engine seaplane that lands on its belly instead of floats. It's large enough for six people, or a few people and a dolphin. Since they only have a few wild rescues and releases every year, the CEO decided we should offer tourist flights. He had a good point. The aquarium already owned the plane, so the plane might as well make us money. So unless there's an emergency with a wild marine animal that warrants the plane, our pilot can give tourists a sightseeing flight. The customers love it, because they get to ride in a plane that rescued a dolphin. It's a great money-maker, but the best is the Make-A-Wish kids.

Brett is the pilot, and he's always been a little skeptical of me, probably because I criticized his preflight check one time when I got to ride along to cut a net off a dolphin's fluke. I've seen my *mamá* do enough preflight checks that I have a good idea of what all goes into verifying that everything is ready. He was cutting corners to save time. All I did was politely ask if he was going to finish the preflight check. He mumbled something at me, got out and checked the rest, and ever since I've been mostly ignored by Brett, even when he shows up at *mi familia*'s, my family's, gatherings. Think about it. If you were a crabby fifth cousin or whatever he is, wouldn't you at least exchange pleasantries with the young lady that you also work with?

It's a small *milagro*, miracle, that I'm not scheduled to work today, because it would look totally sketchy to call in sick and then call Brett to schedule the courtesy flight I won at last year's employee appreciation picnic. But since Brett is already a little huffy about me, I figure I have one chance to make this work. I can't make up something about a marine mammal needing a rescue at Grand Bahama. First of all, that would be a lie which God and Tanner would not approve of, and secondly, it would have to go through a whole report process and the Marine Rescue Team would all be summoned and I'd get fired for making a false claim. And obviously I can't tell him we have to rescue my brothers, because he'd insist on getting law enforcement involved. If I act like I just decided this morning I want to use my courtesy flight for fun today, he won't see the urgency and Marco will have located a huge wreck and shot my family.

One thing I know about Brett is that he studies weather for fun. I overheard him tell Robin that he wanted to be a meteorologist in the Air Force, but he scored so high on some test they made him a pilot instead. So he mastered piloting, retired from the service, flies for us, and spends all his spare time watching the weather. In the breakroom when most people check their email or social media, Brett watches the clouds and looks up weather reports.

I may not study the weather like Brett, but who doesn't find an approaching storm fascinating? And while riding with Officer Cruz, I heard a staticky voice say that a storm is brewing off the east coast. If I can convince Brett to take a look at the clouds, I can tell him to drop me off at Grand Bahama for a couple hours and that I plan to take the evening ferry back home to Florida. On the way, we'll see Marco. Brett will radio the cops, and everybody will sleep well tonight. That would of course be Plan A. Stop Marco, save my family, get Marco arrested, and then go dive for *Dos Hermanos* another day. All without a lie.

I knock my knuckles on Brett's office door, which is adjacent to the small hangar, located across the street from the aquarium. I nose my head around the slightly open door and see the clock. 10:22. We have to get going.

"Come in." Brett is staring at a weather radar map on his computer screen, but he turns to look at me. He sniffs and looks back at his screen. "Hi, Ruby."

"*Buenos días*, good morning, Brett. You're watching the storm, too?"

"Mm hmm."

"I heard this storm is getting the meteorologists riled up. Did you hear that the belugas in the Arctic are going crazy, so they think this will be a big hurricane?"

Nobody has heard that, so just as I hoped, it gets Brett's attention. He moves his hands from hovering over his keyboard and mouse to push away from his desk. The office chair swivels and he looks at me like I just told him I let Baby free. "Where did you hear that?" His tone suggests that it's the stupidest thing he's ever been told. Lots of sea life acts differently before a hurricane, but belugas are way too far north to care about a hurricane in Florida.

"I thought marine mammal behavior can be an indicator of an imminent hurricane." The tourists ask me about this all the time, but I have to tread carefully to get Brett on my side.

"Yes, to some degree. But the Arctic? What did you hea-"

Here's my chance to move the conversation in the right direction. I interrupt him with an excited gasp, like I just had a brilliant idea. "Have you ever flown near a hurricane?"

Brett relaxes back into his chair and gets a faraway look on his face. "Twice."

"I bet this is the perfect time to try to see one. Wouldn't it be? Just when the storm is brewing, but before it's too big?" I jab the radar map with excitement.

Brett nods. "Yeah, it would be."

I snap my fingers and raise my eyebrows. "Oh, I still have my courtesy flight, and I'm off today. Want to check out the storm? I bet if we fly to the northwest edge of Grand Bahama, we'd get a good view and still be safe."

Brett studies me for two seconds, opens the calendar on his computer, looks at his office phone, which is not blinking about any voicemails, and shrugs. "Well, today is open so far. You sure you want to use your courtesy flight on this? You could save it for another time and bring a friend, make it a date."

"A date chaperoned by you, ol' Brett?" I tease. I have to tease, partly because thinking of being on a date chaperoned by Brett is hilarious, and partly because if I think too hard about a date, I'll think about Tanner. Right now I have to get above the ocean. "Nah, I'd like to see the water by Grand Bahama today."

"Aren't you supposed to schedule the courtesy flight at least a day in advance?"

"I didn't hear about the hurricane until this morning."

His eyes shift to the staticky announcement on the old school weather radio in the corner, and he nods in agreement. "Ok, let's take a look at this storm." He walks past me and begins the preflight check.

That was easy.

While Brett does a thorough, albeit quick, preflight check, I sneak my diving gear into the plane and I discreetly stow my waterproof backpack, which is full of snacks and water bottles that I packed in about two minutes at home. I double check that I have the most necessary diving gear that I grabbed from Ruby Sunset in about four minutes. Then I buckle myself into the copilot seat, because it would feel awkward to sit in the back by the animal rescue gear when we're not on a rescue. Well, we are, but Brett doesn't know that yet. As far as he's concerned, I'm just an eager passenger who will take pictures of the clouds on his phone's camera while he flies. I scarf down a granola bar while he finishes the check.

When he climbs into the pilot's seat and closes the door, we both put on headsets so we can communicate without shouting over the noise in the cabin. Brett requests Flight Following from air traffic control, gets his assigned frequency, and speaks some rapidfire pilot lingo as we start taxiing. I still can't believe how quickly he agreed to my plan, and I pray that the storm is big enough to hold his attention, but not too big to hinder my efforts to stop Marco.

In twenty-two minutes we're about two-thirds of the way to Freeport, Grand Bahama and I haven't seen any sign of *abuelo*'s boat. Brett and I have said very little on the flight. There hasn't really been opportunity. Air traffic control keeps pilots around here busy with ongoing instructions. We're N013AH, but air traffic control, or ATC, says, November 013AH. November is what pilots and ATC call the letter N. N013AH is the seaplane's tail number, like a license plate on a car. You wouldn't think traffic in the sky would be such an issue, but ATC has given Brett plenty of instructions. Go higher to make room for a million flights going to and from Orlando. An international flight is cruising at 31,000 feet, so don't do anything obnoxious. Considering we're flying at 3,500 feet, I can't imagine how obnoxious we'd need to be to distract that flight path. It's like the flight attendants who announce that lighting a flame in the airplane lavatory is a federal offense. Who even thinks of that until they plant the idea? Whatever. It's interesting to listen to the radio. If not for riding with my *mamá* as a kid, I wouldn't be able to pick up any of what Brett and ATC are saying. It's like a whole language that sounds fast and staticky until you get used to what they're talking about.

I've flown enough with my *mamá* over the years that I can usually follow what the ridiculously fast, staticky voices are saying, but several of the ATC guys down here have French and Bahamian accents, and it's a lot to decipher. Brett takes it all in stride, so I watch the clouds and the water below. We're flying high enough that I really can't see any boats, but I keep straining to see as much as possible. Meanwhile I pay close attention to the GPS coordinates on my dive computer. At the rate we're flying, we should be there within four minutes. I haven't figured out how I'm going to convince Brett to land, but the sky is getting darker and the airspeed indicator tells me we're slowing down, which makes me think the wind is getting stronger.

In between correspondence with air traffic control, Brett mumbles things about the clouds, wind, and air temperature that I can hear through my headset. He really is into the weather. I can't deny that it is interesting, but right now I have bigger things on my mind. Marco. My *familia*. Len. Tanner and Latin *Vulgatas*, Vulgates.

"This storm won't be too big," Brett says as I snap a few pictures of the clouds on his phone.

"You don't expect much damage?" Since we aren't pressing the switch to talk to ATC, our small talk is limited to our headsets.

"Nah. The whole nation won't remember the name of this storm. Just a medium-sized one," he says. He sniffs. "So, any particular place you want to go today?"

He knows I'm up to something more than the weather. *Act natural.* "Well, we could see if there's any action toward the northwest coast of Grand Bahama. Toward Freeport." Action referring to weather or criminal, of course.

Brett nods, clicks some buttons on his screen, talks to ATC, and slightly turns the control wheel.

"I'll get some live footage for you. The video might go viral. People love watching stuff like this online."

Brett snorts, but I don't know why. My *mamá* makes a modest side paycheck from her flight videos. Especially when she's close to a storm. Those vids get tons of views. Really I'm talking and filming just to waylay his suspicions. Behind the camera, my eyes scan the sea below like I'm searching for buried treasure, because of course, I am.

We cruise into a mass of clouds. Thick clouds. Ugh. "Can we descend for better visibility?"

"Who made you copilot?" Despite his irritation at me, he mumbles that we might as well see something. We start to descend. I hone my eyes on the surface of the water and bite my lip.

"Geese," Brett mutters. I look out the window. We're flying right through a flock of geese. Everybody who knows anything about flying knows that bird strikes are about as rare as shark attacks on humans, and that usually when a plane hits a bird, the only bad thing that happens is that the bird dies. But still, I can see why Brett is nervous, because if the bird hits just right, the pilot gets killed and the plane goes down. We're in a small plane, and sometimes birds damage small planes. It's the difference in diving when you see no sign of sharks versus diving with a couple sharks following in your peripherals. That's the amount of nerves Brett probably has right now.

"Freeport, this is N013AH, I'm at eight hundred feet, trying to get below the clouds."

"November 013AH, acknowledging your altitude change. I can't see you anymore, but we'll stay in radio contact."

I hone my eyes on the surface of the water. I check my dive computer. Almost there. My foot bounces with nerves and I scan my eyes across the turquoise and blue tapestry.

I check my watch. Getting closer. And then I see a vessel. I grab a pair of binoculars and try to focus on it. It's hard to lock in on it because we fly above a bank of clouds so the boat is briefly blocked from my sight. It's Reg's maritime enforcement boat, but it's to the south. I grab a map, check the coordinates in my notebook, do some quick figuring in my head, and realize that the cops are probably just arriving at the first location on the list I gave them. So I know where the cops are, but how long will it take them to get to the last location on the list? Can Brett talk to them and get them in the right place?

"Brett, go a little north."

"Are you air traffic control? And what are you looking up on your map and notebook?" He sounds about as suspicious as a seasoned dolphin by a crab trap.

I point. "Look at the clouds over there. Let's check them out."

Brett is trying to look out the windows to see what I'm so interested in, but he's focused on his display screen, too. I check my dive computer. Yeah, we're really close now. Peering through the binoculars, my eyes dart around the surface of the water. And there's *abuelo*'s boat, moving toward *El Enrique*. Or *Dos Hermanos*. Whatever it is. I put down the binoculars and check the map again. There's no denying that Marco is close. I shut my eyes. This is the first time I've wished mechanical issues on someone. If the boat breaks down, he can't get to the treasure. My treasure.

Brett clears his throat, which sounds aggravated even through the headset. "What are you really doing here, Ruby?"

I look at him and think fast. I have to beat Marco to *Dos Hermanos*. That seagull has no right to Tanner's and my prize. And whatever he did to convince Axel to tie up Len needs to come to light. "Brett, you saw that cop boat just to the south of us, right? You gotta call them. Radio them and tell them to rush to some coordinates that I tell you. It's an emergency."

Brett furrows his eyebrows. "There are a few things wrong with this. You're not my boss. I have no plans to get involved with any legal shenanigans. You should've called 9-1-1 if there was an emergency, not me. And law enforcement uses a different radio frequency than we do."

"Brett, I'll never ask another favor from you again. Somebody down there has at least one gun aimed at my brothers and *abuelo*. Probably two or three guns. Please. Can't you call ATC and have them give a message to the maritime cop boat? I'm not dragging you into legal shenanigans. And I did call 9-1-1. They need my help. They're in the wrong spot. They need to get to that boat." I point to *abuelo*'s vessel.

Brett takes almost thirty seconds to circle and observe both vessels. He even descends a little to get a better look. Finally he addresses me again. "Your *abuelo*, Francisco, is on that?"

I bob my head up and down so fast I get a little *mareada*, dizzy.

He sighs. "You'll have to call 9-1-1, Ruby. ATC isn't going to relay a message to law enforcement."

I clutch Brett's phone and clench my jaw at the thought of calling 9-1-1 again today. Going through dispatch and explaining this messy situation will take forever. I remember Reg's business card and dig it out of my bag. I punch in Reg's number and listen to the rings. More rings. Voicemail. I groan.

Brett glances at me. "9-1-1 isn't working? Cell service must be down."

"I'm trying to call the cop, or Coast Guard specialist, whatever he is, directly, but he isn't answering." Voicemail again.

"You have a cop's direct number?"

I wave the business card. "I told you I already dealt with 9-1-1 today."

I dial a third time. No answer. So much for being able to update Reg.

"Try 9-1-1," Brett says.

Much to my chagrin, I dial 9-1-1. At the dispatcher's prompting, I start my explanation. "I'm in an amphibious plane, tail number November 013AH. I received a tip regarding criminal activity on a watercraft. I request that you advise law enforcement to search for the suspect at the following coordinates."

"Go ahead with those coordinates."

I rattle off the numbers. Dispatch double-checks the numbers even faster. I say, "Roger." Dispatch assures me that the situation will be addressed, so I hang up because I'm tired of empty promises.

I watch the maritime police boat through the binoculars, expecting them to immediately turn. After two of the longest minutes of my life, they haven't even moved. "Brett, they're not changing direction. Didn't they get the message?"

"You requested one favor."

"Don't you want to be a hero?"

"Your bossiness is unbearable. If I had a parachute, you'd be gone."

"This is an emergency. I am not being bossy. ATC has been bossy with their nonstop instructions. I'm just trying to stop-"

"Quiet, please."

I clamp my mouth shut and dial Reg's number again. Voicemail again. How could I be so close, but so unable to help? Marco could be aiming to shoot. Or forcing my brothers to dive in to steal *Dos*

Hermanos. Unless they're actually on Marco's side and chose to go with him.

Brett glances at me and circles the police boat again. "What do you claim is going on down there?"

It won't do any good to mention *Dos Hermanos* or treasure diving, so I'll start with the shocking fact. "This morning I watched Marco, this old sketchy guy who has known my *familia* for years, use a gun to force my brothers and *abuelo* onto *abuelo*'s boat. Looked like there were at least a couple other guys working with him. I gave the cops some coordinates where I think he might be taking them. But that's *abuelo*'s boat," I point, then dramatically gesture out the other window, "and there's the maritime specialist boat." Three miles away, and mostly out of their sight.

"Marco?" Brett's shoulders tense.

"Marco Gonzalez. You know him?"

Brett's eyes narrow. "I wouldn't trust him with a goldfish."

"We need to alert the cops. They're not moving yet."

"And Miss Bossy, how do you suggest I tell the cops the coordinates that you magically know?"

"Fly low and get their attention." No it's not kosher, but if 9-1-1 dispatch can't even get them to listen, what other option is there?

No surprise, Brett grunts his scorn. "Right, and lose my license and go to jail for assaulting the cops."

"Not so low that you'll threaten them. Low enough that they'll tune into the civil radio frequency to ask us what's up."

The maritime specialist boat still isn't moving, other than fighting the wind and the waves. It is way too small to take on a big storm. Looks like Reg should have picked a big enough boat to handle a storm. His oversized ego will have to make up for the undersized boat.

Meanwhile, *abuelo*'s boat starts lurching back and forth. It's not progressing in any direction, just bobbing around. I watch this strange jig for a minute and then realize that Marco must be fighting for control of the steering wheel. They're fighting.

"Brett, look." I point and he follows the direction of my hand.

"Yeah, I see. Too many captains on a vessel and they look like a heap of drunken sailors who didn't learn how to steer."

"How long before you think Marco will shoot someone?" I hope that my charged question will spur Brett to dip lower and get the cops to tune into us.

"How big was the gun you saw?"

"A handgun. A pistol, I think it's called."

"Somebody didn't go to hunter safety." Brett dips the plane a little lower.

"No, I was too busy helping lead scuba dives." Brett gives me an unimpressed look. "You know if you swoop in and play the hero, you and the aquarium will get tons of positive press."

"Just what I want." His voice is as dry as sand on a scalding parking lot. Despite his attitude, I notice we're descending.

We circle the cops in a downward spiral once, twice, three times, so low I can see Officer Cruz watching us. I wave frantically, but the windows are so small that he probably can't recognize me. We dip lower. Low enough that I gulp. I see Officer Cruz hand something to Reg. His phone. Reg stares at the screen and then looks up at us. I dial Reg's number again.

Another plunging swoop makes me bite the inside of my cheek to keep from screaming.

"This is Officer Reg, Coastguard Maritime Specialist."

"Reg! It's Ruby Salazar. I'm in the amphibious plane."

"The gutsy seaplane with tail number November 013AH?"

"Yes! Thank you for finally answer-"

"You are threatening three law enforcement officers. Depart the area immediately."

I look at Brett and point up.

"Give him the message while we have his attention." Brett continues to circle, still low.

I fake a commanding voice. "Law enforcement, this is November 013AH. Thank you for answering your phone. I'm reporting a tip for criminal activity at the following coordinates."

"Ascend your plane immediately." I see Reg aiming a gun at us. For crying out loud.

Brett sees the gun and ascends a little, I'd guess about thirty feet. High enough that we've backed off, but still low enough that I can see their jackets flapping in the wind.

Brett grabs his phone out of my hand. "This is November 013AH, my copilot Ruby is ready with the coordinates of the distressed vessel."

So now I'm upgraded to copilot? I know he's just trying to sound professional and credible, but I'll take it. I can see that Reg is *enraged*. I can't believe we're so close I can watch all this. I'm pretty sure the geese around us think we've lost all sanity. It's much more of an adrenaline rush than I was planning for today.

Brett hits the Speakerphone option and I hear Reg's voice. "Go ahead with the coordinates."

I rattle them off while I watch Reg pace around the deck of the boat eyeing us, still holding a gun. "Brett, go higher! He's gonna shoot!"

"He won't shoot us. We need to be more scared of the storm than of him."

"November 013AH, depart the area immediately."

"Maritime Enforcement Officers, assume the coordinates and perform a welfare check." Wow, did Brett really just backtalk them? Maybe we will get shot down.

A snort comes through the radio followed by, "In this storm, nobody's doing a welfare check. Ascend your craft before the wind takes you down or your resistance requires me to shoot."

Brett says an unsavory word and swoops up so fast I feel queasy. He's old enough I'd think he'd be sick from all this. I refocus my eyes on the deck of the boat. I'm pretty sure Officer Cruz and the other officer are in a scuffle with Reg. Brett sees it too. "Young cops having a stag fight down there. Ruby, you're gonna get me fired but I can't let Marco kill your *abuelo*." And just like that he swoops down again, except this time the cop boat is moving. In the wrong direction.

We both watch the maritime boat turn toward the island. Are they really going to call off the arrest until after the storm? My family could be slaughtered by then, and I'll never know their motive for stealing my treasure.

CRASH.

Glass and feathers spew into Brett and me. Without thinking, I cover my face with my arms, then peek out at Brett to make sure he didn't get knocked unconscious or anything. He's ducking his head under an elbow but looks alive, even if he is covered in shattered glass. At least it's not blood. If not for the deafening and blinding wind on my face, the bird guts in the cockpit would totally make me gag. I can't believe how fast that happened. I don't know if the windshield being knocked out will affect the flying ability of the plane. I only hear engine sounds from one side. All my life I've heard the rare but horrific stories of birds and planes. It's every pilot's fear, but it has a one in a million chance of actually happening.

Brett punches buttons on the radio and then speaks to the emergency frequency operator. "November 013AH. Declaring an emergency. My windshield is out. An engine too. I need to land. Water landing. I'm coming down."

"Roger. Can you make it to the runway? You're twelve miles from a runway. Clear to land." I can barely hear the radio over my thumping pulse and the roar of the wind filling the cockpit.

"Lost an engine. I have no windshield. Too windy. Glass everywhere. Not going to make it to the runway. Am I clear for a water landing?" Brett's fragmented sentences are making me a little panicky.

"November 013AH, I don't see any other activity at your location. If you have visibility, descend. Head into the wind, parallel to the waves. Land on top of or behind a swell."

The wind and rapid descent are like being on a roller coaster, complete with my screaming. "Ruby, enough," Brett shouts. "I can't hear the radio." So I bite my lip and grip my seatbelt with both hands. I've lost track of Brett's phone. I envision the water landing from Gary Paulsen's *Hatchet* and gulp. *Please don't let Brett die. Please let this be smooth.*

In seconds we're coasting just above the turbulent surface of the water. Brett tips our nose up, and as the plane's belly touches down, we make a sudden spin to the left, then to the right. We bounce and catch air, then hit water again. I'm getting splashed from every angle.

The wind and waves are so rough I'm wishing Brett had opted for flying twelve miles to a real runway, even without a windshield. Every rescue I've been on, the water was gentle and the landings smooth, so I'm rethinking my idea to fly near a hurricane. Through the stormy waves, Brett keeps cool and regains control of the plane. For a couple dizzying minutes, we twist and bob on the surface before acclimating to the rhythm of the waves. A swell from the side drenches us. My heart hammers in my chest and I turn to Brett. "You okay?"

He nods. "This is November 013AH. I'm on the water."

"Roger. Are all souls safe?"

"All souls are safe."

"Roger. I'll alert the Coast Guard to meet you. I see there's a Coast Guard Maritime Specialist boat very close to you. Will request they move to you now. Wait for assistance to arrive."

"Roger."

"So the cops will get here first and arrest you for dive-bombing them?" I ask.

Brett sighs. I taste blood in my mouth and realize how hard I was biting the inside of my cheek during landing. Or maybe a stray glass shard cut my mouth. Brett and I both start to shake glass off our limbs and torsos. It's scary sitting five feet above the waves, bobbing along like a pelican. Especially in this wind.

"It looks like our cop friends are choosing land over us," Brett says. I look to where he's pointing. Sure enough, Reg's boat is getting smaller.

"Why would they ignore our emergency? Isn't that against their code?"

"Their boat isn't up to the storm. Better for them to get to safety and let a bigger Coast Guard vessel help us."

"Was it a goose?" I ask. The feathers and guts are gory. I wonder if I'll ever eat poultry again. Thankfully the wind is circulating the air enough that the smell of guts isn't overwhelming. The sight of a webbed foot sticking out of the windshield gasket turns my stomach though. At least it was a quick death.

Brett inspects a few feathers stuck to the ceiling of the cockpit. "I can't tell. Could be."

"Can we motor back to *abuelo*'s boat and check on them?" I know I sound desperate.

"You want me to motor our damaged plane into a crime scene?"

"Pretty sure we're already at the crime scene. We did swoop at those cops who know our tail number. They'll report us before we get back to the hangar."

"Thanks for the reminder." Brett mumbles a curse word. "You're going to get me fired and blacklisted."

I check my dive computer and do a double take when my eyes focus on our GPS coordinates. Are we really that close? We're like five feet from 26.57, -78.89!

I clear my throat. "Well, I brought my diving gear. You know how much I like to explore underwater. Mind if I go for a dive?"

Brett throws up his hands and roars, "Why not?" Then in a mimicking high-pitched voice says, "Brett, let's fly into a hurricane. Brett, fly so low the cops shoot at us. Brett, collide with a bird and make an emergency landing. Brett, while you wait for the Coast Guard to arrest us, I'm going diving!"

I know, I know, it is crazy. But it's also my best chance to beat Marco at his game. To beat my family. To stop this *insanidad*, insanity.

Brett is ticked, but if I react with an equal amount of frustration, it'll only escalate this situation, so I wave my hand as if I'm shooing away a fly. "I would've brought gear for you if I had thought you'd want to join me." Brett grunts and shakes his head. I ignore his grumbling.

I crawl into the back of the plane and grab my gear. I wear swimsuits like most ladies wear undergarments, and today is no different. Under my shorts and t-shirt I've got a modest enough swimsuit that changing back here isn't weird. It's a little tricky getting into my wetsuit when the waves keep jostling the plane, but after a lot of shimmying and

Pilates moves, I'm ready. I pull on my dive gloves and hope the cut on my hand doesn't sting too badly when I get in the water.

I'm so focused on the prospect of being this close to the mysterious coordinates that I barely listen to Brett's radio conversation with the Coast Guard. My ears tune in when I hear them confirm that the nearest Coast Guard Maritime Specialist vessel wasn't big enough to handle the waves. Hopefully by the time Marco arrives, I'll have seen the shipwreck, and the Coast Guard and cops will be here to meet Marco the seagull.

Descending into the dark water is like a sanctuary. Down here there's no storm, no shattered glass or bloody feathers, no guns aimed at my pilot or my family. There's no rapid talk on the radio, no waves bigger than rescue vessels. It's just me and the marine life, and hopefully *Dos Hermanos*. Actually, hopefully not *Dos Hermanos*. Because that would mean my family knew where she was all along, which would stink worse than rotting fish.

The buildup to finding this wreck has my heart racing, but I force myself to take slow breaths to ration my air. Brett mumbled his chagrined agreement to keep an eye on my dive buoy. I didn't tell him what I'm looking for.

Everybody has something they like to search for. Brett likes to chase storms. Runners chase times. Actors chase roles. Surfers chase waves. Gardeners are after plants and chefs are after recipes. Doctors search for cures and comedians live for laughter. Some divers chase species, some are after World War II wrecks, and some are obsessed with Spanish galleon wrecks. Everybody has their passion, and here I am so close to mine.

The coral here is obviously old. When the military purposefully sinks a decommissioned craft, a new, young coral reef will start growing almost immediately. Within two years, it's a diving haven full of color, fish, and young life on the brink of blossoming into a strong ecosystem. But the coral here is full of healthy, middle-aged growth. Well-established and sprawling as far as my dive light will show. Like a huge family reunion, this coral has generations upon generations of growth. A sure sign that it's had something to grow on for a long time. A sign that something might be under it all.

I check my watch again and stare at the numbers. 26.57, -78.89. The safe. The wreck. The fourth on Tanner's and my list. And I'm here. I rack my brain for any memory of us motoring over this spot, watching the sonar light up with a clue that something worth investigating was concealed below. We checked out a handful of spots near Freeport, but the only memory of the day that's surfacing is what happened before Tanner and I set out that morning. Tanner's dad put a hand on each of our shoulders and said a prayer. He asked God that we would be safe and find what we needed to find. Looking back, I wonder if that prayer from four or so years ago will help me today. Maybe that prayer helped me get to this moment. I sure wish Tanner was here to explore with me.

Suppressing a sigh that would mess up my regulator, I decide to give the praying thing another try. It still feels awkward, so I repeat in my mind what Len said that day about finding what I need to find, and I tack on Brett and my family to the safety part. It can't hurt. Everybody dies eventually, but I'll take all the help I can get now. Tanner was good at trusting God with results. Maybe I should pray about that, too.

Descending is easy compared to ascending. You mainly need to pay attention to where you're going down, what time it is, how much air you have, weather conditions, and constantly checking all your gear. But you don't have to worry about decompressing until you go up. One of the most dangerous parts of going down is where you might wind up. The current below the surface can drag you a long way from your boat, and you might not even notice until you come up and can't see your boat anywhere. My shot line has a dive buoy and an anchor, so as long as the anchor made it all the way down and landed in the sand, I can follow the rope down to the bottom. Once I get to the bottom, I need to either stay close to the anchor or hook a secondary line from the anchor line to myself. If you haven't dived before, it might sound unlikely that a person could get lost on the bottom of the ocean, but believe me, surfacing to no boat is a diver's worst nightmare. And sometimes it happens. And since I've already defied the odds by getting an engine knocked out by one bird and the windshield knocked in by another *and* I'm down here solo diving, I'll follow all the rules. If I don't, I might not make it to *Dos Hermanos* before Marco. I might not make it at all.

Thinking of Marco makes me wonder about the storm cooking above the surface. Down here, the only sign of an imminent storm is that the fish are hungrier than usual. They're zipping around like sharks to a fresh kill, stocking up before the hurricane shakes up their lives. Down here it won't be bad, and storms are part of the cycle, but the fish still have a bit of a pre-storm ritual. Nothing will get too ripped up like on the coast though. It'll all bounce back.

The colors down here resemble a fireworks show, and I'm so enamored that I'm surprised when my finned feet touch the seabed. In front of me stands the tallest wall of coral I've ever seen. I reach up and press the record button of the camera on my head strap. Brett snorted when he saw I was taking a camera down.

My wrist computer shows that I'm seventy-two feet below the surface. Enough sunlight filters through that without my flashlight, I can see the mass in front of me is ship-shaped. But not like a ship that made a ginger descent. Picture a ship smashed into the seabed, partially tipped on its side, and covered with the Hanging Gardens of Babylon. There's no doubt that I'm staring at a ship, but it'll take some exploration to determine which ship. Judging on the importance of this location to my family, this baby has already been claimed.

Shipwrecks need to be authenticated by historians and archaeologists, and for one this old, the archaeologists need to compare the wreck with documents that state the vessel's dimensions, what it carried when it went down, and how close the wreck is to the vessel's intended route.

It can be quite the process to authenticate an artifact from a galleon, and it's the artifacts that can determine the ship's name. Most galleons didn't have bells to identify them, and if their names were etched into the bow, they certainly aren't legible after their centuries-long seawater soak. Sometimes a diver might take a photo of a bronze cannon, and the markings on it can be matched with records. On the other hand, a silver bar for instance, would have to be brought up, recovered, and treated in a conservation lab. Once the corrosion is carefully cleaned off, the serial numbers on the bar could be matched with records. The country that has the matching records helps determine the ship. If there are ceramics, the archaeologists can figure out where they originated, which can be anywhere from England or Spain or Peru. Dates on coins can give an idea of when the ship went down and time stopped for all on the galleon. All the clues work like puzzle pieces to identify the wreck, and the name of the ship is usually the last part of the discovery.

I clip the line of my spool, which is basically a giant version of *abuela*'s old sewing machine bobbins, to the anchor line and let it unreel as I resume swimming, staring, taking it all in. I watch fish, anemone, and hard and soft coral in every color and shape. I let the current tug my body along the hull of the ship, my secondary line unreeling as I go. At the front of the ship, I swim parallel to the bow, which is an awkward diagonal up because of the angle the ship lays, looking for any etching, feature, or clue of what ship this is. With all the coral, it's unlikely to see much, but not unheard of. Especially since there's less coral on this side, probably because the underside receives less sunlight.

I check my dive computer and aim my flashlight at a sparse area on the ship. Spotting something that catches my eye, I fin close enough that I could touch the bow. I look up and down, realizing I'm right by the center of the bow, and a distinguishing feature spans into the dark ahead of me. A mast. *El Enrique* had four masts. *Dos Hermanos* had three. I need to count the masts.

I stare at the weathered hull with reverence. I begin swimming all the way around the ship, savoring the experience. My heart races as I slowly turn my head so the camera can't miss the wreck. Four masts. *El Enrique.* It feels like I'm being cheated that I can't confirm the galleon's identity. This isn't like Shackleton's *Endurance* with her name clearly inscribed and preserved. There's no unique dolphin carving, and certainly no plaque like Robert Ballard left at *Titanic.* The mystery continues, but I'm relieved to find the remains of four masts. They aren't upright and stately, but the rubble shows where four masts once stood. *Dos Hermanos* is still out there, waiting for me.

With the huge coral reef here, it's kind of amazing that low-flying planes hadn't seen it before *abuelo* and the twins were first here, but why would a pilot suspect anything unusual about this coral reef compared to all the others? Florida and the Bahamas have thousands of sunken ships, thousands of reefs, and thousands of deeper, darker depths. Only a small percentage of us want to investigate every single dark spot to see what's there.

All this time I resist the temptation to swim 4.2 seconds north-northeast. That's like five hundred feet. But swimming five hundred feet away without a safety tether could be the end of my days. A current could drag me off course, or much farther than what I planned. Surfacing that far away, especially with big waves, could mean I'd never again see *abuelo*'s boat or Brett's plane. But still. Five hundred feet. How can I be so close but so far? But do I really want to find *Dos Hermanos* like this?

After circling the wreck several times, and carefully unwinding and rewinding my secondary line, I check my dive computer and see that if I start heading up now, I could actually avoid a deco stop. I'll do a short safety stop to be on the cautious side, but I won't get bent from this time and depth. I think about what awaits me at the surface and I resist the *tentación*, temptation, to stay down here. A storm. Brett. Marco. Cops. I shudder, and it's not from the water temperature.

During my safety stop, I keep thinking about how annoying it is that my family never brought me to *El Enrique* before. Like they thought I'd blab her location or steal artifacts or something. Why would they keep it a secret from me? I completely understand keeping it on the down low, but why couldn't they tell me? And why is Marco risking prison time and threatening their lives to find *El Enrique*? Everybody knows that my brothers found her just like everybody knows about Mel Fisher and *Atocha*. Unless he's planning to drown us all out here, blame it on an unfortunate diving accident, and then take what he wants, it doesn't make sense that he's after this.

If he knows that *Dos Hermanos* is apparently 4.2 seconds north-northeast of this wreck, why is he wasting time here? Why not go 4.2 seconds north-northeast of this coordinate and have his henchmen check that out?

Bewildered and frustrated, but relieved that it isn't *Dos Hermanos*, I finish my ascent. Above me I can see the belly of Brett's plane, and a larger vessel that looks like the underside of *abuelo*'s boat. I have no choice but to leave the calm and face the storm.

I emerge and instantly get slapped in the face with a wave. When I recover, I spin and see Brett staring at me. He's gripping the yoke, or the steering wheel, and grimaces as another wave rollicks the plane. I push up my mask and turn toward the larger vessel, which I immediately recognize as *abuelo*'s. Marco points a gun at me. Where are *abuelo* and my brothers?

A wave swells to my left, so I duck dive under it. When I come up, Brett's plane is still surfing and the wave slaps against *abuelo*'s boat.

"Leave Ruby alone, Marco." Brett's voice is a low warning growl. I didn't know the guy had such emotions. I'm treading fast in the rough water and turn to see his face. Brett's nostrils are flared, and his eyes are fixed on Marco like a shark on its prey. What's he so mad at Marco about? Brett doesn't care about treasure. And since when does he stand up for me? The churning waves and wind parallel the tension between Brett and Marco. I swim to Brett's plane and grab onto a wingtip float for stability.

"Leave her alone? What do you think I'd do to her?" Marco asks. I spin back to study his face. For a lightning-fast second, Marco's steely eyes soften as he looks at Brett. Marco's hands holding the gun even drop half an inch. Then Brett snorts and Marco's eyes narrow again. He refocuses on me.

A dozen thoughts tie up my tongue, and while I'm flubbing, Marco says, "Ah, Ruby, I've been waiting for your arrival." He is such a creep.

Act unfazed. "Oh, hi Marco. What are you doing here?"

He cracks his icky, untrustworthy smile. "Tell me what you saw down there, Ruby."

I don't have a plan, but I am surprised when a prayer comes to mind. *Dios, guíame. God, guide me. Um, please. And thanks.* "Marco, I know how much you like your free civilian life. You know, cooking what you want to eat, driving your cool sports car. The Coast Guard is on its way to help Brett, and you don't want them to see you brandishing your gun. Being arrested is no fun." Believe me. I know from an *itty bitty* experience a few years ago.

Marco's lip curls into a snarl. "Look at this storm, Ruby. Nobody's coming to help you."

I don't believe that. The Coast Guard wouldn't leave Brett and me out here. The storm isn't that bad. Yet. But I'll stall for time as long as I can. "Oh, have I introduced you to Brett yet? Brett is the pilot at the aquarium. He's helped rescue three of our dolphins, an orphaned whale, and a juvenile beached shark, if I remember right. Brett has over twenty years of piloting experience, and he always takes time to perform detailed preflight checks." I turn and wink at him, just to be annoying. He glares at me. I keep talking. "Brett, this is Marco. He and *abuelo* go way back. When I was little, Marco used to go diving with us all. You watched my *mamá* grow up too, didn't you, Marco?" I turn and face the gun again, but Marco has let his guard down just a little. Since it's working, I'll keep going. "So anyway, Marco helps out at the dive shop from time to time and is a pretty strong influence for the whole diving community. Now that you two have met, maybe you'll want to work together or something." Surely Brett wouldn't join organized crime, and from Brett's reaction before we landed, they've already met, but I'll play the role of the chatterbox until the Coast Guard comes.

"Enough, Ruby," Brett spits out. "Get yourself out of the water and dry off before the jellyfish sting you to death."

I duck dive under another wave, look at Brett and stop myself just in time before I almost admit that the jellyfish aren't a problem right now. He probably thinks if he can get me up on a wing, near one of the plane's fuel tanks, Marco would at least hesitate to shoot at me. If he missed me and hit a fuel tank, I could just picture the plane exploding and burning him up too since the plane and boat are only two wavelengths apart. Maybe it would only happen that way in a comic book, but who would take the chance? Not that Marco couldn't easily back up and then explode us if he wanted to blow us up. Of course if he wanted us to drop off the face of the planet, that would be his perfect opportunity. But if he shoots us all, how's he going to find a prized wreck? Since apparently doing the work himself isn't his style.

Brett steps down from his seat, braces a foot on the wing I'm hanging on to, and extends a hand. I reach up, push myself up on the wing and grab his hand. With my air tank, dive weight, and fins, I'm heavy and awkward to heave out of the water, but without too much floundering, I manage to get my knees on the wing. Without a goodbye or any explanation, *abuelo*'s boat turns and motors away, fast. Brett springs himself back into the plane, making room for me to stand and get in the plane. Brett helps lift my tank as I step up, and I see an approaching vessel. "Nice of Marco to wait with us until help arrives," I say with a shake of my head. Brett only grunts, and it kind of freaks me out that he's so rattled by Marco. I mean, of course I'm rattled by him, but Brett's a macho guy who shouldn't be worked up by an old creep.

Within a few minutes, the Coast Guard is close enough for us to hear them talking from a megaphone on their boat. I'm standing, facing my seat, and I reach around and grab my waterproof bag from behind the seats. I can't wait until we're on the bigger vessel. A big swell is coming toward us, and I hug my seat. For a second I think the plane will ride on top of the wave like it's been doing so far, but a gust of wind pummels us, and the cockpit dips down. The plane jolts from the impact of a big wave. Now it's Brett who screams, but in the scramble to keep our faces out of the water that whooshes into the cockpit, I don't even hassle him for screaming. The nose of the plane drops further and water floods in. Brett grabs my wrist, yanking me out of the cockpit and away from the plane in a sort of dancing deer leap, in which he's jumping forward and I'm flying backward. I use the term flying optimistically here. Tripping, much like my life theme of stumbling, would be more accurate.

I'm certain the suction of the plane taking in water will drag us under. The Coast Guard crew hurries around on their deck and prepares to rescue us. They're a no-nonsense bunch of heavily muscled guys, all helmets and uniforms, harnesses and rapid jargon. By nothing short of a *milagro*, miracle, and the aid of my fins, I kick just out of the suction of the sinking plane, Brett and me both tugging each other toward the Coast Guard boat. N013AH sinks into the big blue. We stare, open-mouthed, and in three seconds we can't even see it anymore. I didn't even try to add a new tourist attraction for the Ruby Sunset guided tours. I think I'm shaking. Finally Brett turns to me and says, "Ruby, never ask me to take you flying again."

7

I guess I would've expected a ride with the Coast Guard to include some interrogation about us dive-bombing the maritime officers and maybe some questioning about Marco. Surprisingly, they only seem to be interested in our safety. They want to hear all about the plane crash and why I'm in diving gear. To that, I tell them that I had reason to believe that my brothers were in danger at certain GPS coordinates, and that I dove down to see what I could find. Understandably, they look pretty confused but either they don't think my explanation is important or they think I'm delusional, because they don't push the subject.

The captain glances over his shoulder and says that the storm is coming from the Bahamas, but that we should make it back to Florida before it hits the coast. But now what? Is my family locked in the storage cabinets in *abuelo*'s boat? Dead in the sea like Brett's float plane? And why does Marco care about *El Enrique*? Does he read *abuelo*'s dive logs too?

Back in Florida, the tourists and newbies on the coast are preparing for the storm. The Florida lifers aren't too concerned, but the clouds on the horizon are looming and building. According to the TV in the police station's waiting room, the meteorologists are having a hay day. Brett listens as he and I wait with our Coast Guard escort for our maritime specialist questioning. During a commercial break, the Coast Guard officer explains that his job is to keep us alive and now we are subpoenaed for questioning. A minute later a cop enters the waiting room and shakes hands with our Coast Guard officer. We all stand and the Coast Guard officer carries my air tank. Brett is polite enough to carry my fins. I'm dry but still in my wetsuit and sandals, still carrying my bag with *abuelo*'s dive log and my clothes.

The cop leads Brett and me and our stoic Coast Guard hero into what he says is the sheriff's office. I realize that this questioning will be my chance to spill the beans on Marco, and it makes me tremble. Unlike the officers, I'm uncomfortable being here.

A friendly looking sheriff, rude Reg, and Officer Cruz are already here. Our Coast Guard officer stands sentry at the door. I wonder who flew Reg and Officer Cruz here so quickly.

Thankfully there's a nice window so I don't feel so trapped like Baby, but the air conditioner is too cold and the overhead lighting too fake. Brett hands me a cup of water from a dispenser in the corner, but it lacks flavor and doesn't quench my thirst. Diving is dehydrating, and I know I haven't had enough water today, even though I downed two water bottles on the Coast Guard boat. My lips are cracked, but I'm so mad at Marco and my family right now that I numbly answer the sheriff's initial questions. I roll the paper cup back and forth between my palms and stare at the tiny whirlpool that continuously tries to form but doesn't due to the changing direction. Brett elbows me and I jump. "Sorry. Can you please repeat that?"

The sheriff leans over his desk with a look of concern and determination. I glance at nice Officer Cruz who gives an encouraging nod.

The sheriff says, "Miss Salazar, tell us why you were in the aircraft identified as N013AH with Brett this morning."

My palms crush the paper cup, spilling the cold water on my knees. I would've liked to change on the Coast Guard boat, but with the blanket and snacks they gave me, I didn't prioritize dry clothes then. I wish I had, but I ignore my now itchy knees and take a deep breath, before letting the truth spill out. I start with the day on the beach that Marco asked me if *abuelo* had applied for the treasure diving grant, and I don't leave out a single detail. I tell them about Marco's offer to buy the coordinates from my brothers, about the mysterious phone conversation at 4:23 this morning, and Marco knocking my phone into the water. I describe finding Len and meeting Officer Cruz. When I get to the part about Reg refusing to let me on his stupid cop boat, I let all the scorn in my voice show and I lock eyes with him. Reg struggles to resist rolling his eyes at me, which gives me some satisfaction. I know, I know, I'm being immature. Back to the story.

I say that my pilot *mamá* couldn't come over today and tell how I convinced Brett to get me to the coordinates. I go into extreme detail during the dive-bombing scene, making sure to highlight all our attempts to talk to Reg before Brett desperately resorted to buzzing the maritime officers. By the time I get to the part where Marco roared away from his own crime scene, my knees are bouncing and my voice shakes. The sheriff, Officer Cruz and even crabby Reg stare at me with what I optimistically hope is some level of respect. Brett has a thoughtful look on his face, and he doesn't seem completely annoyed with me.

I sigh and let my shoulders slump. It's been a long day. The sheriff's hands are balled together in front of his clean-shaven face, his chin resting on his thumbs. His bushy eyebrows, which were furrowed during my whole story, lift slightly. "You must be exhausted. Do you have any leads about where Marco is now?"

I shake my head.

"Is there another target on this list of coordinates you have? Would he have any reason to go back to Ruby Sunset or The Dive Shop?" he asks.

I shrug. "I guess it depends on what he's looking for. I don't know how it would benefit him to kill my brothers and *abuelo*. Everybody knows they found *El Enrique*, so it's not like he can claim the discovery. And even though the ship is full of valuable metals and stones, it's impractical to haul up very much, plus it's completely illegal. It takes tons of cleaning and authentication, and unless he only wanted to sell one item, he'd be heaping suspicion on himself. All that stuff is more valuable right where it is."

"How so?"

This is a frequently asked question among customers at Ruby Sunset, so it's easy for me to answer. "Wealthy divers happily pay a month's mortgage to swim around a wreck. Tourism, you know, it's my family's livelihood. And it's not like you're snorkeling, cracking open a treasure chest, grabbing a handful of diamonds, and selling them in town. Unearthing that stuff, without damaging the coral or the integrity of the ship that you don't want to collapse on you, is painstaking. If you could possibly convince a court to let you take anything, you'd still be a long way from being rich." The sheriff is listening intently, so I go on. "If you get anything more than a handful, you gotta make it buoyant somehow. Then would come the cleaning and authentication, which is only done by nautical archaeologists, who are few and far between and work at museums and universities. Then by the time you pay taxes to all the countries and jurisdictions who need a share and shoo away all the nosy reporters, you get to have your name on a placard next to the item in a museum. For the good treasure divers, it's about the challenge and the history. There are only a few greedy ones, like Marco, who give us all a bad rap." I look at Reg and sniff. He looks unamused, but next to him Officer Cruz bites back a smile. I look back to the sheriff. "But I don't know what Marco would need *El Enrique* for."

The sheriff taps his thumbs on his chin, leans back, glances at Officers Cruz and Reg, and looks down at his notes.

I take a deep breath and decide I might as well spill the last inkling of information I have. "In *abuelo*'s dive log, I read something this morning."

The sheriff snaps his attention back to me. "Go on."

"A big wreck lies 4.2 seconds north-northeast of *El Enrique*. He thinks it might be *Dos Hermanos*."

His bushy eyebrows inch up. "And *Dos Hermanos* is?"

"A legend. For years people have even suggested that maybe it was *un mito*, a myth, a story to stir up excitement and get people's noses away from other wrecks. *Dos Hermanos* was a Spanish galleon that carried the world's heftiest load of jewels and precious metals. Nobody knows why she went down, and for decades all we knew was that she's somewhere between West Palm Beach, Florida and Freeport, Grand Bahama. No direction, no details. Just somewhere near Grand Bahama. My diving buddy and I did tons of research, and I mean tons of research, to find *Dos Hermanos*." I stop, suddenly remembering something. We read it in a book. At the time I skimmed over it since it seemed to be more about *El Enrique*. When *El Enrique* sank, one of two survivors was a teenage boy. A crew member. He made it to land and some natives helped him. The boy and the natives didn't speak the same language, but when he was reunited with other Spanish speakers, he reported that he saw another vessel sink, about twenty-five to thirty-five rods away. To the northeast. I do some quick mental math. One rod is sixteen and a half feet. Thirty rods would be a little more than sixteen times thirty, so I'll simplify to three. Let's see, same as eight times six. Forty-eight. Add the zero for multiplying by ten, so four hundred eighty feet. About five hundred feet. In GPS, a second is 101 feet, so 4.2 seconds would be a little over four hundred feet. So the crew member from *El Enrique* could have seen *Dos Hermanos* sink.

"Is there something more?" The sheriff is intent on my face.

I swallow. "Well, I just remembered something I read that could back up the idea that *Dos Hermanos* is 4.2 seconds north-northeast of *El Enrique*."

He blinks. "Do you think Marco will take your family there?"

"Or just claim it himself."

"If he already knows these locations, why do you think he has your family hostage?" The sheriff's brows are furrowed in confusion.

"On his own, Marco can't find them. All he can get is other people's reports, so maybe he's coercing my family into telling him their information."

"And why can't he find the shipwrecks himself?" He sounds genuinely curious and equally concerned.

"A few years ago Marco got bent. He can't dive anymore."

"Bent?" The sheriff is confused.

"You know, the bends. Decompression sickness. His was bad enough that he's not supposed to dive again."

The sheriff nods and says, "Ah, the bends. I follow. Marco isn't supposed to dive again? Ever?"

I shrug. "I guess it messed up his lungs badly enough that the doctors said he shouldn't try at his age. He's kind of a case study. He didn't get bent so badly that he's dead or paralyzed, obviously, but he's smoked most of his life, and his bends were pretty bad. They couldn't get him in a barometric chamber right away because of a storm on the coast, so it all added up and for the rest of his life, he's safer above the surface."

The sheriff and everyone else in the room studies my face. For a full minute, everybody is quiet. I watch the clock.

In the chair beside me, I can sense Brett's tension leaving. With this whole story in the light, hopefully they'll give him a break and nix the part about him threatening the cops. All the law enforcement guys tell us to wait in our seats while they discuss some things among themselves in another room. I can't tell if this is a good thing or a bad thing, but I turn to Brett when they all leave the room. "What will the aquarium do?" On the boat ride back to Florida, the aquarium was alerted that their plane was sunk but the employees were safe. Good thing Brett followed all the protocols for taking me out on my complimentary employee tour.

"Fire us, maybe." His ankle is propped on his knee and he blows out a breath. "Ruby, now I see that you needed help. But next time, please don't get me involved."

"Yeah," I mumble as I drop my chin. I'm getting used to being alone. We don't say anything more, and I gulp down a few paper cups' worth of water. Several minutes of clock ticking and air conditioning fan sounds later, the cops walk back in and return to their seats, with our Coast Guard guy back in the corner.

The friendly sheriff with the bushy eyebrows looks at me and says, "Miss Salazar, we think Marco may target you next. Based on what you've told us, it makes sense that he'll be after you. We're assigning Officer Cruz to escort you home. I'm assigning him as your main contact with law enforcement. You need to be the eyes and ears of this situation. If anything concerns you, tell him right away, even if it doesn't seem related to Marco. The more information we get, the sooner we can find him and your family. Do you agree to report all suspicions to Officer Cruz?"

"Wow, I'm glad it's not Reg." I clamp my hand over my mouth. "Sorry. It was the first thought I had." Reg rolls his eyes. Officer Cruz chuckles, trying to hide it by clearing his throat. "Um, sure, I guess."

The sheriff speaks. "Miss Salazar, this is a firm yes or no situation. We believe you could be in danger of Marco. Do you or do you not agree to work with Officer Cruz and communicate your relevant observations to him?"

"Yes, sir." I nod. "Just one question."

"Yes?"

"Is he my bodyguard now? Meaning, he's going everywhere with me?"

"No. Let me clarify. He'll escort you home, and if you have any errands to run this evening. I imagine you're hungry?"

I nod.

He continues. "If we had a bigger department, I'd have you go about life as usual with constant police protection. With the full-time protection of an undercover cop, we could lure Marco to make a move and then arrest him. But with all the budget cuts, I can't afford an assignment like that while searching for Marco." He gives an apologetic look.

I swallow. "I don't think I'll be able to sleep a wink thinking of Marco *persiguiendome*, hunting me. The undercover thing sounds like a good setup."

"Yeah, it does, if it were more feasible." He sighs. "Do you have family in a different city you can stay with until we find Marco?"

My mouth scrunches to the corner of my lips as I think. "My parents are on the Gulf side, but Marco knows that, so I don't know how much safer that would be."

The sheriff props his chin on his fists again and considers this. "There's a full security crew at the aquarium." He taps his thumb along his jawline. "Marco knows everyone in your family? And where they live?"

"And work," I add with pursed lips.

"And he knows about your close association with the owners of The Dive Shop?"

I nod.

He sits back. "For now, I'll have Officer Cruz get you home safely and we'll have extra patrols around your neighborhood at night. Work as much as you can, and I'll talk to the aquarium security as soon as you leave. Be very careful. Don't go anywhere alone."

Siempre tienes a Dios. You always have God. I whisper a thank you to the friendly sheriff.

He nods, then turns to Brett. "Brett, we're not pressing charges, but next time you need to call for help, leave the dive-bombing to Hollywood."

"Thank you, sir."

"Reg will bring you back to the aquarium to retrieve your personal vehicle, and I'll send a statement from our office and the Coast Guard to the aquarium explaining about the crash. Here's my direct number if you have any trouble." He hands Brett a business card. Really? It's that simple?

The sheriff turns back to me. "Miss Salazar, what else do you need? You have keys to your house, car, the dive store? Like I said, Officer Cruz can get you fed and home. You'll have his direct number as well as mine, in case he can't answer. I'll make sure an officer stays in your neighborhood. As long as you're staying in town, try to return to your routine while we get to the bottom of this."

I nod, taking this in. How will I return to my routine when I don't know where my family is, or if they're alive? They expect me to act normal when *abuelo*'s boat has been stolen, after I swam down and saw *El Enrique* with my own eyes, and a plane sank right out from under me? I blow out a breath, making my bangs puff up. "I have house and car keys in my bag here. The dive shop has a keypad lock and I know the code. My car is at the aquarium's hangar, so I should bring it home. One thing that would help is a phone. My *mamá* calls me every Monday, Wednesday, and Friday. If I don't answer and she calls *abuelo* or the twins to check on me, she'll get all mom-worried."

The sheriff nods and says, "Yes, I'll get a new phone assigned to you. Write down your number." He slides a notepad and pen to me. "Anything else?"

I jot down my phone number and the all-important account PIN and shake my head. "Not that I can think of."

"Be safe. Remember, it's not your job to be the heroine or find Marco. I need you to stay near Officer Cruz and your aquarium security, get back to your routine as much as possible, and be alert to anything out of the ordinary. We'll be in touch." He shakes my hand, tells me he'll have a phone brought over by tomorrow morning, and asks Officer Cruz to bring me to my car and then follow me to my house.

For the second time today, I'm riding in a cop car. The adrenaline rush from the day is wearing thin, and I desperately want to shower and go to bed. The clock in Officer Cruz's vehicle says 6:52. My stomach growls and I rub my eyes.

"Miss Salazar?"

"Huh?"

"I asked if you've eaten. Do you have food at your house or do I need to bring you somewhere to eat?"

"I think there's quinoa and fruit in the kitchen." If not for the worry of Marco and my family, I'd probably be asleep right here in the cop car.

"Quinoa?" Officer Cruz asks.

"You know, the high-protein seed. Kind of like rice, sort of," I say.

"No, I know what quinoa is. But after this wild day you've had, you only want to eat quinoa?"

I shrug. "A quinoa and fruit salad. Or just sleep. Why? What do you eat after a wild day?" He probably has more wild days than I do.

Officer Cruz's eyes widen and he says, "When I have a rough shift, I unwind with a protein shake, four fried eggs, a baked potato, a steak, medium rare, and half a grapefruit."

"All at once?" I'm only five foot, four inches, so he's got close to a foot on me, but wow, that's a lot of food.

He glances at me. "Yeah. I don't eat much during a shift."

"I'm just impressed. Are you that hungry now?"

"I'm pretty hungry now."

"We have eggs and potatoes at home. I think there are still a bunch of oranges if they'll suffice instead of grapefruit. We can check the freezer for steak." I yawn.

"You don't have to feed me." He looks a little embarrassed.

"No offense, but I'm not cooking for you. My kitchen talents only recently expanded to include quinoa. I used to live on sugar and fruit. I'm just saying you can eat our food if you need to. As long as you can cook it yourself."

He chuckles. "No offense taken. But my shift isn't over, so it's just snacks in my car for dinner tonight. I'll drop you off at your car and then patrol your neighborhood."

"Til when? Is it safe for me to go to sleep?"

"I'll do my part in keeping you safe. Try to get some rest. I'm on duty until ten tonight."

"Then who will babysit me?"

"Having a police escort is not being babysat. It's a sign of importance, like the queen."

"Or it's a sign of suspicion." I yawn again.

"Not in this case." He pulls into the hangar parking lot. "Are you awake enough to drive?"

"With a cop following me, I think I'll be good."

He smiles. "I'll check in with you during the days, and at night-"

"Please not Reg!"

"Nope." He laughs. "But I'll tell him you said that." I roll my eyes. "At night you can call the sheriff or Deputy Parker if anything happens."

"Is Deputy Parker as nice as you?" As soon as the words are out, I feel myself blush under my dark complexion.

"I'd say so, and he's better looking. Plus he's been on the department longer than I have." He pulls up a contact in his phone and copies the deputy's number on a piece of paper for me.

"Is that supposed to make me feel better?"

"Miss Salazar, we'll all do our best to keep you safe. Until your new phone arrives, turn on your porch light if you need me. If I see it on, I'll stop and check on you, and I'll tell that to Deputy Parker, too."

"Thank you. Um, why do you keep saying you'll do your part to keep me safe?"

"Because I will. But it isn't just up to me or any other cop. You need to rely on God too."

I tilt my head. "You're a Christian?"

"I am. Are you?"

"Sort of."

His eyebrows crinkle. "Sort of?"

"Yes, but my faith is a little shaky. Pray for me." I blush again and look down. I'm such a *mensa*, a dork. Is it even legal to ask a cop to pray for you?

"Sure will." His voice is serious.

"Officer Cruz, do you think Marco killed my family today? Or is he holding them hostage somewhere?"

He looks away for a minute and puffs out a breath. His large eyes look back to me and he says, "Usually when a person is last seen with a gun to the head being taken to a secluded location, it's a pretty grim outlook. However, in this case, your family has information that Marco seeks, so he has reason to keep them alive."

"So I need to find where he's holding them?"

"Absolutely not. You need to act normal and let us find them."

"Does 'us' mean you and Reg?"

"If your family is as far from the coast as you suspect, we need the Coast Guard. That means Reg."

"Is he always condescending, or did I overreact?"

Officer Cruz tilts his head. "Reg takes his job seriously, as he should. And he's right that civilians aren't supposed to join in on missions like we had this morning. But he lacked compassion when he spoke to you. Reg is good at strategy and problem-solving, but he's not the officer they send to tell a family their loved one died."

"That part of the job must stink." Since I was with Tanner when he died, an officer didn't have to tell me. There was no question when the life went out of his eyes there in the ocean. I was pretty messed up after that, and even though I was with Tanner's family when the cops told them, I didn't hear a word they said. *Recuerdos estúpidos,* stupid memories. I shake my head and look back at Officer Cruz. "Death is so stupid," I say. My voice is almost a hiss, catching me off guard. "The only good thing, and I mean the only good thing, is the tissue donation, even though I hate that term. Tissue donation." Like a human life can be boxed up and doled out.

Officer Cruz swallows hard and nods, serious and deep in thought. He stares straight ahead for a full minute. Finally he speaks, but his voice sounds like he has to force down a wave of emotion. "I'll get your car door for you and when we get to your house, I'll help you carry your diving gear in. We can do a walkthrough of your house together before I get back to patrol."

I'm exhausted but I barely sleep. I blame the storm, but I know that the fear for my family is the biggest thing keeping me awake. Plus there's being alone while Marco is on the loose. All night long, as soon as I finally convince my mind to rest, that I can't do anything to help until I've slept, a howling gale outside the window puts me back on high alert. The palm fronds clack against my window, and the neighbor's dog must think the storm is Armageddon, so he barks like it's his duty to save us all. The heart of the hurricane is north of here, so all we're getting is rain and wind, and no lightning, which is a good sign. This type of storm is what sends tourists home and excites the newbies. The long-term Floridians always have a bigger storm story to one-up small threats like this. I'm not worried about flooding in this storm, but the wind is going to pose a big problem for finding my family. Hopefully it blows through the area quickly.

I know Officer Cruz said it's not my job to find my family, but what kind of granddaughter and sister would live idly while her family is missing? I'm thinking of a plan. Marco obviously wants something from *El Enrique*. But what? And since he was literally waiting there when I surfaced, he must know that's where she lies. And where could he keep my family? I already untied Len, and Marco would be a fool to tie up my family in Ruby Sunset where he knows I'll go. Unless it's a trap and he'd bring them there and then lie in wait to nab me too.

I roll over and look at my clock. 3:10. Another sleepless night. How long before I lose all sanity from exhaustion?

I grab my journal off the nightstand and flick on the lamp. Time to make a list.

- Check in with Len.

- Keep reading *abuelo*'s dive logs for clues.

- Tell Officer Cruz to check Ruby Sunset.

After making a list, an action plan, my brain finally lets me settle into a halfways restful sleep. At least until 6:00 when my alarm startles me awake. I groan, turn off the alarm, and force my legs under me, because if I don't stand I might fall back asleep, be late to work, and miss important observations to report to Officer Cruz.

I can't help but wonder if Brett will be at work today. Will the aquarium's insurance policy replace the plane? Will Brett's boss be totally ticked? I should arrive early for my shift in case they need to question me about yesterday. I don't want to be questioned, but if it must happen, I'd rather face it head on and get it over with. Like cleaning a barnacle cut, it's best to just take it on and get it over with.

Shuffling to the kitchen, I take some leftover quinoa from the fridge and slice berries, a peach, and peel an orange. I skip the kiwi this morning because I don't have the energy to peel it, but I sprinkle in a handful of pumpkin seeds. Like I told Officer Cruz, my main sustenance used to consist of highly processed foods that required a toaster, but then I got healthy and broke up with the microwave. Not that I'm super crunchy, but Janie got all healthy when she joined the aquarist program and convinced me to join Pilates with her, so I didn't want to be the only unhealthy one there. Most women don't make drastic changes like this until they have a cancer scare or get old and their metabolism slows. The turning point for me was eczema and stomach pains. About that time August teased me that I was spending two hundred dollars a week on fake food, and I realized he was right. So I asked him what I should have for breakfast, and he said I should eat produce. I probably wouldn't have listened to him, except the super fit ladies at my Pilates class all said the same thing, so here's my clean, crunchy breakfast. Ready to fuel me for a wild day.

I drag myself through a form of my morning routine, even doing some stretches and brushing my teeth without any thought. Working at an aquarium means there's no point in showering before work, especially on a rainy day, so I step into my sandals, grab the car keys, and open the door. On the little decorative table by the door that once held a landline telephone, I see one of *abuelo*'s Bibles. I consider opening to a Psalm, but I don't think I'd be able to focus with this exhausted brain fog cloudier than the early morning humidity. As I turn to lock the doorknob, a police cruiser crawls by. I check the doorknob, then turn and give a small wave at the guy who must be Deputy Parker. He parks at the curb and rolls down the passenger window a few inches.

"I'm Deputy Parker. You're Miss Ruby Salazar?" he calls through the rain.

"Yes, sir," I say, jogging to the car. If Marco is spying on us like the Russians and the Chinese, he'll figure out the cops are guarding me in no time.

"I didn't see any trouble at your house overnight. You're heading to work now?"

"Yes, sir."

"I'll follow you there. Have a good day. Here's my number if you need me." He stretches across the front seat and hands me a business card. It's the same information Officer Cruz gave me, but I accept it with an appreciative smile.

"I don't have a phone yet."

"Oh, yes. Sheriff spoke with the phone store, and the storm shattered a couple of their windows, so it could be another day or two before we can get you a phone. You can make calls from work, right?"

"Yeah, the aquarium has phones. The storm broke windows on a commercial building?"

"Crazy, isn't it? One of only a few damage reports we received during the night."

Seems suspicious to me, but I don't voice my thoughts. Not until I know enough for it to make sense. Marco wouldn't have reason to vandalize the phone store, other than to keep me from getting a phone, which I could totally order online. It's probably not related. But still. I slip Deputy Parker's card in my pocket, hoping to keep it mostly dry.

"Thanks for, ya' know, patrolling or bodyguarding or whatever you call it."

"That's my job. At ten, Officer Cruz will be back on duty."

I nod. "Cool. Thanks again. Have a good day. I mean, stay safe, and I hope you don't have to tell anyone their loved one died." Could I be more awkward?

Deputy Parker shakes his head and says, "Only a couple hours left, but in this line of work, I never know when the unexpected will strike."

I shudder.

"Anything you want to share with me? Ideas you had in the night about where Marco may have taken your family? Any suspicious activity?"

"Not yet. I'm thinking on it. But I should get to work now."

"Keep it under the speed limit. Let us know if you think of anything." He stresses the word *anything*, and I can tell he means it.

"Keep it under the speed limit? I thought you wanted me to act normal." I can't believe I just joked with a cop that I sometimes speed. Rain drips down my forehead.

Thankfully he chuckles and nods. "Nice one. Be safe. Have a good day feeding the animals."

"Thanks." Only the animals' trainers can feed them, because the rest of us peasants could untrain them if we tossed them their dead, cold fish. All it would take is accidentally giving a cue or not giving a cue and all the training in the world could be undone in a flash. I sigh. Measuring the fish is important too, but sometimes I think it would be more gratifying to be a trainer. But those are the most sought-after jobs and the hardest to get, so for now I'll stick with the dirty work that pays the bills.

Deputy Parker follows me as I drive to work. It's only three minutes out of the way to go by The Dive Shop. I glance at the clock and realize I'll still be early to the aquarium if I make sure to talk for only ten minutes. Parking in Len's lot, I breathe a quick prayer. *Um, querido Dios, dear God, ayúdanos a encontrar a mi familia, help us find my family.*

Deputy Parker pulls in next to me and rolls down his window. "Pit stop?"

I nod. "I want to talk to this shop's owner for a minute. See if he's heard anything about Marco."

Deputy Parker nods, but suddenly his radio announces some serious alert and he narrows his eyes. He listens for a minute and looks at me with an apology in his eyes. "They need more officers on this call. I don't want to leave you, but it's like Sheriff explained to you yesterday. If we had a bigger department, I could make sure you get to work safely."

"How about I call you from the aquarium to let you know I made it?"

"That'll do this time. I'm sorry."

"Good luck on the call. Thank you." I duck through the rain and he backs out.

The customer entrance is unlocked even though it's before opening time, but knowing Len and his prompt schedule, it's probably a good sign.

"Hi, Ruby. What's up?" Len peeks out from behind a lineup of air tanks. Looks like he's testing regulators and gauges.

"Hey Len. You're looking good compared to yesterday morning."

"Yeah, the doc examined me and said I'm no worse for the wear. This goose egg on my head sure hurts though. How about you? What'd you do after you left here?"

Oh to summarize yesterday in ten minutes. I look at him and blow my bangs to the side of my forehead. "To sum it up, I convinced the aquarium pilot to fly us over toward Freeport where Tanner's and my coordinates predicted Marco might be. We saw *abuelo*'s boat, but the law enforcement boat wasn't in the right spot, so we swooped down to get the cops' attention, almost got shot at, hit some geese, and made an emergency landing on water. While waiting for the Coast Guard, I dove down to see if our coordinates were right, came up to Marco aiming a gun at me, watched the plane sink, and got rescued by the Coast Guard a minute after Marco raced out of his crime scene."

Len's jaw drops. He rubs a hand across his cheek and says, "Wow."

"Any idea where he has my family?"

Len looks like it takes a minute for my question to register. He blinks. "So you were in a plane crash yesterday after you left here? And you still don't know where your brothers are?"

"Not a crash, an emergency water landing. Brett landed as smoothly as possible in the storm, even with no windshield and an engine knocked out. *Mamá* would've approved." I nod, remembering. "And nope, the twins are missing. *Abuelo*, too."

"Ruby, I'm so sorry." Len's hand is still on his face, like he has to hold his jaw closed to control his surprise. "That must be awful for you." He blinks and asks, "Do you want to come stay with Tara and me?"

Tara is Tanner's *mamá*, but it would be totally weird to sleep in Tanner's old room. I've never spent a night at their house, but it wouldn't take Marco long to find me there, and I do not want Len and Tara even more involved in this mess. As nice as it would be to stay with them, my second parents, Tanner wouldn't be there. But I'd be in his house. I swallow. My face must show my thoughts, because Len says, "Sorry, maybe that wasn't a good idea. Grieving is a long process. Tara might not be up to it either."

I wave my hand. "It's fine. I just wondered if you know why Marco would be after *El Enrique*?"

"*El Enrique*? Why would he care about that wreck? Unless he only wanted to grab a handful of jewels and sell the pieces all over the world at random times for the rest of his sorry life."

"My thoughts exactly."

"No way would the courts or the public let Marco, or anyone else, get her rights if the twins got murdered. Anybody could see through a plan like that."

That makes me feel better, so I'll cling to it. They might still be alive. Somewhere.

"Hey, Ruby, I'm gonna pray for you, for this whole situation with your *familia*, right now." Then he bows his head and puts a hand on my shoulder and prays a monologue to God. He doesn't seem embarrassed or nervous or awkward. His words and attitude are so...fitting. Yes, fitting. They're comforting, yet also pleading and respectful at the same time to the God of the universe. Why can't I pray like that?

After the amen, I look at him. "So he got that from you."

"Pardon?"

"That ability to talk easily to God. You sounded just like Tanner." I'm seriously having flashbacks here. I mean, Len's obviously *papá*'s age, and Tanner only inherited a few physical features from Len, but the voice and heartfelt prayer took me back. Back to diving and skimboarding with Tanner. Back to him coming to the aquarium on my lunch break to bring me food when I forgot it. Back to him insisting that I ice my ankle after spraining it while running on the beach. Back to swapping Latin phrases and trying to stump each other. Back to sarcastic commentary while watching old reruns. I smile at the wave of memories, then look back to Len.

"Tanner prayed with you?" His face takes on a nostalgic look.

"Every time we dived. Every time we came up. Every time we researched. Sometimes it was so often he drove me crazy." I shake my head slowly, realizing that I was the crazy one to not want to lean on God.

Len swallows hard and asks, "Did he pray the day he died?"

I nod, unable to speak because of the lump in my throat, because of the lump I can see in Len's throat.

Len swallows again and squints his eyes. "I guess it was his time then."

We're both quiet, but in a minute Len speaks again. "It's a mystery of life, why some people die so young." He takes a shaky breath. "But God has a great plan. He sees the whole timeline. We only see a few decades."

Yup, Tanner got it from him. The unshakeable *fe*, faith. What would it be like to treasure God that much? I clear my throat. "I have to get to work now, but if you think of anything, could you let me know? Call the aquarium or stop by the house. I don't have a phone right now."

"I can do that. Ruby, you can pray, too."

I manage a small smile. "Tanner said that, too."

Len smiles and his eyes brighten a bit. Then he looks serious again. "Are the cops looking for Marco? And your family?"

"Yup, they're doing what they can."

"That's something," Len says with a lilt of hope in his voice.

"Too bad Marco is about as evasive as a weasel."

Len nods in agreement.

"Hey, one more thing," I say.

"What's up?"

"Do you think my brother teamed up with Marco to tie you up, or did Marco force him to tie you up?"

"I sure hope he was forced into it." He shakes his head. "But wreck diving, the obsession with treasure, sometimes goes to people's heads. Makes them greedy. And greed is the root of so many heinous crimes."

I nod, letting his words sink in. "Hey, I gotta get to work, but I hope your head keeps feeling better."

"Thanks. I'll be praying. I don't want to get involved, but I'll help if you need me."

"Pretty sure you're involved already. They tied you up first and Marco might use you to get to Tanner's and my coordinates."

Len nods grimly and opens the door for me as I step back into the morning rain and humidity. "Keep me in the loop, Ruby."

I step to the side as one of Len's newer employees, a middle-aged guy walks in. "Morning, Roger," Len says. The guy nods at Len, avoids looking at me, and walks into the shop.

I assure him I'll probably be around to pick his brain more, and then I finish the drive to work, arriving fifteen minutes before my shift. Probably not long enough to help talk Brett out of trouble with the boss, but I can still try. Good thing for the letter from the sheriff.

Ten feet from Brett's office I see half a dozen or so people dressed in business attire. Maybe some of the high ups in the company got off their yachts to check on their business. I step closer and see a couple people holding out microphones. So Brett made the news? Wait 'til they see my footage. The camera was still rolling when we hit the geese. That reminds me that I need to ask Brett to see the video on his phone. It's not like it could make him much crabbier at me than he already is.

My boss's boss, Jerome the Operations Manager, is just outside Brett's office. Jerome is almost everybody's boss, except for the rich ones who own the yachts and don't know the employees. He's the boss we all know, and he does a good job. Robin likes him, I like him, and I can't say that I've heard any of the employees ever upset with him. I'm not saying he's perfect, but he knows the business, his employees, and the animals. From what I can tell, he tries to make the best decisions for us all. He turns and notices me. "Ruby!"

The crowd of suit-clad people and a few microphones jump in my face.

"Can you tell us why you and Brett were flying yesterday in the storm?"

"Tell the audience what you were thinking when your plane went down."

"How do you explain Brett's threatening flight pattern near the maritime officers?"

I hold up my hands and push through the crowd into Brett's office. His arms are crossed and he's standing about six inches behind the doorway, but he steps back enough to let me in. "We'd like to talk to our boss, Jerome, first. In private," I raise my voice over the crowd. No idea where that came from. And I'm not really sure I want to talk to Jerome. But it probably has to happen, and the sooner we get the media coverage over with, the sooner I can find my family. Jerome politely tells the reporters to wait for him at his office and that he'd like to make the statements for the media. Good. See, he cares about us all and doesn't want Brett and me to say something condemning.

As soon as the door clicks shut, Jerome turns to me. "Ruby, thanks for coming over right away this morning. How are you both feeling after yesterday?"

"Could be worse," I say.

Brett grunts and cocks an eyebrow at me. "My wife started a mid-life crisis when I told her what happened. So if I take a leave of absence for Cancun, you'll know why."

"I can imagine it was a terrible scare. On behalf of the aquarium, we're glad you're safe and sound."

"Thanks. Sorry about the plane," I say.

"Hey, that's replaceable. Lives aren't. I'm working with the Coast Guard to arrange a debriefing for both of you." He goes on for a few minutes about that, then tells us to keep our lips sealed when it comes to the media. "They'll take a perfectly innocent statement and turn you and the aquarium into a devil. So let me handle the media, like you just did when you came in." He smiles, then talks a few more minutes about that and offers to walk me to my end of the aquarium.

"Ruby, one question I have for you is why did you go diving when Brett and the plane were in distress? I saw the police report. Solo diving during a storm when a seaplane was in peril on the surface? What were you diving for?"

Just as I feared. Someone will get to the bottom of this. But the media is after Jerome, and if he knows the whole story, they'll weasel it out of him. So I shrug and say, "You just never know what you might find. The coral was super pretty down there."

Jerome gives me a curious look, like he knows there's more to it, but I check my watch and say, "I gotta start weighing fish. You know how antsy the seals get."

8

— · —

Hours later I hose sludge off my boots and step into the break room for lunch. Thankfully it's somebody's work anniversary or something worth celebrating so there's a baked potato bar today. The diners at the aquarium are ridiculously overpriced, and I didn't pack a lunch in my morning haze, so the potatoes are a welcome sight.

I fill my potato with salt and pepper, chives, diced peppers, and sour cream and claim a small table in the corner of the break room. The hurricane rains are already slowing, and the air is starting to feel more like the usual level of humidity. I swipe the back of my hand across my sweaty forehead, fork a bite of potato into my mouth, take a swallow from my water bottle, and then remember about praying. *Um, querido Dios, dear God, thanks for this food that I didn't plan or pack. Please help me find mi familia. Let them be safe. Por favor, please. Amén.*

I check the time – twenty-seven minutes left of break – and grab *abuelo*'s dive log out of my bag. I took the three most recent logs off his shelf, hoping for some kind of clue as to why Marco was at *El Enrique*. With my right hand I eat the delicious potato and with my left hand, I page through the same journal where I found *abuelo*'s confession that he most likely knows where *Dos Hermanos* is.

Page after page after page contains normal entries. Then an entry dated three weeks ago catches my eye. It's only a few pages after the *Dos Hermanos* confession entry.

Location of dive: 4.2 seconds north-northeast of El Enrique

Depth: 86 feet

Observations: She's a beauty. As old as El Enrique *and covered in coral. A shipwreck, no doubt, measuring 145 feet long. She lies on her starboard side with her bow pointing straight at Grand Bahama. Decks contain the usual cannons and weapons covered in barnacles. Lower decks contain wooden crates of coins and gold chains. Under a layer of mud in the lowest deck I found stacks of bars, most likely silver. This is a remarkable find. Absolutely remarkable. Precious metals fill the whole wreck.*

Still need confirmation that this is Dos Hermanos, *and Marco is tracking me like a communist spy. The minute he corners Ruby about this, the game will be over. She wants* Dos Hermanos *more than anybody, and she deserves it, even if she's as greedy as Marco. If she knew how close Marco is to making the claim, she'd put herself in grave danger to beat him. And this is why I hurry. This is why I'm acting like a seagull. Because if I don't find Dos Hermanos and quietly make a claim, Marco will seize the opportunity and the whole world will be all over it. It will crush Ruby like the paralyzing bends. If I find Dos Hermanos first and ward off Marco's threats while Ruby searches, she'll still have a chance. And when she goes to make a claim and finds out she's second, at least she'll be alive. She'll never forgive me, but she'll be alive. And not in prison from her greed.*

The baked potato in my stomach feels like a lead weight. *Abuelo* thinks I'm as greedy as Marco? And he's racing me? The table rocks and something bumps my knee. I jump, slam the dive log shut and gasp. Officer Cruz is sitting across the small table, his wide brown eyes staring at me.

He holds his hands up apologetically. "Miss Salazar, I didn't mean to scare you. I was asking what you're reading, how the day is going. You didn't respond for almost a whole minute and you jumped a mile when I sat down."

I blink and take a few breaths, thinking about what I just read. My mouth feels dry and I think I might be sick. *Abuelo* doesn't trust me to be smart or fast enough? He thinks I'm as greedy as Marco? So he would classify me as a seagull? We used to be a team. I swallow, which takes way more effort than it should. "Yeah, sorry. I guess I was just focused."

"I see that." Officer Cruz studies me for a minute and then takes something out of his chest pocket and passes it to me. "A little gift from the sheriff. He sweet-talked the phone store into setting it all up for you. Your contacts and messages should be in here."

A sheriff who can convince the phone store to help their customers? He'll get my vote. When I can think about normal life things like voting for the sheriff, that is.

I make myself focus on Officer Cruz rather than *Dos Hermanos*. "A new phone. *Gracias*." I didn't realize how often I was relying on my phone to check the weather and tide reports until I didn't have one. Most of my coworkers and friends spend every spare minute scrolling through mindless stuff on their phones. Drives me crazy. If I have something I need to look up, I will, but I don't want to be hypnotized by a screen. I only have time for one addiction, so I'll take treasure diving over reposting pointless posts any day. Not that I'm totally anti-tech. The dive apps can be pretty fun, and they're a great place to share fun diving pictures and collect information. Other than that, my phone is usually my connection to *mamá*, and I'm surprised she hasn't flown over here herself to check on me. "What day is it?"

"Tuesday the fourteenth."

"Did my *mamá* call the sheriff's department last night?" If she couldn't reach me, *abuelo*, or the twins, would she assume the worst and call for a welfare check?

"No, but we called your parents. Part of an abduction investigation involves questioning family about where the person, or in this case, people, might be."

"Did my *mamá* say whether she and my *papá* will come stay with me?"

"Not that I know of." Officer Cruz's eyes focus on mine. "But you could call her, let her know you don't want to be alone." He nods his head toward the new phone.

I nod slowly. "Okay." I check my watch. Six minutes left of break. "You don't mind?"

"Not at all. Want me to step out while you call?"

I shrug. "You can stay." It isn't like *mamá* and I talk with overt emotion or anything. It only takes a few seconds to unlock the phone and find my contacts in this updated version of my old phone, and *mamá* answers on the second ring.

"Ruby, are you okay?" Her voice shows her concern.

"I'm alright. Officer Cruz is keeping a pretty close eye on me." I look up, embarrassed, but he smiles easily. I feel myself blush. *Change the subject. Look away from his cute smile.* "Are you okay?"

"I'm stunned. My *papá* and sons were last seen at gunpoint. I feel like I can't get to you soon enough." *Mamá's* voice is more stressed than I've ever heard. "Your *papá's* been offshore this week and I haven't been able to talk to him. He's scheduled to come back on Thursday. I canceled my flights for tomorrow and am coming to see you this evening."

"You are?" I can't keep the surprise out of my voice.

"Of course. This is an emergency. I would've come sooner, but the sheriff only called me a few hours ago. I've been worried sick." I hear a plane or car door in the background close. "Just having my mechanic check my plane while I pack the essentials, and then I'll be on my way."

"Do you need me to pick you up at the marina?" She usually docks her plane at the marina a few miles from our house, not the one with our boats by Ruby Sunset that's walking distance away.

"That would be great. I'll call you when I land. Probably around 6:00. Love you."

"You too." I hang up and avoid Officer Cruz's eyes for a minute. I glance around the break room, realizing that my remaining coworkers have assumed the last-minute-of-break-hustle. Lunch bags zip shut, water bottles are quickly filled, and chairs scrape the floor as they're shoved in. I stand. "I guess I better get back to work, too."

Officer Cruz holds up a hand like a crossing guard. "Actually I need to ask you a few questions."

I pause halfway between sitting and standing. "Um, maybe I should let my boss know first."

"I talked to Jerome and Robin. When a cop needs to question you, that takes priority." He doesn't say it arrogantly. More like he's explaining the basics to me, like when I was telling him about treasure diving. His attitude is so much different than Reg's. More like August. Kind, helpful, probably even trustworthy.

Officer Cruz is still sitting, so I lower back into my seat. He and I are the only two left in the break room. He gives a little smile and slides a small notepad out of his pocket and clicks a pen. Great. Let the interview begin. "How is your day going so far?" he gently asks.

"Pretty good. My quinoa and fruit salad charged me up for a wild day." I smile lightly and he chuckles.

"Glad to hear it. Maybe I'll have to try quinoa with fruit." He laughs and then gives a little grimace. "Someday."

I laugh, but only until I feel guilty to be finding a ray of happiness while my family is missing. I bite my lip. Officer Cruz senses my internal battle and gets back to business. "What else can you tell me?"

"Deputy Parker introduced himself and said the neighborhood was quiet overnight."

He nods. "I heard that too."

"I had a hard time sleeping even though I'm so exhausted. I want to figure out where Marco has them."

He nods. "Any ideas?" His eyes track to *abuelo*'s dive log on the table.

"I'm reading *abuelo*'s most recent dive logs, looking for any clues." I blush again. *Abuelo*'s logs are way too personal to share with just anybody. But Officer Cruz is here to help, and his honest eyes make it way too easy to spill the truth. I remind myself that it's his job to get the truth out of me, and he's in questioning mode. His aim is probably to get me to fork over *abuelo*'s log so he can pass it on to Reg.

Here's why I'm afraid of saying too much. If the cops get all involved in these valuable dive sites, it could ruin treasure diving for everybody. All it takes is one foolish move to get the public overly involved, and some obnoxious activist would stir up the media's interest, and stupid laws would pass, and treasure diving would be over. I'd rather solve this quietly and alone. Just find Marco and my family and leave the wrecks in their mostly unknown resting places.

"Dive logs?" he inquires.

I lift the dive log a couple inches off the table, showing him what I'm talking about while keeping it firmly in my hands. "Lots of divers these days record their dives in apps, but some people, like *abuelo*, still write down details of the dive in notebooks. A paper notebook, not on a laptop."

He nods. "What kind of details do you record?"

"The date, coordinates, depth, water temperature, cool stuff you see, any reminders you want for next time you dive there." I shrug. "Stuff like that."

Officer Cruz looks interested. "Cool. So, it's details you'd want for the next time you dive in a spot?"

"Definitely. It can save a lot of time researching."

"Do you keep dive logs?" He's good at questioning. This feels more like interesting conversation than police questioning, which will make it way too easy to say too much.

"I use a dive app and a notebook. The app is handy for capturing the logistics, like the time and depth, and for storing that information with pictures I take underwater. Then when I get home I like to write about it and reflect on my thoughts about the dive."

Officer Cruz lifts an eyebrow. "You reflect on your thoughts about the dive?"

I shrug. "About how fun it was, what kind of stuff I thought about down there."

"Like what?" He actually seems curious.

"Different stuff, I guess." My shoulders lift in another shrug. "It's quiet down there, so it's a good chance to think."

Officer Cruz looks thoughtful. "Diving is how you unwind after a wild day?"

I smile. "That's one way of putting it."

"Maybe I'll have to try that sometime, too." He pauses and then asks, "You bring phones scuba diving?"

"In the right hard case you can, to a point. I like to take pictures and put them on the dive app." I shrug. "Just me, but I still prefer a dive computer on my wrist for the super important stuff, like dive times and deco stops."

He nods, taking this in, not taking notes. "Do most people use their phones now instead of the dive computer?"

"Among younger people, yeah, if they can afford the hard case."

His brown eyes are steadily on mine. "How expensive are the cases?"

"A few hundred bucks. I got mine for wholesale price through the shop."

He looks surprised and then looks at *abuelo*'s log again. "You were very intent when I walked in. Have you found anything helpful?"

My blush gives me away. Officer Cruz's eyes widen not exactly suspiciously, but definitely with an uncanny look that makes me feel like he's a hovering parent reading my mind. There's no sense trying to hide it now. I flip through the log until I find the page I was at, skim over it again, and then slide it across the table to him.

He reads the entry, and raises his gaze to make eye contact with me for a second, before reading it again. Flipping the page, he scans the next entry, and leans back in his chair. "Let me guess. Is this where you dove when the plane went down?"

"No. I was at *El Enrique*."

He leans forward in his seat, studying my face. "So your *abuelo* beat you to the wreck you wanted to find first?" His voice holds a mix of bewilderment, like he's trying to figure it out, and defensiveness, like he knows this would upset me and he feels bad for me. I appreciate his understanding tone.

I blow my bangs up, feeling defeated. "Looks that way. Unless this wreck turns out to not be *Dos Hermanos*."

"Do you think Marco knows your *abuelo* found *Dos Hermanos*?"

I bite my lip. "He must, so that's why he abducted *abuelo* and the twins. I think I should go there in case he's holding them hostage."

Officer Cruz holds up a hand. "Oh no, no, no. That's our job. We need you to share your observations and ideas with me, I pass them on to the sheriff, and we take care of the dangerous part. Your job is to live like normal, and my job is to keep you safe. That's a lot harder to do if you're in the thick of it."

"Pretty sure if cops are hanging around, Marco will disappear into the woodwork. The guy's a scoundrel. Me living like normal includes my irresponsible, impertinent ways, meaning I'd probably try to track him down. I mean, I've never been in a situation like this before, but if you want me to act like Ruby, I'm not sitting back while you and Reg steal all the excitement."

Officer Cruz's eyebrows pop up. "I told the sheriff you'd be difficult." His shoulders slump and he sighs. "Just my luck that he'd assign me a stubborn one."

"What do you mean by that compliment?" I ask sarcastically.

"Meaning I wish I could go undercover and accompany you on your investigations. From a distance, Marco would think I'm your friend, not a cop. He'd be more likely to do something illegal in front of me if he didn't know I'm a cop."

"Are you certified to go undercover?"

"The short answer to that question is yes. It was a lot of extra training and it doesn't happen often, but yes, I am allowed to work undercover."

"That's so cool." Did I say that out loud? I blush.

He laughs it off. "It can be cool. But it's not going to happen, unfortunately, as the sheriff explained."

"Easy. Just accompany me on my investigations when you're off duty."

He laughs, and his expression says, "Yeah, right. Some of us need sleep and decent amounts of food." But then he tugs his collar, clears his throat, thinking. "Hypothetically speaking, if you were going to recklessly do some amateur sleuthing, what would you do?"

I lock eyes with him and share what I came up with during my restless, unproductive night. "I'd start by checking out Ruby Sunset. I haven't been there since the morning Marco took them. I'd also go to The Dive Shop and see if Len knows anything else."

"I thought you talked to Len this morning."

"Deputy Parker told you? Yeah, I did, but obviously a lot can happen in a day. Maybe by now he's heard something."

Officer Cruz narrows his eyes. "Let me guess. You'll do this right after work today."

"I thought this was hypothetical."

Officer Cruz gives me a wry look. "I'll meet you after work, but only so you don't get killed."

"I thought the sheriff said you couldn't go undercover on this investigation."

"Well Miss 'Follow Me When You're Off Duty,' it'll be after my shift. All legal. I don't want to do anything to get you in more trouble." His brown eyes challenge mine, but a glint of humor keeps it lighthearted.

"Good. I gave up my illegal ways a few hours ago." In an effort to hide my smile, I purse my lips, but Officer Cruz sees through my tough exterior and laughs.

It's awfully hard to focus all afternoon. My mind is on a roller coaster, or more like two roller coasters with intertwined, damaged tracks. *Abuelo* raced against me. To keep me safe from Marco. Because I'm as greedy as Marco.

A boy on the sinking *El Enrique* watched *Dos Hermanos* struggle in the storm, so it's probably the wreck *abuelo* found. In all the time that *abuelo* and the twins took paying customers to *El Enrique*, they never bothered to take me or even tell me where it was. Like they didn't want to share the monumental experience with me.

When Marco got greedy to find Tanner's and my wreck, *abuelo* swooped in and found her first. Why didn't he just tell me to hurry up and find her? Why steal the joy from me? To punish me for being a seagull?

Then Reg acted like I was the scum of the population and unworthy of helping solve a crime I'm very much linked to. And why does Officer Cruz have to be so cute and nice and willing to watch my back? He makes it hard to think straight.

I hose off the deck at the dolphin tank for my last time today. There will be two evening performances, but I'm off in twenty minutes. On my way to the staff shower room to change, I go check on Baby through the glass. Since I'm not her trainer, I'm not supposed to visit her above the surface, but she and I have a game we play through the glass. Well, partly through the glass.

I give four soft knuckle raps on the glass and glance over my shoulder to make sure the tourists are still occupied with the seal show in the other tank. In just a minute Baby swims over to me. I set down my pail and flatten my palm against the glass and she pokes her rostrum against the glass in front of my hand. I move my hand, making a big circle, and she follows with her rostrum. I silently clap and she nods up and down, making me laugh. I grab the pail, extend my other arm, and point. She swims off. I sprint up the steps and toward the tank deck, my pail bouncing against my leg the whole way. Baby is getting so fast, and she has a straight shot, but I still give it a full effort.

Janie sees me approaching, smiles, and looks the other way. She always turns a blind eye to this particular shenanigan, for which I'm grateful. I see Baby's dorsal fin emerge and she hops onto the tank deck. Beat me again. I smile and look around. The coast is clear. I walk to her, telling her what a good girl she is. I grab a live fish out of my pail, a rare treat for a captive dolphin and toss it in the water in front of Baby. She whistles and takes off after the fish, an Atlantic mackerel caught by yours truly. Baby chases the foot-long fish for half a lap and grabs it in her teeth. She swims back to me, looking pleased with herself. I laugh and toss her another fish. Footsteps behind me make me freeze.

"Ruby?" It's Robin.

Oh no. Caught red-handed.

I turn slowly. "Hi Robin. I'm on my way to punch out and change."

Robin looks at Baby, then at my now empty pail and eyes me suspiciously. She gives a slow nod. "You could apply for a trainer position, you know."

"I've thought about it. Can we talk more later? I gotta pick up my *mamá* from the marina."

Robin gives a knowing smile. I thought Janie was the only person who knew about my illegal play sessions with Baby.

I bite my lip and swallow. "Thank you."

Robin walks on and over her shoulder says, "Be safe, Ruby. See you tomorrow. We could always use another trainer."

I prefer to shower at home rather than work, but I do like to rinse off my feet before leaving, and as usual, the hem of my shorts get a little wet too. I'm toweling off my legs in the shower room and look up when Janie walks over, eating from a bag of shelled pistachios. She's part of the shows this evening and is still in her wetsuit, so this is probably her dinner break. I step into my wet sandals and fling the towel over my shoulder. Janie and I have been friends since we had pimples and braces, and I know she's been worried about me. "Are you doing okay? Do you want me to come over to eat with you or spend the night so you're not alone?"

"*Gracias*, but my *mamá* is coming into town tonight. I don't want to drag you into my stress fest." Janie dated August for a while, and even though they broke up on mutual terms, I think she feels awkward hanging out at our house, even if August is lost at sea right now.

She swallows a few more pistachios and nods. "I'm glad you'll have her. But let me know if I can do anything, Ruby. Friends are supposed to be for times of stress, like all those overpriced greeting cards say."

I smile. "You can pray, I guess."

She nods and says, "Already have been, girl. Go chill if you can."

Chill? Try not to sweat like a high school wrestling team is more like it.

9

Under my instruction to act natural, and considering I have no clue how to act natural a year and half after my boyfriend died, a day and half after my family has been abducted, and an hour and a half before my *mamá* flies in, I pick the oranges I can reach on the low branches of our orange tree. I showered after work and put deodorant on four times, but I'm already a sweaty mess. Florida is for the cold-blooded.

My pail is almost full when a squad car pulls into the driveway. I wave and walk toward the car. Officer Cruz steps out and my breath catches. Man, he's cute, with his happy smile and clean-shaven face. Tanner had a goatee. I blink. I have to stop comparing the two.

"Hi." I swallow. "So, you're off duty?"

"Yup, just helping a friend." He chuckles.

I smile. He closes the driver side door and offers to help me pick oranges.

"You can use your squad car off duty?"

"The short answer to that complicated question is yes. Working for our department, I can. And depending on what you have planned, it could come in handy."

"I choose my friends wisely."

He laughs.

"Maybe you can reach those." I point to the branches out of my reach even with *abuelo*'s ladder.

Officer Cruz nods and smiles. "Sure." He has to be close to six feet tall, making me wonder if somewhere in his lineage was a tall German despite his Latino features. I hold the ladder for him while he steps up and gathers the fruit. "Reminds me of my grandparents' yard," he says.

"They have orange trees?"

"They did. Best oranges beneath the Florida sun." He passes down the pail and three oranges tumble out and roll down my sweaty arm. "I miss them. And those oranges."

"I'm sorry you lost them." I let go of the ladder as he steps off the bottom rung.

Officer Cruz nods. "Thanks. And I'm sorry about Tanner."

I nod. Somehow that one simple acknowledgement of Tanner's death calms me. By mentioning his name, it's like he's promising to make this whole secret investigation as easy on me as possible. I smile and he takes the full pail from me. "You want these in the kitchen?"

"Yeah, I'll get the door. Thanks."

He follows me into the entryway, wipes his army boots on the rug, walks to the kitchen, and sets the pail on the counter. "So about tonight," he says.

I look at him, the kitchen island between us.

"We don't think your house is bugged, but outside of these walls, we have to be super careful about what we say out loud. Your house and my car will be the safe spots if we have something confidential to say. The department has no involvement with my being here. This is just me taking a few hours of personal time to help keep you safe. Like we're friends hanging out."

I nod.

He glances down at his hands gripping the edge of the island counter and looks back to me. "And another thing. I don't want you to feel like this is a fake date. I'm not using you to get evidence."

"You're not?"

Cruz's wide eyes bore into mine. "It probably feels that way." He rubs his chin with his knuckles. "Yes, I want to make sure you're safe, but um..."

I wait. Glance at the clock. And wait some more.

Finally he meets my eyes again and says, "I think you're crazy to go all Nancy Drew with Marco. I don't even like the idea of this, helping you when I'm off duty. If someone gets killed, I'll probably get blacklisted. This is insane." He shakes his head. "But I can't let you walk into a fire alone and I know you're going to walk into it." He takes a breath mid-vent. "Anyway, I don't know why I decided to accompany you. I'd probably hang out with you even if I wasn't a cop, but you better not get us killed."

That was confusing, but I muster a smile. That was like the opposite of a compliment sandwich. *You're insane, you're cool, and you're putting my life in danger.* "Thanks."

His eyebrows furrow a little, like it wasn't the answer he was expecting, but he steps back to the door. "Are you ready to go?"

"Yes." I feel like a *mensa*, dork, who's trying to be cute in my white denim capris and navy short-sleeved top with peek-a-boo shoulders. Janie or anybody else would look cute, but I feel out of place. I twirl my favorite dolphin necklace and stand there wondering which shoes I should wear. Sandals would probably go better with my outfit, but Officer Cruz's black army boots have me wondering if I should be prepared to run or fight. "I'll just grab socks. Be back in a second."

I hurry to my bedroom, grab a pair of clean socks from the dresser, glance in the mirror and ignore a flashback to Tanner's and my first date, when the sound of his voice at the door talking to my parents sent my heart into overdrive. Knowing now isn't the time to get all mushy, I return to the entryway.

"You can just call me Cruz, by the way, when I'm off duty."

I start to put on my socks, and of course I can't do it gracefully with a cop watching me. "You can call me Ruby when you're off duty."

He chuckles. "Miss Salazar does feel awfully formal for such an irreverent young woman."

"Irreverent, huh? Talk about rude. Wait, Cruz is your first name?"

"Yes. Cruz Sanchez."

I gape. "You should start a boat tour service called Cruz's Cruises!" He laughs.

"Seems like a pretty good backup business plan to me."

He laughs harder. "I'll remember that. If law enforcement doesn't work out, I can get into boat tours. Cruz's Cruises." His hearty laugh makes me forget about all the craziness for a lighthearted second. Then he's back to business. "To keep this as kosher as possible, despite the insanity, we'll drive separately. I'll hold your door for you because *abuelita* taught me to be a gentleman. If we wind up in a tight spot and need to hurry, hop in the squad car. The passenger door has a safety lock on it. If we're in a situation where you have to ride with me, there won't be time for manners, so climb through my door."

I look up from hopping on one foot with a sock halfway on and meet his eyes. Yup, he's serious. "Climb through your door? Can we slide across the hood too, like in *The Dukes of Hazzard*?"

"You know *The Dukes of Hazzard*?"

"*Abuelo*'s favorite." Finally both of my socks are on.

"My *abuelito*'s too," he says. "My job is to keep you safe enough that you don't have to slide across the hood. But if you do, I've found rolling is easier than sliding." He laughs.

I kneel down to tie my shoe and realize he's still serious. "How did you figure this out?"

"Lots of bruises."

"So you've practiced?"

"I'm a boy who was raised on *The Dukes of Hazzard*. Of course I've practiced."

This time I laugh as I finish tying my other shoe and stand up. "I'm ready."

"Do you need, like, a purse or anything?"

I laugh. "If I'm acting natural, I'll need this." I grab my waterproof phone and wallet case, sling it around my neck like a lanyard, and let him open the door. My waterproof backpack is still in my car from work. We both lower our sunglasses and step into the post-hurricane haze. The blazing early evening sun casts an orange glow behind a veil of clouds. I could probably do without my sunglasses, but they're such a common fixture on my face that I keep them down. Cruz stands by me while I lock the door and clip the key to my lanyard.

"Where would you like to eat?" he asks. We stand by my car door for a minute and watch a teenager with a beanie ride a bicycle past. Way too hot and humid for hats like that.

"We're going to eat? I thought we were recklessly amateur sleuthing."

He gives me another wry look. "Yes, but aren't you hungry?"

Starving. "Do you like Lettuce Eat?"

Cruz gawks. "The salad place?"

"Yeah, that one."

He fails to hide his grimace. "Never been there. Do they have sandwiches? Or meat?"

I laugh. "We can go to a steakhouse. They have salads."

He looks like he has to try really hard to agree to my request. "We can go to Lettuce Eat. With any luck, they'll be closed and I can take you to my favorite steakhouse."

Cruz opens the driver door for me and I lower down to the seat. It's about five hundred degrees through my white capris. Bring on the air conditioning.

"Are you a vegetarian?"

"No. Not at all. We can get steak."

He quirks an eyebrow. "I'll take you to Lettuce Eat. If I was actually undercover, I'd act like I was taking you on a date. On a real date, you gotta please the lady."

"But you're not undercover."

"After the way you talked to Reg, I don't want you mad at me, so whatever you need to eat to stay happy will be worth it."

"Thanks for the compliment."

He laughs and strides over to his cruiser and we drive our vehicles across town.

When we arrive at the Lettuce Eat parking lot, Officer, I mean, Cruz, meets me at my door. "So you have quinoa and fruit for breakfast and salad for dinner?"

I step out of the Civic. "The ladies at my Pilates class have me eating so healthy that a candy bar gives me a headache." I used to love a greasy meal at Taqueria del Ray or *abuela*'s homemade *menudo* with all the extra grease she used.

Cruz shakes his head. "Are you saying steak and eggs aren't healthy?"

"Not at all. But look at your biceps. You need all that protein. I'm a foot shorter than you and can get all my protein from quinoa with a side of steak, not the other way around." Then I tease, "If you eat your whole salad like a big boy, I'll let you pick out a yogurt and granola parfait for dessert."

He chuckles and I think about how good it feels to make someone laugh. It's been too long.

After an uneventful, but enjoyable meal together at Lettuce Eat, we stand between our vehicles for a minute.

"What's the fastest you've driven that?" I ask, nodding toward his squad car.

I expect a casual, maybe even bravado answer. Instead Cruz trains his eyes on me for a beat and then shakes his head. "Well, fast, but not every chase has a good outcome, so I don't like to think about it."

"I'm sorry." I hope he can hear the contriteness in my voice.

"I know. But it isn't all excitement for cops."

I nod.

Cruz forgives me with a ready smile and says, "So we're stopping in to check on the shop?"

Three minutes later I park in front of Ruby Sunset. Cruz opens the door for me and I step around a *charco*, a puddle. Acting confident, I unlock the front door and Cruz locks it behind himself after we both enter. The store looks the same as when I left it. The main lights are off, and the security lights are still lit. Everything in the aisles is arranged as usual, and the floor is swept, still tidy from the closing duties two nights ago. Or three nights ago? I'm losing track of time since the abduction.

I lead the way to the register. "The other morning I checked the cash register, safe, and *abuelo*'s desk in the office."

Cruz looks all around, his right hand ready to grab the handle of his gun on his hip. While eyeing all the doorways and probably twenty other details, he asks, "What did you find?"

"Nothing helpful. *Abuelo*'s wedding ring, our birth certificates and scuba certifications and insurance stuff."

"Where did you find the combination for the safe? The numbers that turned out to be GPS coordinates where you found *El Enrique*?" He's standing by me now but is in total FBI detective mode and is still peering around.

"August and Axel made me memorize them a few years ago. After I already got into the safe, the numbers were inside it without any notes."

Finally Cruz looks at me. "How did you figure out it was GPS coordinates?"

"I already told you twice."

"I have to ask a lot to check for consistency."

"*¿Crees que soy un criminal?* You think I'm a criminal?"

"I'm gathering information. *Y tu historial no está tan limpio.* And your record isn't squeaky clean." He doesn't say it arrogantly, but he's cautious. About the whole investigation, obviously, but apparently me too, despite his smile and comment that he might hang out with me for fun. But my night in jail was a one-time thing, and it's not like I killed someone or did anything terrible. It was only underwater trespassing, and not serious enough that anyone pressed charges against me. *Abuelo* and Tanner got me out the next morning. But I can see why Cruz would be suspicious of me if he looked up my name and found that. Oh, and there was also sneaking into the library, which is different from breaking and entering. It was during the pandemic when everything was closed for months, and I was desperate for a fresh supply of print books to flip through. I used the keypad to unlock the door (it's not my fault the code was easy to crack), disabled the alarms, didn't do any damage, and spent the evening reading. It was great until on my way out, somebody saw me. I got caught and fined. If this is what Officer Cruz is finding about me, no wonder he's suspicious. Repeat trespasser, right here. So much for not using me to find evidence.

I sigh. "When I was mad at Reg for taking off with my information, I was staring at the list of coordinates Tanner and I scoped out. Since I'd just been in the safe, the numbers stuck out to me."

Cruz nods, finally approving my story since it's so consistent. "Does anything look disturbed since you were here last?"

"Not so far, but let's check the office." Cruz watches while I unlock the office door, but he pulls on my shoulder and lets himself in first, gun ready. He doesn't get knocked over or tackled as he flicks on the light, so I follow him in and look around.

"Looks good in here," I say.

When I lock up Ruby Sunset, Cruz hovers like a bodyguard but takes a half-second to check his watch. "We have enough time to talk to Len before we need to pick up your *mamá*."

The second I climb out of my car at The Dive Shop, Cruz asks, "So Len didn't hesitate to call the police on your brother who tied him up?"

"Correct, but I don't think my brother, either of them, would tie someone up. Unless Marco was wagging a gun over their heads. I hope not, at least."

Cruz nods sympathetically as we step into the store. Len is helping a customer, so I peruse the aisles. Gotta keep up with the competition. Mmm, I see a mask that is two dollars cheaper at Ruby Sunset. Cruz isn't acting very natural, unless natural means bodyguard or FBI agent.

The customer leaves and I step to the counter. Len eyes Cruz. "That's Cruz." I want to say that he's my unofficial undercover cop who is off duty, to assure Len that part of me will always love Tanner, so I wave my hand and say, "A cop friend who's helping with the case."

Len doesn't respond awkwardly like I expected. I suppose he's made new friends since Tanner died, too.

To my surprise, he steps around the counter and Cruz gives him a bro hug. Suddenly I remember Cruz gripping his shoulder on the morning Len was gagged. These two are not being introduced for the first time. Evidently they're tight, which surprises me because of how close I got to Tanner's family. If Cruz is such a good friend of theirs, how come I never met him?

"How's Benji?" Len asks Cruz.

Cruz gives me a sidelong glance, then lasers his big eyes on Len. He sighs, smiling as he nods. "He's good. *Gracias.*" Cruz squeezes Len's shoulder and I wonder who Benji is and why Cruz thanked Len.

Cruz steps next to me and his rock-hard bicep bumps into my shoulder. Feeling majorly self-conscious, I turn to Len. "How's your head feeling?"

Len pats the spot that had the goose egg and says, "Getting better." He gives me a look like he wants to ask about Marco, *abuelo,* and the twins, but doesn't want to give away family secrets in front of Cruz, even though he was one of the first responders.

"It's okay. I've pretty much filled Cruz in on what happened. He's one of the main officers on the investigation."

Len looks relieved that the cops are on my side.

"Have you seen or heard from Marco since all this happened?"

"No," Len says. "And I've been listening like a dog to everyone in the shop, hoping to pick up some clues. My guess is Marco is watching us like a panther, but we won't see him."

"That sums up Marco. I'm going crazy not knowing about my family's well-being."

"I can't imagine what you're going through. It's hard enough on me, and they're not even my brothers or *abuelo*. Your *mamá*'s on her way?"

"How'd you know?"

"She talked to Tara this afternoon." Len's wife Tara and *mamá* have always been pretty good friends.

"Oh, right."

"She's worried sick, of course. I think Tara invited your *mamá*, and therefore you, to eat with us tomorrow night."

"Sounds good." Almost like old times, but without *papá*. Or Tanner. "Did she say if she's gotten in touch with my *papá* yet?"

"Not yet, last I heard."

I nod. "We better go pick her up at the marina now, but hey, let me know if you hear anything."

"Absolutely. We're praying without ceasing, Ruby."

"I know you are. Tanner would've too."

He smiles at me with steady eye contact.

"I've prayed more in the last couple days than in the last couple years."

"Well that's a silver lining." Len turns to Cruz. "And you're welcome to join us for dinner tomorrow too, Cruz."

Cruz glances sidelong at me. Again. I'm starting to feel like a fish in a bowl. A cop friend in my former boyfriend's house. Len is being really chill about this, but then again, since they know each other, maybe it isn't so weird. "Thank you, sir. I'll talk to my boss and Ruby about it and maybe come over. I appreciate the offer." They shake hands and we leave the store.

I walk to my car, but Cruz pauses a few feet outside The Dive Shop's door. He stands still, but his eyes are glued to his peripherals, like he senses something. I kneel down to act like I'm retying my shoe and sneak a peek in the direction he's looking. To the north side of the shop is a line of palm trees and the edge of the property. I see a tiny lizard dart across the sidewalk, but nothing weird. After a minute Cruz says over his shoulder, "Wait in your car. Lock the doors. I need to check something out."

I obey, my adrenaline surging as I watch him walk to the edge of the building. I don't have any desire to watch another person die. Cruz isn't gripping his gun, and I wish he would, to be ready. What if Marco is waiting for him? I peer around the edge of the building through the windshield, but I lose sight of him.

Two minutes later he returns and my breathing slows to normal. It was a long two minutes. I lower my window and he says, "Just some kids loitering."

"How did you know someone was there?"

"I heard something." He says it like it's no big deal. Clearly he was trained for this.

"You're sure it was just kids and not Marco?"

"Yeah, they're not a concern."

"Thanks for checking."

"I want to solve this case too, Ruby." He lets out a breath.

"You seem really committed to your job, even when you're off duty," I say.

He glances at me. "Yeah, I like helping people. This is a weird case. The mystery is interesting." He's quiet for a minute and then says, "And hanging out with you is a bonus."

"Do you flirt with all the girls you help?"

He looks a little offended. But I can't help wondering. "No, and I wasn't trying to flirt. I mean, not exactly." He shakes his head. "Never mind."

Now I'm a little offended. And abashed that I assumed he was flirting and I couldn't tell the difference. "Sorry. I didn't try to make it awkward."

He shakes his head again. "Let me try again. I'm enjoying hanging out with you. Some civilians are bears to work with. You're mostly easy to work with. Nice, willing to cooperate with law enforcement, you haven't sworn at me or told me how much you hate cops, or told me that as a taxpayer, you're firing me. So yes, hanging out with you is a bonus."

Oh, that definitely wasn't flirting. How embarrassing. So the fake date really is a fake date. I feel deflated and look out the windshield, wishing I could *derritir*, melt, into the seat. "Let's head to the marina." I roll up my window and mentally kick myself on the short drive to the marina. I park, with Cruz just behind me, and I see *mamá* walking around her plane, doing a post-flight check.

She glances our way as Cruz's squad car pulls into the parking space next to me. After my blundering conversation, I really want to disappear, but Cruz the gentleman opens my door for me. I avoid eye contact and slip past him, mumbling, "*Gracias.*" Now *mamá* is staring, probably grateful that I'm not being arrested. Since Cruz is off duty but still in his uniform, I don't even know how to explain. I hurry toward the dock so we don't look "together." Hopefully *abuelo* and the twins will be the conversations of choice.

Mamá steps from the float of her plane onto the dock and strides right to me, arms open for a hug. I step into her arms and squeeze back, swallowing the realization that I miss seeing her and *papá* every day.

But they chose jobs on the Gulf, so I can't get too comfortable with the idea of having her close. "Thanks for coming."

"I wish you would've told me it was an emergency." She's still hugging me.

"Would you have canceled your flights and come yesterday if you knew it was an emergency?"

Silencio, silence. The hug loosens.

I step back. "Doesn't matter. You're here now. And we've got to outsmart Marco and find them. I'm glad you have your plane."

"What's law enforcement doing to find them? And what leads do you have?" *Mamá* sets her carry-on sized travel bag at her feet and finger combs her hair, redoing the ponytail. She keeps her dark hair a little longer than mine, and her complexion is beautiful as always. When the twins were younger, she often was mistaken as their older sister. By the time I came along a few years later, people realized she was the *mamá*, but she definitely has the youthful look that Hispanics are known for. Now that I'm an adult and she still doesn't have a single gray hair, we might get mistaken for sisters. Especially if this stress keeps up and I get wrinkles from all this hullabaloo. She finishes her ponytail and turns her attention to Cruz, who steps up next to me.

Mamá wipes her palms on her khakis and extends a hand. "Tonia Salazar. I'm Ruby's *mamá*."

"Cruz Sanchez. Nice to meet you. I'm a cop."

Mamá looks curious. "Has the sheriff assigned a few of you to take turns watching my girl?"

"No, unfortunately, but only because of the budget and the number of officers we have." He gives a humorless laugh. "I'm technically off duty."

Mamá tilts her head. "So you're friends?"

"Cruz is afraid I'll get killed when I go all Nancy Drew, so he offered to watch my back."

"You know my daughter well enough to see trouble brewing."

"Thanks, *mamá*."

Cruz laughs.

Mamá nods. "So let me get this straight. Not enough officers, *no hay dinero*, not enough budget, so you're working off duty to keep my daughter safe." She shakes her head. "*Pues, gracias*. Anyway, thank you. And thanks for the police escort now. It's a hot walk back to my *papá*'s house, so the ride is appreciated."

"Happy to do so." Cruz takes *mamá*'s bag and leads us up to the parking lot.

As we stride toward the vehicles, *mamá* links arms with me and says, "I have some ideas for how to find them."

I meet her eyes. "Good. Because I'm out of ideas."

I unlock the Civic with my key fob, and Cruz loads *mamá*'s luggage in the backseat. Before he can go all gentleman and open her passenger door, she climbs in, so he opens my door. I cautiously glance at Cruz's face and he gives a little smile. Whew. Maybe I didn't wreck our budding friendship. But I know now not to make anymore flirting comments. He's just nice to everybody, and he doesn't want me to die. Just part of his life's work.

"I'll meet you at your house and listen to your amateur sleuthing."

10

— · —

Back in our yard, *mamá* heads straight to the orange tree. Cruz sets *mamá*'s luggage by the front door and strolls over to the orange tree. "So you're a self-employed pilot?" Cruz asks *mamá*.

"Correct. The oil rig companies contract me to fly their workers to the rigs and back. Tourist sightseeing flights are a nice paying side-gig. That alone covers my liability insurance."

"Insurance can be a doozy," Cruz says. "Can't live with it, can't live without it."

"Exactly." She turns to me. "You must've picked the oranges today?"

"Yeah, they're inside."

Mamá smiles. "Can't wait to eat one. Cruz, do you live in town?"

Cruz nods. "Just outside of town. I live with three roommates on Barracuda Avenue."

"Three roommates? Sounds like a busy house." *Mamá* begins walking around the yard, checking on all the plants. Cruz and I follow.

Cruz chuckles. "We have different work schedules, so there's a lot of in and out. We don't have to worry about too much time together, which is good. Two of the guys work days, and me and the other guy have alternating schedules. The rule of thumb is to be quiet in the house because no matter what time it is, somebody's probably asleep."

I listen to the conversation. *Mamá* asks, "*Cuatro hombres*, four guys, and the house is quiet?"

"They don't always follow the rule of thumb."

Mamá and I laugh. *Mamá* plucks off a few wilted flowers from the bed of pink and purple pentas blooms that *abuela* planted when I was little. She straightens up. "So Cruz, what leads do you have for my *papá* and *mis hijos*, my sons?"

Cruz's tone turns serious. "Mrs. Salazar, we have many officers working on this investigation. A lot of it has to be kept confidential, but anything I can tell you, I will." He pauses as *mamá* huffs at his tight-lipped response. "I'm sorry I can't tell you more, but I need you to be patient. It might take a few days before Marco will make a move. He's probably watching Ruby and waiting for his opportunity to strike."

"That's what scares me," I say.

"The watching or the waiting?" he asks.

"The watching. And the striking."

Cruz nods. "Me too."

Mamá quirks an eyebrow. "Well let's get to work then."

Cruz eyes us both, realizing *mamá* is serious. He swallows. "*Hablamos adentro*, let's talk inside."

I lead Cruz and *mamá* into my bedroom and we surround my desk. I point to the large map on the wall. Taking a pack of neon sticky flags from my desk, I place a yellow flag on West Palm Beach, by the marina. "Here's where Marco abducted them." I do some general measurements and eyeball the coordinates to what I'm pretty sure is *El Enrique* and place a pink flag there. "Here's where *El Enrique* is and where Marco aimed a gun at me. And now the aquarium's plane lies right next to *El Enrique*. Hopefully that won't mess up Ruby Sunset tours." I gulp, knowing what's next. Doing some more general measurements, I say, "And here's where *abuelo*'s dive log says *Dos Hermanos* is." I feel my nostrils flare.

"Wait, what?" *mamá* asks.

"You heard me," I grunt, not masking my anger.

"Since when does my *papá* care about *Dos Hermanos*?"

I blow on my bangs and dig into my bag, retrieving *abuelo*'s log. I flip to the page that I wish I hadn't seen, no, that I wish hadn't been written. I scan my eyes over *abuelo*'s familiar handwriting, feeling the stab of pain all over again. Closing my eyes, I hand it to *mamá* and she begins reading, whispering the passage aloud. "*Still need confirmation that this is* Dos Hermanos, *and Marco is tracking me like a communist spy. The minute he corners Ruby about this, the game will be over. She wants* Dos Hermanos *more than anybody, and she deserves it, even if she's as greedy as Marco. If she knew how close Marco is to making the claim, she'd put herself in grave danger to beat him. And this is why I hurry. This is why I'm acting like a seagull. Because if I don't find* Dos Hermanos *and quietly make a claim, Marco will seize the opportunity and the whole world will be all over it. It will crush Ruby like the paralyzing bends. If I find* Dos Hermanos *first and ward off Marco's threats while Ruby searches, she'll still have a chance. And when she goes to make a claim and finds out she's second, at least she'll be alive. She'll never forgive me, but she'll be alive. And not in prison from her greed.*"

Hearing *mamá* read this aloud reminds me of *abuela*. I speak both languages without much of an accent, from what I'm told. *Mamá* speaks both languages, but her English has an accent, and I secretly love it.

Mamá looks at me with crinkly eyebrows, then at Cruz. "You saw this already?"

He nods. "Ruby showed me at lunch today."

Mamá quirks an eyebrow at me. "You're sure being cooperative with the police."

I give her a tense "please shut up now" smile.

She turns back to the dive log. "Your relationship with *abuelo* will take a hit from this."

Duh. *Way to state the obvious.* I swallow hard. "I don't get it. If the race was on, why didn't *abuelo* ask me to help? He and the twins know how hard Tanner and I worked to find her."

Mamá nods. "Marco must have given a serious threat, but that makes me wonder..."

Cruz and I wait a minute. "Wonder what, Mrs. Salazar?"

"It makes me wonder why my *papá* didn't get law enforcement involved right away." She eyes Cruz. "Unless someone has some cops on his side."

Cruz's eyes pop and a vein in his neck bulges. "You're accusing someone in our department of working with Marco?"

"I'm not accusing anyone. I'm asking questions. If my *papá* felt that Ruby had been threatened, why not go straight to the cops? Why would he meet Marco at the marina?"

"I've listened to all sorts of reports, and one consistency is that when a gun is aimed at your head, you'll go along with *instrucciones estúpidas,* stupid instructions." Cruz thinks, then asks to read the dive log entry again. He reads, *mamá* studies the map, and I stare at a picture of Baby that's taped to the bottom left corner of my laptop. Why does life have to be so complicated? Dolphins get to swim and play all day. Cruz clears his throat and turns to *mamá*. "Maybe Francisco is as skeptical of law enforcement as you are and that's why he didn't report Marco's threatening actions."

Mamá narrows her eyes, her brows still knitted. She tugs the bottom hem of her business polo shirt. "I wouldn't say we're skeptical of law enforcement. I'm just asking questions to gather facts." She's ticked. And skeptical of law enforcement, but I won't call her out on it.

"And that's always a good idea." His tone shows that he's trained in calming people down. "Another thing to consider is that Marco's threats were vague enough to not warrant police involvement."

Mamá arches an eyebrow.

"Marco is good at that," I speak up. "He's so weird. Sometimes when I do my nature journaling, he corners me and tries to pry for information. It's just nosy enough to be creepy, but not illegal enough to call for help."

Cruz and *mamá* look at me like I just said I'm swimming to Cuba. They speak at the same time in a jumble. *Mamá* asks, "When were you going to tell me about any of this?" Cruz asks, "Nature journaling?"

Cruz's question has a shorter answer, so I start with him. "I study critters in the tide pool. Sketch them, write down observations. It's peaceful." I shrug and turn to *mamá*. "The last time you called me for the 8:00 p.m. check-in, your call was just in time because it's what got me away from Marco and his creepy eyes and icky hand on my arm." Cruz stiffens and I feel his eyes lock on my face. I squirm at the memory.

"How long has this been going on?" *mamá* demands.

I shrug. "I only get to nature journal a few times a month, depending on how the tides and my work schedule land. But ever since Tanner died, if I'm there, Marco usually rears his ugly head."

Mamá and Cruz frown so deeply I regret bringing it up. "Look, I'm just saying that I could definitely see Marco saying something to *abuelo* to imply harming me without actually saying it. And *abuelo* is so protective that a vague threat toward me might cloud his smarts.

I don't take Marco's claims too seriously, but maybe *abuelo* got into protective patriarch mode when he said something."

Cruz nods and then asks, "Why is Marco so involved in your family in the first place?"

"He and *abuelo* used to be good friends, until he got bent and *abuelo* wouldn't let him in on *El Enrique*," I say.

"Like you explained to the sheriff," Cruz says. "So you think Marco is still salty about *El Enrique*?"

Mamá clears her throat, but awkwardly, like she's trying to avoid attention even though it makes Cruz and me look at her. She adjusts her ponytail again. Straightens her shirt hem again. She's got a cat to let out of a bag.

"Is there more?" Cruz prods.

Mamá looks between Cruz and me and lets out a breath. Her blush is deeper than her complexion. She looks at me and whispers, "Marco is almost like family."

"Huh?"

"Marco and my *mamá*, um..." she trails off.

"This sounds bad."

Mamá lets out another breath. "Marco and my *mamá* had a baby together. They were teenagers. *Papá*, your *abuelo*, helped her and the baby when Marco refused to take responsibility."

I gulp. "Don't tell me you're Marco's baby."

Mamá whips her head back and forth, her ponytail going crazy. "No, no, thankfully. Definitely not. Francisco is my biological *papá* and your *abuelo*. One hundred percent."

"Phew." A new thought comes to me. "So who is your half-sibling? *Abuela*'s first baby?" The thought of *abuela* with anybody else, especially Marco, sends a shiver up my spine. Eww.

The look on *mamá*'s face reveals that she knows exactly who it is but doesn't want to say. I rack my brain and draw a blank.

"That's irrelevant right now," *mamá* says with a wave of her hand. "You wanted to know why Marco is always trying to top my *papá*. There you have it. *Papá* helped raise his baby and won *abuela*'s love. His baby is beside the point."

"I'm not so sure of that," Cruz says. We look at him. "If Marco is still mad that Francisco married your mother, that baby and your parents' marriage could be a driving force of Marco's anger against all of you."

"I understand what you're saying, but my half-sibling moved to live with relatives in Georgia when I was still quite young."

Wait a minute. Brett once mentioned he grew up in Georgia. I blurt out, "It's Brett isn't it?!" The strained moment between Marco and Brett in the ocean. It makes sense now. Brett was angry because his own father rejected him, and for a rare, soft instant, Marco felt guilty.

Mamá's face pales as much as her complexion will allow and her mouth forms a wide O.

So it's true? "Brett is your brother? My *tío*, uncle?" *Tío* Brett. I bet he'll love it when I call him that. "He knows I'm his *sobrina*, niece?"

Mamá shakes her head as if erasing evidence written on an Etch A Sketch. "How did you figure this out? A minute ago you didn't even know about *abuela*'s firstborn."

"And he said he wouldn't trust Marco with a goldfish. Does he know Marco is his biological father?" I'm thinking fast and out loud.

"Brett was shaped more by *papá* than by his biological father, thank the Lord," *mamá* says. "He wouldn't work against us. I know he wouldn't."

I pull the chair out from under my desk and sink into it. Brett is my uncle? "*¿Por qué hay tantos secretos en esta familia? Why are there so many secrets in this family? Abuela* and Marco?" I shudder.

"Ruby, slow down," *mamá* says. She turns to Cruz. "Is Marco mad about *papá* and *mamá*? Yes. Is Brett going to team up with Marco to harm *papá* and the boys? No. I am confident of that."

Cruz takes notes in his notepad. So much for not using me for evidence. "Well that does provide some background as to why Marco is targeting your kids and Francisco."

Mamá nods. "So we're back to the question of where he has them."

"And what he's getting from them," Cruz adds.

"He can use them to dive," I say.

"But why not send down a camera?" Cruz asks.

I shrug. "Lots of reasons. But the main one could be that he wants to be a bully." I swallow. "He knows nothing would divide our family like them finding my wreck."

Cruz nods sympathetically.

I point to the dive log and turn to *mamá*. "So you think we need to go to these coordinates where *abuelo* says *Dos Hermanos* is?"

"And take him on ourselves?" Alarm etches *mamá*'s voice.

"Absolutely not," Cruz says. "May I take a picture of this page?"

"No, but I'll write down the coordinates for you."

His jaw tightens, but no way is the dive log getting broadcast to all the officers, especially Reg. At least *he's* not my uncle. "Hey Reg isn't Brett's son, is he?"

Cruz looks amused by my concern but *mamá* shakes her head. "Brett only has daughters."

"Good. I do not want to spend Thanksgiving with Reg."

Cruz throws back his head and laughs out loud. *Mamá* says, "Who is Reg? It was easier before you knew." *Of course. Don't tell Ruby anything. Just let her keep tripping her way through life, kept out of the family loop.* My nostrils flare again, but my eyes return to my map.

We spend the next fifteen minutes looking at the map while Cruz takes notes and *mamá* and I ask questions. *Mamá* says she's going to the kitchen to get iced tea, and I stretch back, yawning. Cruz turns to me and whispers, "I'll give you and your *mamá* some time together. Call me right away if you feel threatened or receive any tips. I'm back on duty tomorrow morning. I think we've hit a wall tonight, but you and I both need some sleep."

I walk him to the door. *Mamá* hands both of us glasses of iced tea and announces that she's going to sit on the patio with hers. "I need to head out in a few minutes, Mrs. Salazar." He hands her his card. "If you think of anything else that could be helpful to the investigation, please let me know." *Mamá* agrees, thanks him for the help, and walks through the living room to the patio.

Cruz and I step outside and he gives me a cautious smile. "You okay?"

"I'm just glad Reg isn't my relative."

He almost spits out his iced tea as he forces down a laugh. "I'm more relieved you're not my relative."

I punch him in the bicep, but his serious gaze makes me wonder if he's implying that he's interested in me. Remembering how foolish I felt when I thought he was flirting earlier, I shove that thought to the back of my mind. He's probably thankful he's not related to me because I'm a repeat trespasser and an obsessed treasure diver with a stalker.

Thankfully he lets the moment slide. "I need to go pick up my nephew, but I'll check in with you tomorrow at the aquarium."

"See you then."

He hands me his empty glass and I watch him step into his squad car. Why does he have to be so cute? To make matters worse, he smiles and waves before he backs into the road.

A minute later *mamá* meets me on the front porch. *Mamá* says, "I do feel better knowing they have a cop escorting you everywhere."

"Not everywhere. The sheriff said I should go stay with family out of town, but when I told him Marco knows where you live, he said I might be safer at work with the aquarium security and he'd have his officers patrol our neighborhood extra when I'm home."

"And Officer Cruz volunteered to take you out to eat tonight?" *Mamá* purses her lips in an attempt to hide a mischievous grin.

"He was looking for evidence."

"Seems likely." Mothers shouldn't be allowed to tease their adult daughters like this. That's what brothers are for. Not that it matters. If she had heard our earlier conversation, she wouldn't be hinting at this.

11

I've got to do something. *Mamá* is antsy too, but she's too busy working on her own plan to notice me devising one of my own. So it's just Cruz I have to work around. *Mamá* will shrug me off if I say I'm taking a walk or going to work early. But Cruz is on to me. He knows I'm not satisfied with the brief responses that law enforcement can give to my twenty questions.

It's been three days and I haven't seen a trace of Marco or heard a word from my family. *Mamá* has spent the days flying in a grid pattern above the ocean and listening to half a dozen radio frequencies all evening, searching for any trace about their whereabouts.

Cruz sends me messages, telling me that his agency is, in fact, finding some clues but that he can't tell *mamá* or me. I've had it with waiting. It's time to take action.

"Miss Salazar, did you hear me?" Cruz asks.

I snap my attention to him. "Hmm?"

"Don't do anything yourself. We're getting close to finding them." He's sitting across from me at our dining room table. *Mamá* is in *abuelo*'s office down the hall looking through his dive logs, and we can hear the rapid jargon of the voices on the frequency she's tuned into. "I need you to stay safe."

For the eightieth time of listening to this pointless talk, I just nod. "Got it."

"Ruby, I'm serious."

"I know. I've never doubted that you're taking this seriously."

"But you don't think I'm trying hard enough." Cruz's gaze is challenging.

Silence.

He sighs. "Look, if I wasn't sworn to secrecy, I'd tell you a couple details and you'd believe me. But please, just believe me anyway and don't put yourself in Marco's path."

Silencio, silence. Does he read my mind?

Cruz sighs again and stands. He pauses at the door, gives me a serious look, and then walks out the door without another word. I'll need to act now before he stops my plan.

"*Mamá*, I'm going on a walk!" I call down the hallway.

"Ok. See you soon!" Her voice carries down the hall louder than the staticky radio voices. Cruz backs out of the driveway. The coast is clear.

I have a theory. There's no way that sixty-something Marco is able to subdue my *abuelo and* the twins, even with a gun. So I'm thinking one of two things: either he paid off some corrupt fishermen to subdue each of them in various fishing boats, or he dumped them in the ocean. And when I watched him escort them onto *abuelo*'s boat with a gun, there had to have been at least one accomplice, probably two or more. If it was only Marco, the twins would've fought back.

My theory and plan have led me to do something completely Ruby. Here I am, at the tide pool with my waterproof backpack, acting natural. I'm sketching details on a crab, watching the clouds over the ocean, and writing Latin words to try to slow my racing heart. *Per ardua ad astra.* Through adversity to the stars. I wonder if Tanner's prayer from the storm long ago will apply now. I hope so. I'm sure that Marco has been watching and waiting for me to be convenient. The shark.

Five feet, four inches and alone, I know I'm easy bait. It's only a matter of time before the shark swims in for a bite.

I nod to a couple of tourists who walk past me and take about a thousand pictures of everything. They make their way up the coast, and I squint into the distance, wondering if my backstabbing family is out there and how much longer Marco will take to do his dirty business. Could he have paid off some cops to give him more time?

Another ten minutes creep by and I fill two more pages in my nature book. I'm feeling like bait on a hook. I just want the anticipation to be over. Finally I hear footsteps behind me.

"Ah, Ruby."

I turn and stand. "Marco." I swallow. It's now or never. This is my chance. I have to help my family. "You have my family. I have *Dos Hermanos.* We both have what the other wants."

For a millisecond Marco maintains his usual shrewd look, but he quickly covers his hunting shark face with a look of startled surprise. "You're saying you'd like to join forces? You help me, I help you, yes?"

I muster up my most defeated look, lower my eyes, and extend my right hand to Marco.

He doesn't shake it. "You're a few days late, Ruby."

I stare. Is he bluffing? He's too good at covering the truth for me to decipher what's really going on. "So you already found *Dos Hermanos*?" I'll act unfazed. "She's a beauty, isn't she?"

Marco narrows his eyes. "She is. The live footage your brothers took was crystal clear. I took footage to the nautical archaeology association first thing this morning to begin authentication." He might as well have twisted a fish hook out of my skin. The only thing that keeps me from throwing a toddler-sized tantrum is the fact that I don't believe Marco.

"If you found her, where's my *familia*? Shouldn't you bring them back to shore now?"

Marco gives his nasty smile and reaches into his chest pocket for a cigarette. "They helped me, Ruby. We found the shipwreck together. And this beauty is gonna have my name next to her in every museum and record." He props the cigarette between his lips and lights it.

I take a step back. "What do they get out of the deal?"

Marco fixes his creepy gaze on my face. "Your safety."

It's a crafty plan, but I think it's too cliché for Marco, even if *abuelo*'s dive log affirms it. I still don't believe him though. Like I told *mamá* and Cruz, I think Marco is more talk than show, even if he convinced *abuelo* he'd actually hurt me. But I'll give him an inch. "Thank you for the thoughtful gesture. So where are they now? Can I bring them some banana bread?"

Marco shrugs. "I'm not their bodyguard. After I made the initial claim with the historians, I assumed they'd get back to the shop. They didn't want to slow down their business too much."

I nod. "Well congratulations, Marco. I'm a sore loser when it comes to *Dos Hermanos*, but good job."

He gives me a tight-lipped smile and I nod in return. For a minute I study Marco and wonder how a heart gets so hard. Finally I say, "I thought you might hesitate to be seen in public."

"The public doesn't know I'm a celebrity yet. Once the wreck is confirmed and the press release goes out, you'll have to work through a crowd to talk to me."

"It'll change your quiet lifestyle." *El Enrique* really changed our home life. "But I meant I'm surprised you're in public right now because I think there's a warrant out for your arrest. The last you were seen was forcing my family onto *abuelo*'s boat with a gun. The cops have been looking for you and them."

For a second Marco looks nervous, but he puffs his cigarette and says, "Wasn't me. I don't know who reported that, but it ain't true."

"Oh, my mistake." I point my index finger like I've just remembered something. "I believe the last you were seen was right before Brett's plane sank, and you left us in peril."

"I was busy. Your brothers found something and I had to get to them fast."

"Glad you had a convenient excuse to ditch us."

Marco gives me a long look and just when I think he'll finally say something or shove a knife to my throat, he walks away.

I let him get a headstart, and then I follow. He's moving fast and doesn't even look back to check that I'm not following. The sun sits low on the horizon now, so I'm able to trail him. I purposefully wore black clothes and dark sneakers. Three blocks away in an old alley he climbs into the passenger seat of a pickup truck that I don't recognize. The license plate looks like it was dug out of a junkyard. I expect the truck to take off immediately, but when it doesn't, I get enough courage, or stupidity, to sneak up close. There's a guy in the driver's seat, but I don't recognize his shadowy figure through the open windows. It smells like vehicle exhaust, cigarette smoke, and dead fish. What goes on in this alley?

When I get just behind the tailgate, where I would totally get run over if they put it in reverse, I can pick up some of the conversation. "So what do we do now, Marco? The pigheaded brothers still won't say a word and the old guy is weaker every day. I told you I ain't gonna kill anybody, so unless you find your stupid shipwreck soon, I'm out." The voice sounds like a voice I've heard before, but I can't place it.

Marco grumbles. "I'll figure it out. Let's go to the marina. We'll bring 'em their rations. They'll dive for me tomorrow. If they keep refusing, I'll get the girl too."

It's time to make a split-second decision. Thanks to the dark and my flexibility, I gingerly step onto the bumper and climb into the bed of the truck, staying low. Looks like I'll be going with. I lay down as flat as I can between piles of stuff.

After a nearly carsick-inducing ride to the marina, the truck stops, but the engine stays running. I know I have about two seconds. In the same heartbeat that I hear the passenger door swing open, I vault out the back end and crouch down. I duck walk behind a nearby car and peer around the bumper, orienting myself in the marina's parking lot in the dark. Marco opens the tailgate and grabs an armload of stuff out of the bed. During my ride back there, I guessed there were a few small duffel bags and tackle boxes, but I tried to stay as still as possible. While he grabs his stuff and kills the truck engine, I slip off my shoes to make my feet quieter, and I run to the dock, hoping I don't step on a fish hook. Even in the dark, I recognize Marco's catamaran boat, but *abuelo*'s vessel is not in sight. I hear footsteps. In another heartbeat, they'll be close enough to see me in the dark. I have to board the boat.

A catamaran is like a big pontoon built for the ocean, and Marco's isn't huge, but it does have a cabin and a few other places I'll be able to hide in. In my bare feet, I carry my shoes and my bag with my journal, one of *abuelo*'s dive logs, a couple water bottles, and some other stuff I grabbed from the dive shop and Cruz's squad car yesterday. Hustling up the metal rungs of the rear ladder, I roll my body over the ledge and slink my way along the length of the boat. Without stopping, I set a Pringles can next to the steering wheel. Inside the chip container is a two-way radio with the Talk button taped down. Obviously it's only a matter of time until someone tries to eat the chips and discovers there are only a couple inches of chips on top of a radio, but hopefully I can get a little information before that happens.

Just as I hear footsteps up the ladder, I back my body into an underseat compartment along the side of the vessel. The fact that it's empty enough to accommodate me is enough to make me whisper a prayer of thanksgiving. I feel a rope and what is probably a tool box, but I'm surprised it isn't way more cramped in here. I seriously cannot believe I pulled this off so far. When Marco finds my sandy footprints on his boat deck, I'm toast.

In just a minute the boat engine rumbles to life and I feel us move out of the slip. In the dark compartment, I slowly unzip my backpack and feel around for my flashlight. I'm debating whether I should surprise Marco and his accomplice right away and try to subdue them, or wait until we're closer to wherever he's holding my family. I also have to consider the unnerving fact that my footprints will give me away eventually, but probably not until morning. The chip container will probably be the first giveaway. I whisper a prayer that we'll be to the destination before then. I need to formulate my plan. Maybe a couple plans with backup plans. A flowchart, even.

I place the earbud to the other two-way radio in my ear and turn off my flashlight. Even if it's spooky, I can think in the dark, and I need to save my battery power for when it'll matter most.

For a few minutes through the earbud I hear Marco and his accomplice banter back and forth about how foolish or intelligent Marco's plan is. The conversation, if I can call it that, leaves both guys huffy. I can see from their dialogue that trying to reason with them and talk them out of their plan will probably not work. Not that I'd be able to talk them off their crime high even if they were willing to listen, but I'll still cross that plan off my mental flowchart.

I hear the accomplice tell Marco he's going to get some sleep in the cabin. With only one guy to take on, I consider that it could be the perfect chance to gain the upper hand. If I subdue Marco, then when his crime partner gets up, it's more likely I'd be able to overpower him. But I imagine that if I tackle and overpower Marco, he will yell and wake up his friend, and then I'll have to act on adrenaline and a prayer to overpower them both. But then what? How would I convince them to cooperate and tell me where they're going?

I decide it might be better to wait until we're closer. I click on my dive computer, the super watch that does everything, and see that we're going east. Toward *El Enrique* and presumably *Dos Hermanos*. There are a lot of small islands east of Florida. My family could be on one of them.

I let my watch go dim and readjust my body. I've been sitting in a ball, with my knees by my chin, but I discover that I can let my legs stretch out a tiny bit. I put my sneakers back on so I'm ready for the wild day. I let my head rest on the rope. The rumble of the engine is calming, so I let out a sigh and try to force my heart rate to slow down. I should save my energy for what's to come.

It turns out that having your family abducted is a great motivator to pray, as evidenced by the fact that I'm still on my praying streak. The only problem I see with this is that God can tell that I'm turning to Him in distress, but He probably wants to know why I've basically ignored Him during times of peace. *Okay, I get it. Lo siento, I'm sorry. I really need to prioritize You. I promise I'll try. Starting now.*

I know, I know, I fumble through prayers. Tanner was good at praying. I wonder if Cruz is better at praying than I am. If he is, and if we can have any form of friendship after this is all over, maybe he can help me with the prayer thing.

My clumsy prayer goes on for a few minutes, but it's hard to focus in the dark. I can't let myself fall asleep. In my head, I sing the lyrics of "Country Roads" and I recite the safe combination. I picture *abuelo*'s dive log entries and try to pick up on any clues. I fight back a yawn, but the exhaustion is winning.

"Are these your chips?" Marco's voice in my earbud startles me. I've been asleep. For how long?

"Not mine."

"Huh. Guess I'll have some."

"Not a heart healthy breakfast, but that's never been your priority." The accomplice's voice sounds weirdly familiar, but I don't know from where.

I push myself up to my curled sitting position, knowing that the time is drawing near. From my backpack, I retrieve a fishing net and unroll it. I unbuckle my belt and double check that my pepper spray is in the front pocket of my shorts.

God, what should I do? If I hurt these old guys too badly, I'll go to prison. There's no way I can afford a decent lawyer. But I can't let them hurt me either. Please let this go well.

The rustling sound of chips is so loud I turn down the volume on my earbud. Here we go.

The next minute feels incredibly long. I know what's coming, but I have to wait until the exact moment it happens to act. I adjust my dive headlamp at the top of my forehead and check that my dive mask is firmly over my face. I hear the chip container being jostled around, some swearing when my two-way radio is found, and aggressive footsteps all around the deck of the boat. My sandy footprints must not be the only mess on the deck floor, because it takes longer than I anticipate for someone to approach my cubby.

I click the headlamp on and position my feet and knees so I'm ready to spring out. When the cubby door whips open, I aim the dive light right into the eyeballs of Marco's accomplice. His eyes instinctively squeeze shut at the bright light, so I jump out and tackle him with the fishing net. Fishing nets are the whole reason divers carry knives. Getting tangled in a net is an impossible mess. The guy howls and thrashes back, but I've got him down, his shoulder blades pinned to the deck. He's pushing and punching fast, so I grab the pepper spray from my pocket and aim it at his face. It makes contact with his eyes, and he howls again, partially sitting up and grabbing his face with both hands. While his hands are at his face and his shoulder blades are off the ground, I yank the belt off my waist and wrap it around his elbows and torso. I pull the belt tight and jam my knee into his back. Holding the belt taut with my left hand, I pierce a hole in the right spot with my dive knife, and fasten the belt. Knowing I need to do something about his thrashing legs, I lean over his body and reach for the rope that made a decently comfy pillow. By sitting on his knees, I manage to tie a knot at his ankles.

That's when a hand clamps down on the back of my neck and a piece of cold metal smacks my head. This is it. I'm done. I swallow, my pulse throbbing in my head. My last few heartbeats. *God, I just want to help my family.*

"Ruby, put your hands on your head." Slowly, I raise my hands, and then without warning I vehemently ram my elbow behind me, knocking him in the diaphragm. I hear the wind go out of his lungs and I twist my body around to face him. I flail my hands toward him, trying to grab his wrists, but he lifts the gun with surprising steadiness. I have a half-second or I'm toast. And since I'm as good as done anyway, I take the chance. I lean over and drive my shoulder into his chest. Marco stumbles backward. I take a step back and ram again, this time making him fall down.

He curses, struggling to point the gun at me again. Why isn't he shooting? Ah. Of course. He still needs me to get to *Dos Hermanos*.

Just like when the twins and I used to wrestle, I get behind Marco, yank his elbows into a full Nelson, and slam his chest into the ground. The gun clatters to the deck of the catamaran. Pinning him down with my fists and my left knee jammed into his back, I stretch my right leg out as far as I can, straining to reach the gun with my toe. If I get the gun, it'll give me the upper hand. They don't need to know I've never shot a gun before. I keep pressing Marco's chest down and stretch my leg...a little more...almost...ugh! To reach the gun, I'd have to leave Marco. At least it's out of his hand. For now.

Disgusted, I hook my toe onto my backpack strap and drag the bag to me. The move is a gamble. He pushes his torso up and heaves his body and I fall to the side, hitting my shoulder on the deck, but my knee and knuckles dig deeper into his back, forcing him back down. He vigorously pushes up again, like a bucking bull, and I lose my hold. My shoulder crashes into the deck again and I belly flop. Marco makes an angry huff as he comes up on his knees, turns, and reaches out to grab me. I roll out of his reach and shove my backpack, which slides under the steering wheel. So much for using the handcuffs I snagged from Cruz's squad car.

Marco stands up and curses again, lunging for me. I bob and weave like a boxer, luring him toward the back of the boat. The next time he lunges, I duck, then kick his knees, making him fall onto the corner rail of the boat. He desperately flails his upper body, trying to grab anything to keep him in the boat, but momentum and gravity work against him and he falls like a rock into the water. I gape. I think I just bypassed a step in the flowchart.

Marco comes up spluttering, "Please don't leave me."

"I'm not as heartless as you. And you have information I need." I grab the life ring from the hook on the opposite wall, toss it about ten feet behind him, and then tie the rope around a rail on the back of the boat with a bowline knot. "I'll tow you."

I run to the steering wheel and slam the accelerator forward, thankful that the motor is still on and far enough from where Marco landed to not shred him to pieces. I look behind me and see Marco scramble to grab the life ring. I watch just long enough to make sure he's secure. I don't want to do too much damage to the old guy, but obviously he isn't afraid to play dirty, so I need to keep him at a safe distance.

I return my attention to the steering console and what lies ahead of the boat. Marco's GPS is directing me to a programmed coordinate. ETA is in eight minutes. From the screen, it looks like a dot of an island. Hopefully where my brothers and *abuelo* are. I peek at the accomplice who looks like he's trying to fish something out of his jeans pocket. Probably a lighter or pocket knife. I walk over and give him another small dose of pepper spray. Guilt gnaws at me for doing it, but there are a lot of lives at stake right now, and the mace will only hurt, not injure. The guy swears and rubs his eyes vigorously, so I can't get a good look at his face to remember where I might know him from. I reach into his pocket and confiscate his pocket knife, then run back to the steering console.

As the catamaran cuts through the blue waves, I formulate the next step of my flowchart plan in my mind. When we approach the island, I'll slow the boat, drag in Marco, and handcuff him. Then I'll rescue my family, and we'll go back to Florida and turn in Marco and his sidekick. I'll deal with my family and my treasure on a different day.

A speck of tan and green becomes visible, and I begin seeing an expanse of coral under the catamaran. I find the handcuffs in my backpack and stow them in my pocket. When the depth finder says we're at about ten feet deep, I pull back the accelerator all the way. I grab a dive knife and walk to the back of the boat. Marco looks a little waterlogged, but no worse for the wear, so I decide to act quickly before he can outthink my plan. I reel in the life ring rope, hand over hand, and when he gets within two feet of the boat I say, "Don't fight and this'll be easy."

"Ruby, you don't know who you're dealing with. You're about to find that you're in over your head."

I know he's desperate to scare me, which doesn't scare me, but he does get my attention. "Speak, old man."

"Your boyfriend, the cop, he's working with me too. He gave me your coordinates."

I don't even blink. "And?"

"Your *abuelo* called me on our drive over this morning. Your family offered to pay me for the coordinates." He fakes remorse, like it hurts him to tell me this. Then he smirks and says, "But the price they offered me is too good to pass up."

Whatever. I'll play along. "How much did you pay Officer Cruz for them?"

Marco gives me his evil shark smile. "Oh he didn't sell them to me. It's a favor. We help each other out, you see. Always good to have a few dirty cops on your side."

He's just trying to distract me, and I think I can use this to my advantage. I paste a stunned expression on my face. "Officer Cruz is a dirty cop? And you have the coordinates? You promise? You're not lying?" I fix a cold stare into his dark eyes and wedge the toes of my shoes under the bottom rung of the rail.

"Never," he says.

I hold back a snort. With my left hand holding the cuffs in my back shorts pocket, I extend my right hand toward him. "Promise." I brace myself, knowing that he plans to yank me into the water. The instant our hands almost touch, I flick mine to the side, then lunge for his wrist. He jerks back, but I'm ready and I have a firm hold. I let him pull for a couple seconds, and when he lets up the slightest, I pull with everything I've got. Bracing against the rails, I have leverage, but he has gravity to his advantage. I can't get him out of the water, but I can tell he's tiring. I let him pull again, and when he lets up, I awkwardly clip a handcuff to his wrist in record time. My hand and forearm muscles are on fire, but if I let go now all is lost. I dig my nails into his wrist and secure the other handcuff to the handrail.

Marco hollers like an angry dog, calling me names I won't repeat here. I consider giving him a squirt of pepper spray, but since it probably won't make him be quiet, I decide to save the rest of my pepper spray for an attack. I glance behind me and make sure that his accomplice is still cooperating inside my fishing net. For now he's not fighting. It's no question that the clock is ticking before he and Marco get the upper hand again, so I grab the gun off the deck and hurry back to the steering console.

The path toward Marco's GPS coordinate says we'll arrive at our destination in one minute. Based on what I overheard, I think my family is floating off the coast of this utopian island, so I put the motor at trolling speed and turn the boat parallel to the coast. I keep a vigilant watch on both bad guys, holding the gun as if I know what to do with it, and do a constant sweep of the area with my eyes. For the first four minutes I don't see anything unusual. Then, a flash. It's brief, barely enough to catch my attention. It's maybe sixty feet ahead of me, and as we close in, I see the sun glinting off dive masks. My stomach clenches tight at the approaching sight of people. My *familia*. A dozen thoughts fill my mind. How glad I am to see them alive. How hurt I am about *El Enrique* and *Dos Hermanos*. How hungry and exhausted they must be...and no doubt dehydrated and sunburnt to a crisp. Have any sharks bothered them? Will they have energy to climb into the boat?

I'm close enough now to make out their profiles, and they barely look up. "*Abuelo*!" I shout. "August, Axel, I'm here for you!"

At the sound of my voice, they numbly glance my way. Marco and the accomplice grumble to each other.

I stop the boat about five feet away and lower the anchor. I lean over the boat, almost close enough to touch them.

"Ruby?" August murmurs through cracked lips. Oh, he is badly dehydrated.

"Stay with me, August. All of you. I'll bring you water." I run to the steering console and grab my backpack. On my way to the edge of the catamaran, I hop over the accomplice and tell him not to try anything. I unscrew the top off a water bottle and step down the ladder. "Hang on, guys. I'm here. Drink." It looks like they're all tied together with a piece of sailing rope wrapped around their BCDs. They're pretty out of it, so I stretch out into the water. I'm vulnerable right now, so I check over my shoulder again. The bad guys aren't making progress. Still, I need to hurry. I grab Axel's shoulder and pull him toward me, and since they're all tied together, they all drift closer. In a daze, the twins help spin the group so *abuelo* comes closest to me. I thrust the water bottle in front of *abuelo*'s mouth and he takes a sip. "*Abuelo, debes beber más,* you gotta drink more." He does. Not enough to rehydrate, but hopefully enough to keep him alive. When he shakes his head, I hold the bottle in front of Axel, then August.

The twins perk up almost immediately after drinking some water, and Axel hauls himself to the boat ladder. "Untie us so we can get in," he says, his voice hoarse. I lean over his shoulder and fumble with the wet rope. I look over my shoulder again, paranoid that Marco and the accomplice are a foot behind me, ready to strike. They're grouching at each other, but Marco is still handcuffed to the boat railing, flopped out on the boat's float. The accomplice isn't even rolling around on the deck.

With the paradise blue sky, summer sun, and ocean breeze, the criminals are out of place. Seeing that they're still under control, I take a shaky breath and flex my fingers. Finally I manage to untie Axel and he climbs aboard. His legs are shaking, so I instruct him to sit down and eat a protein bar. I try not to think of him as the criminal who tied up Len.

He stares at me, eyes dull from dehydration, and I realize I have to unwrap the protein bar for him. I hold the bar to his mouth and as if in a trance, he takes a bite. "Can you hold it?"

Unsure of how long they've been immersed in water, I'm scared to take off his diving glove. What if I find an infected fungus farm on his skin? I grab his hand and wrap his fingers around the protein bar. "Eat. I'll get August and *abuelo*."

August is next closest to the boat, but I tell him to help me get *abuelo* out. I've never thought of *abuelo* as old, but I'm sure this experience has aged him. August waits while I lean over and wrestle with the next knot. It feels like two minutes of fumbling before I get it. I grab *abuelo*'s BCD and tow him toward me. August hooks his elbow around the side of the ladder and braces his body against the boat so *abuelo* can lean on him. Between my tugging on *abuelo*'s BCD and August's torso supporting *abuelo*, my hero heaves himself up the ladder and into the boat. When he's standing, I come alongside him and wrap my right arm around his waist and walk with him to the bench by Axel.

Axel's bar is nearly gone and his eyes look a bit more alive. *Abuelo* sits next to him and I hold the water bottle to his mouth again. He takes a few sips and then a hearty swallow of water. I take a banana from my backpack and peel it for him. I have a few more protein bars, but *abuelo* hates them. Like I did for Axel, I wrap his hand around the banana and tell him to eat. It seems to take a minute for my instruction to process through his dehydrated stupor, so I wait until he takes a couple bites of banana. Satisfied, I return to August.

He's standing on the second rung of the ladder and staggers up the last few rungs. I hold his shoulder to steady him. He sits on the deck floor by *abuelo*'s feet and gives me a blank look. I take another protein bar from my bag, unwrap it, and hand it to August. "*Come*, eat." I anxiously glance toward the guy in the fishing net and Marco again and look back to the men in my family, the guys I've looked up to along with my *papá* for as long as I can remember. For now I swallow the sting of betrayal.

My family begins to regain some strength, so I take a round to check on the criminals. I'm still not convinced that Marco and his reluctant accomplice did all this themselves. The twins are young and strong, and nobody messes with *abuelo*. There must be a third, and maybe fourth, person on their team. Right now I think my best course of action is to get back to the marina, hand over the criminals to Officer Cruz, and take my family to the hospital. I haul up the anchor, make sure everyone is somewhere reasonably safe, and plug in the marina's name to the GPS at the steering console.

It says it's a two hour cruise. Plenty of time for the mace to wear off and the criminals to get the upper hand. What to do next? If only I had a way to keep the accomplice dangling on the outside of the catamaran too. I take a short break from driving to better secure the accomplice. He's just feisty enough that I don't trust the leather belt around his shoulders and fishing net. I retrieve the wet rope that tied my family together, and he cusses at me. "You already have me in a net. Now what?" He flexes against the belt, confirming that an extra rope is a good idea. I wrap a few loops around his wrists, right over top of the fishing net. When his wrists are bound tight, I tie the tail to the railing of the boat next to where he's been laying. He grumbles some more.

"What's your name?"

He only narrows his eyes at me.

Now that I can see his face, I know I've seen him before. Maybe only once or twice, but somewhere. I shake my head. I'll let the cops figure out who this thug is.

Feeling better about the criminals, I check on my family since we're stopped anyway. I hand them each a bottle of electrolyte drink. "I'm taking you to the hospital. Hang tight." They nod, slumping like they just swam the Panama Canal. "Sip on these." I loosen the caps for them and return to the steering console.

One hour and twenty minutes to go. The criminals are under control, my family will be okay, and the sky is blue, but the fuel gauge is bugging me. Why would Marco set off on a long round trip without a full tank? And where's his spare fuel can? The gauge is very low, and when the Low Fuel alert flashes on the dashboard, we're still thirty minutes from the marina. I decide I need to call Officer Cruz. I was going to call him anyway, but I was looking forward to it being a victory call from the marina, not a desperate plea for help when we're fourteen knots away from the marina. But still, at least I've got good news. And I did more in a few hours than the cops did in a week. Reg should totally thank me. Ha. No way would his haughty brain stoop to a level of showing appreciation.

The fumes of fuel carry us another ten or fifteen minutes. I hear the motor putter out of fuel and I check all the usual places for a spare can. Under all the compartments, in the built-in toolbox. Nothing. Idiot. Who travels without spare fuel? "Marco, where's your extra fuel?"

"In the bed of Roger's truck," he growls. Okay, then. I pull my phone out of my backpack. Thankfully the new phone battery holds a charge well and I still have plenty of power. I dial Officer Cruz.

"Go ahead, Miss Salazar." What a business-like way to greet me.

Again humiliated that I actually thought he might have been interested in me, I skip any conversation and get right to the punch line. "Officer Cruz. I have Marco and an accomplice subdued. *Abuelo* and the twins are with me too and are eating and drinking, but they should probably see a doctor."

"Where are you?" *Demanding, much.* "If you just said what I think you just said, this is serious, Miss Salazar."

"Don't let Reg rub off on you. I'm nine and a half knots from the marina. Can you meet me?"

"At the marina?"

"No, right where I am. Nine and half knots from the marina." I read our GPS coordinates to him. "Marco's catamaran is out of fuel."

"Are you safe?"

"Sure am! Wait 'til you see how I got the criminals under control." I smile smugly.

"You disobeyed law enforcement. This is serious. Don't do anything until we arrive. I'll call dispatch right now."

"You're welcome."

"I'm not thanking you."

"Why not? Because I embarrassed you and Reg?"

"Playing vigilante is no game. You could get yourself and your family killed. Or you'll mess up one tiny detail and Marco's lawyer will shred you. You could wind up in prison and he'll get off scot-free."

Another failure.

Still though, what judge would let Marco win? "Nooo," I drawl, my tone showing how unlikely that seems. "I'm just helping you along."

"Don't do anything else. Wait." He sounds furious with me. Just great. I need the cops on my side.

While I wait, I check on my family. August greets me. "You're something, Ruby. Knocking down Marco and his guys. How'd you do it?"

"Did you say guys, plural?"

August hooks his thumb toward the far railing. "He's got Roger here, and at least two others."

"Oh no." So there are definitely more out there. And wait...Roger? As in Len's employee, Roger?

August raises his eyebrows.

"No wonder Marco hasn't been fighting me this whole time. He's probably got his phone and called for his own backup!" I run to Marco who sports his sly smile, even while I'm holding his gun. Not a good sign.

"You phoned a friend?" I try to act nonchalant, but my stomach does a divebomb.

Marco just smiles in return. Hopefully the cops will be quicker than his guys. How long ago would he have called them? I should've called the cops as soon as we got to my family. *You should've let law enforcement handle it.* That's what the sheriff will say. Oh, he's gonna flip out. And what will *mamá* say?

I hear something approaching and I squint in its direction. Does law enforcement use jet skis? I glance at Marco. He perks up at the sound and looks at me. "They're right on time."

My grip on the gun tightens, and I try to lift my hand toward Marco, but it's shaking. Come on, Cruz, hurry. I'd even take help from Reg right now.

Two jet skis race to the catamaran. The guys driving them look way younger and even meaner than Marco. One of the guys addresses Marco. "You want us to get the girl?"

I muster up all the fierceness and grit that my family has complained about my whole life and I force myself to point Marco's gun at his accomplices.

Marco's face curls into a snarl. "Get Roger and me. Her cop boyfriend is on the way. Might not be time to get her now."

I shudder.

The other guy jumps on the deck of the catamaran and aims a gun at *abuelo* but stares at me. "You try anything and the old man gets shot." Expertly pointing the gun at *abuelo*, the other guy rushes at me, elbows me in the face, and yanks Marco's gun out of my hand. So much for that.

I grab my pounding face. *Dear God, what did I do now?* The first guy props himself up by Marco and uses some heavy duty bolt cutter with handles almost as long as my arms. Marco is no longer subdued. My gut clenches. Now bolt cutter guy and Marco both have guns. The first guy, whose gun is still aimed at *abuelo*, raises his eyebrows at me in a challenging way. Bolt cutter guy runs to the accomplice, Roger, and slices a knife through the net, then through the ropes and belt. More guns than I care to count are aimed at me and my family. I sigh. In a moment, all four pile onto the jet skis. I glare at Roger. Len doesn't work with evil people. And I still hate jet skis, or rather the heartless criminals that use them to hurt the innocent. They tear off into the distance, and I can only whisper a prayer that the cops will get them. The cops!

I dial Cruz again. "If you see two jet skis with four guys, arrest them."

Officer Cruz groans. "I'll let dispatch know. Which direction are they traveling?"

"Southwest. They're all armed."

"Ten-four. Dispatch will probably send out a chopper to look for them. ETA to you is six minutes."

12

— · —

R eg's crew and Officer Cruz are towing us back to the marina where the cops can take the twins to the hospital and they'll send *abuelo* in an ambulance, "because of his age." Understandably he took the mistreatment a little harder than the twins. It's a tense ride because Marco is back on the loose and Officer Cruz has every reason to be furious at me. I almost don't want to get back to the marina, but in twenty minutes we're there and I have to face the inevitable.

The twins are escorted to a couple police SUVs for the short ride to the hospital. I grimace at the thought of their skin under their wetsuits. Assuming they've been immersed for more than ten or twelve hours, they've probably got infected sores all over. Coupled with malnourishment and bad sunburn on their faces, they need some serious TLC and whatever else the doctors can do.

A team of EMTs has *abuelo* lay on a stretcher and a slew of questions begins. Officer Cruz and Reg listen intently. *Mamá* waits by my car, fuming, which can be worse than being disappointed. Why? Because *mamá* is too stoic to get disappointed, but she absolutely gets mad.

I stand by *abuelo*'s stretcher for support. Giving and getting support, that is. As the EMTs wheel him to the ambulance, *abuelo* locks eyes with me. He isn't mad or disappointed, I can tell. "Come visit me at the hospital." He reaches out and gives my hand a weak squeeze.

He wants me safe, and he knows Marco won't come to the hospital to nab me. His eyes say all of that. "*Gracias* for getting us." I squeeze back until his hand slips out of mine as the EMTs slide him inside.

"*Te quiero*," I tell him, which is "I love you" in Latin and Spanish. It's easy to say that to *abuelo*.

He whispers, "You too."

The ambulance doors click shut and my *mamá* and Officer Cruz look ready to pounce on me. I should've ridden with *abuelo*.

Mamá pulls me close. "This heart can't handle many more close calls."

"At least the boys are safe."

"For now. What happens when they're released from the hospital? Marco wants you all dead."

"*Deus, salva nos.*" It comes out as little more than a whisper.

Officer Cruz tilts his head, then arches his eyebrows at *mamá*. "Latin?" he asks.

Mamá nods. "When she slows down enough to make good decisions, she's actually very smart." She squints her eyes at me.

"God, save us?" Officer Cruz asks, and I nod.

Mamá gives a half-hearted smile. "Let's go to the hospital. I have the car keys."

Cruz holds up a hand. "It's definitely safer if I bring you."

"Any news on the criminals?" I ask, pointing to Cruz's radio.

"They haven't found them yet," he says tersely. "Lock your car and I'll drive you to the hospital." Cruz walks toward his squad car. I wonder if Marco previously saw him in a squad car and figured out Cruz is a cop? Unless...Marco's venomous words that Cruz is a dirty cop replay in my mind. No. Officer Cruz is not a dirty cop. Is he? Would he violate his oath of honor to make money under the table? Could Len be feeding him information, and that's how those two know each other so well? And with Roger working for Len? I swallow hard and force my legs to walk toward Officer Cruz's SUV.

I don't want to sit in the front by Officer Cruz or in the back where criminals sit. *Mamá* senses my discomfort and says she'll sit in the back with me. When we pull up at the front entrance of the emergency department, Officer Cruzs opens *mamá*'s door. She steps toward the entrance. I scoot out and Cruz holds up a hand. Here it comes.

"You have guts, I'll give you that. But Reg's crew was this close" – he holds his fingers about an inch apart –"to putting an end to the madness. Your *familia* would still be getting admitted now and the criminals would be detained. You stuck your nose where it didn't belong and those four criminals remain at large. And now they're mad as hornets." He shakes his head. "Your safety is definitely at risk now." His warning feels as heavy as a black cloud.

My shoulders slump. Two hours ago I thought I was the heroine. Instead I messed up everything. I don't even open my mouth to apologize. What good would it do? I just want to see *abuelo*. I pull my backpack out of the squad car and follow *mamá*, who walks through the first set of automatic doors.

"One more thing," Cruz's voice, rumbling like thunder, makes me stop. "Now that Marco knows who I am, I can't effectively help you off duty anymore. You might need to find another cop friend."

That stings. But I'll process this end of friendship later, because something bigger is looming. I lock my eyes on his. "Are you a dirty cop?" I demand.

Officer Cruz looks like I snapped him with a wet towel. "Of course not. I'm offended you have to ask."

"Then how do you know that Marco knows you're a cop?"

Shock flashes over Cruz's face and I wonder. He recovers and matter-of-factly states, "Legally I can't tell you. But it didn't take him long to recognize me, remember seeing me with you, and figure it out." He pauses. "What made you think I might be a dirty cop?" His eyes showcase built up anger, like a thundercloud ready to pour.

"Something Marco said." I hook my backpack on my shoulder and walk toward the hospital. If Marco dragged Len into his spell of working with dirty cops and Cruz is part of this whole thing, I might just disappear and start a new life in Bermuda under a fake name.

Cruz steps in front of me. I stop. He hands me a slip of paper, about the size of a business card. I look at it. A voucher for food from the hospital cafeteria. "I'll check on you as soon as I can."

"I'm sorry," I blurt. Is it really that stupid to entertain the possibility that Cruz is a dirty cop and he and Marco are using Len to get information from me? I didn't mean anything personal by it.

"I know. I meant everything I said. That you made rash, foolish decisions. That you completely messed up the investigation. But I also believe what you said. *Deus, salva nos.* And it's definitely going to take God to fix this mess."

The mess that I made. I'll for sure need a new cop friend. I know he's right, but still, ouch.

In the waiting room, *mamá* is restless. She paces back and forth, back and forth, trying to call *papá* every five minutes. She tries his co-workers. Four of them. But they're welding underwater, so how could they answer their phones that are up on the rig? Finally she connects with the foreman of the company contracting *papá* and asks that he relay a message. "Please tell him that my *papá* and the twins were abducted. Our daughter found them and they'll be ok after a few days in the hospital. The criminals are still at large."

A pause. "No, this isn't a joke. I've been trying to reach him for days." Pause. "Okay. Thank you."

She turns to me. "Finally. Now let's find a nurse." She spins and heads down the hallway like she works here. Why is everyone so surprised that I'm impulsive? Like mother, like daughter. Soon a nurse is assuring *mamá* that as soon as the guys are settled in rooms, we'll be able to visit.

"You hungry?" I ask as she looks out the window.

"No. Go ahead. I need to call some customers." As usual. At least she's here.

I follow signs to the cafeteria.

Two mornings later I'm ready to take action again. "*Mamá*, I'm going over to The Dive Shop to talk to Len." The doctor just finished a morning round and assured us that probably one more day for the twins and two more for *abuelo* will be enough for us all to be on our merry way. Then it's back to being hunted.

"Why?" she asks. Axel eyes me. I smile at him and step into the hall, and *mamá* follows.

"To see if he's got any leads. He's been eavesdropping, hoping to hear something helpful." While walking, I look out the hallway window from the third floor. A car is pulling under the awning. "Looks like the Uber driver is here."

Mamá crinkles her eyebrows and keeps walking with me. "Maybe I should come with you."

"I don't know. I always hear that patients need an advocate at the hospital. I shouldn't be gone long, and Marco won't look for me in an Uber." We're silent on the elevator ride down to the first floor. The elevator dings and lets us out near the concierge. We walk to the huge sliding doors and step into the heat.

Mamá looks skeptically at me, then considers the Uber driver. Looks like a young guy trying to pay off college. Seems harmless. *Mamá* isn't convinced. "I think you should call Officer Cruz first."

Like he wants to hear from me. "I'll call him when I learn something juicy."

She steps to the driver window and motions for the driver to roll down the window. "May I see your license?"

I resist a face palm, mainly because I realize how smart she is to check up on this guy. What if Marco sent one of his minions to be my Uber driver? When my driver passes *mamá*'s background check, I give her a little hug and climb into the passenger seat. *Mamá* stops me from closing the door.

"Hang on. Give me your phone a sec."

Gotta love being treated like a fourteen-year-old. I hand her my phone and wait while she no doubt sends Cruz's number to her own phone. This irritates me because it could interfere with my plans, but in keeping up my casual facade, I only smile and say, "Good idea."

She closes the door and heads back through the hospital doors. I ask the Uber driver to take me to The Dive Shop. "Nice day for a tour," he says. "Were you here for the storm we had last week?"

"Yeah, I'm glad it wasn't any worse."

He nods and makes more small talk while we traverse town toward The Dive Shop. What would Tanner do if he were here now? Would we have found *Dos Hermanos* already? Would he play vigilante with me? Or would he be sticking a tracking device to my backpack and following me, in constant communication with law enforcement? What I would give to talk to him again. I sigh and open the bank app so I can pay my driver.

We pull into the parking lot and I transfer the money to my driver. We thank each other and I ask him to wait in the parking lot until I'm in the store. He looks surprised but says he can do that. He starts scrolling on his phone, oblivious that I want him to be attentive to our surroundings. I tell him it's pretty basic manners, that you never know where trouble lies, and I really need him watching, just in case he has to call for help. He looks a little weirded out, so I smile and thank him again.

From the door I look back and wave, and he quickly backs his car out of the lot, probably afraid that one more minute would land him in the center of a crime scene after my "you never know where trouble lies" pep talk. From behind the counter, I hear Len call, "I'll be right with you. Check out the clearance rack for a minute while you wait."

"Hi Len, it's Ruby!"

Len's face pops up from behind the counter and smiles at me. "Oh, hey Ruby! Make yourself at home for a minute."

I study the framed photos and certificates on the wall with posters about the dive tours he offers. My eyes land on a picture of Tanner and me, his arm around my shoulders and our smiles as bright as the sun. We'd just gotten out of the water, our wetsuits dripping and my hair a mess. I feel a lump in my throat. That's the last picture of him.

Len tentatively walks up. A sudden sob lurches out of my throat. "I miss him." Len puts a comforting hand on my shoulder blade and nods. I wipe my eyes. "Sorry. That's not why I came today."

"I understand." Len swallows hard and squeezes my shoulder. "We'll see him again."

I nod and sniff. Len leads the way to the counter and hands me a tissue.

I swallow. "What are you doing today?"

Len points behind the counter. "I just got a huge order that needs to be inventoried, and Roger called in sick."

"Roger?"

"Yeah, a newer employee. Older guy, but he knows diving gear and boats. In a few more months, he might be able to take out tours. For now, he's a big help in the store."

I shake my head fiercely back and forth.

"What?"

"What's Roger look like?"

Len bobs his shoulders up and down. "About so tall," he holds his hand a few inches above his head. "Grayish hair. Why? You know him?"

"If it's the Roger I tied up on Marco's catamaran, he's a criminal. At large."

Len closes his eyes and his shoulders drop. He swallows hard. "No. Didn't see that coming."

"I gotta act quickly. Are you going out on the water today?"

"My tour for this afternoon canceled on me. Tourists, their son got sick. They'll try again in two days before they fly home."

"Does that mean you have some free time?"

"Does that mean you'll help me organize this order and work for me on Labor Day in exchange?"

"Gladly."

For an hour and a half, Len and I work to inventory the new gear and arrange it on the shelves. The work is familiar and peaceful. It's good to let my heart slow down and give my mind time to muse over what's been happening. When we fold up the last of the boxes and walk them to the recycling bin outside, Len asks, "So what do I do about Roger?"

"I heard the cops are on their tail. Four of them. Law enforcement might take care of Roger for you."

"I hope so." He sighs, then looks at me. "Where do you want to dive today? We won't get sunk and abandoned, will we?"

I let out a dry, "Ha, ha," and pull out *abuelo*'s dive log from my bag. I flip to the page and read Len the coordinates.

He nods, his tone teasing as he says, "Do I get to know what might be there?"

"You already know."

He raises his eyebrows high and nods. "Enough said. You got your gear?"

"It's at Ruby Sunset, and I just need to fill up my air."

"Let's grab it and be on our way." His stride reminds me of Tanner, and I love the familiarity.

It takes less than ten minutes at Ruby Sunset, during which Len paces the inside perimeter and stands guard. We load my gear in his pickup and drive to the marina. Len does a standard pre-cruise check while I set my gear in the back of the boat.

During the two hour cruise to *abuelo*'s claim of finding the biggest, most beautiful wreck that's captivated me for forever, I watch the water ahead, the wake behind, and the careless clouds drifting through the sky. The water, wake, and clouds don't have a care in the world. We spot a small pod of dolphins, and they swim parallel to us for a couple knots before turning. I've always wanted to have one of those experiences where a dolphin and a diver help each other. I'd cut a rope from its fluke and a few days later it'd chase off a shark that's circling me. Something like that. I love Baby, but nothing too dangerous happens at the aquarium for her to save my life.

Finally Len idles down the engine and says, "Here we are." If life wasn't such a hamster wheel of busyness, I'd love to learn to navigate without GPS. But in time crunches like Marco is imposing, I'm thankful for GPS.

"Your first time here?" Len asks with trepidation in his voice as I step into my wetsuit.

"Tanner and I copied the coordinates when the sonar lit up. I haven't dived here. According to *abuelo*'s dive log, this is it."

Len nods. "You mean *Dos Hermanos* is right under us?"

"According to the log." My voice is flat. I'm completely deflated. This isn't how it was supposed to go.

Len is acutely aware. He gives me a knowing look. "Nobody deserves it more than you."

"And Tanner," I add.

Len swallows hard. "What's your plan?" All about safety, just like Tanner. With no way to communicate with him once I go down, we have to agree on a dive plan. If I don't surface when I'm supposed to, he'll assume I'm in trouble.

"Let's say thirty minutes down there. Looks like a depth of ninety-two feet. To be safe, I'll deco for five minutes every fifteen feet up. Thirty minutes to get back up. Does an hour from now sound good?"

Len nods and sets a timer on his watch. "Ruby, you said your *abuelo* dove here already. Are you okay?"

I shake my head. "I feel more lost than after Tanner died. Like my own *abuelo* is a treasonist." I clench my fist. "I just, I just want to see *Dos Hermanos* before Marco does anything else."

Len nods and prays for the dive and the Marco situation. I muster a smile and he double checks my gear. All about safety. I flip backward over the side of the boat, grab onto the anchor line, and let gravity and the weights on my BCD pull me down. The clear blue fades to a navy-green that grows thicker the deeper I go. I take slow breaths from my regulator, confusion gnawing at me. On one hand, I'm thrilled that Tanner's and my research was correct. Obviously I would've rather found it with him. I feel conned that *abuelo* dove here first. Why couldn't he let me share the fun? I'm dying to see *Dos Hermanos*, but I'm dreading seeing her since Tanner and I weren't the first to find her. It's dark now, so I turn on my light. This deep I feel weightless, and soon my fins touch sand. Here I am. Still holding onto the anchor line, I slowly turn around, expecting to see the glorious wreck *abuelo* logged. All I see is dark water. Huh?

I keep rotating, blinking and squinting for a better look into the water. I clip a secondary safety line to the anchor line and start swimming a few feet off the bottom. Not seeing a wall of any sort, I check my dive computer. Yup, the coordinates are consistent with *abuelo*'s dive log entry. Did he copy them wrong? But there must be something down here because Tanner and I wrote it down when the boat's sonar alerted us. Something large enough to send back an ultrasonic wave. There has to be something, but where? And what?

I swim a wide circle, moving my headlamp back and forth like a hammerhead shark. Finally I see something, about two body lengths to my left. Swimming over to the odd shape, my pulse quickens. *Steady breaths.* Is this a clue?

I stare for a minute before I confirm what I'm looking at. Two cannons. One is on its side and the other is upside down, partially buried in the sand. A few cannon balls are scattered nearby. Cannons, okay. Where's the ship? I make sure my safety line is untangled and I continue a thorough search. Nothing but sand, sand, and more sand. There's no shipwreck here. I check my watch and see I've only been down fifteen minutes. I hadn't expected to see so little. I spend the next five minutes searching next to the cannons. If the whole ship were buried, *abuelo* couldn't have seen what he recorded, but maybe I'll find a clue as to where the rest of it lies. But five more minutes of searching reveals nothing.

Nothing, unless I'm blind as a bat. Absolutely nothing but two cannons and seven cannonballs. Huh. With ten minutes to spare, I begin my ascent, watching my depth closely so I stop every fifteen feet, just to be on the safe side. Since I wasn't down the full half-hour, I could probably get away with skipping the deco stops, but the stops give me time to think. During my five minute stops, I consider every angle of this. Either *abuelo* lied in his log, or he miscopied the coordinates. But he's always been so careful with details, it's hard to believe he made a mistake. By the time I surface ten minutes before scheduled, I've made up my mind. I have to ask *abuelo*.

Len looks up suddenly from a book when I emerge. He checks his watch. "You're early! What did you see?" The suspense is killing him.

"Two cannons and seven cannonballs. That's it." I shake my head as I climb the ladder and he extends a hand to me. "I don't get it, Len. According to *abuelo*'s log, she should be here."

Len looks perplexed but doesn't say anything. He knows I need to emotionally decompress.

As he helps me out of my gear I ask, "Do you know anything about *Dos Hermanos*?"

Len offers a sympathetic frown. "I promise I don't know where she is."

I nod. "Okay. We can go back now. We should check on your employees and hope Roger didn't come in while you were away."

Len says he's really sorry, and I know he is. For Tanner and me. In a way, this is better. It means I might still have a chance at finding her first. It also means that Marco is looking just as hard.

For the first twenty minutes of the ride back to the marina, we're silent. Suddenly I turn to Len. "Hey, how do you and Officer Cruz know each other?"

Len jumps a foot and swivels his head toward me. His sunglasses block my view of his eyes, but his mouth opens in surprise. He tries to compose himself. "Officer Cruz? Um, Tara and I met him at a restaurant a while back."

That's such a lame answer. Something is up between them.

13

— • —

I peek in *abuelo*'s hospital room, and seeing he's alone and awake, I stride in holding his dive log. He quickly mutes the TV and smiles at me. "How's my *nieta*?" Granddaughter. I love how he says granddaughter. His eyes settle on the dive log and he lowers his eyebrows.

I flip open to the supposed *Dos Hermanos* page and thrust it at him. "I just dove here. Know what I found? Two cannons and seven cannonballs. Explain."

"Where did you find this dive log?"

"In your office at home."

He coughs and reaches for the handle of a plastic thermos with one of those accordion style straws next to his bed and draws a long sip of water. His hands look like what I imagine a leper's skin looks like, but the doctor says the IV antibiotics are working fast and his skin is improving. "Still get thirsty easily," he says.

I nod. He scoots over and pats the bed by his knees. I sit next to his legs and put the dive log on my lap.

He looks at it, takes a deep breath and says, "Ruby, Marco wants *Dos Hermanos* and he won't stop even if it means killing you. I wrote this entry to distract him." He takes another breath. "Unfortunately my plan backfired. After he read this, he abducted the twins and me and forced us to dive for him, with a camera so he could see what we saw. Not surprisingly, the cannons didn't impress him. He anchored us where you rescued us, trying to force us into telling him the real coordinates."

"Did you tell him?"

Abuelo takes another breath, his whiskers scruffier than I've ever seen. Maybe I should bring his electric razor in. He meets my eyes, shakes his head, and drops his voice. "Ruby, I strongly suspect *Dos Hermanos* is either a legend or was destroyed and won't ever be found."

I shake my head. "What? Why do you think that?"

"Look at all the hours you and Tanner searched for her. Were any of your coordinates right?"

Mentally checking off the coordinates for today's dive and the coordinates to *El Enrique* which I saw after the plane crash, I say, "There are two more spots for me to check."

"And she might be there," *abuelo* says. He pauses and glances down at the fake dive log in my hands. "Or she might not."

I narrow my eyes. "Did you go to those coordinates too? To keep me safe? To punish me for being as greedy as Marco?" I don't attempt to mask my frustration.

Abuelo holds my gaze and sighs, knowing he hurt me. "No. I don't steal research."

"Are you just saying this so I'll stop looking?"

"No. The most hopeful lead anybody had on *Dos Hermanos* is the tale from that surviving crew member on *El Enrique* who claimed to see a ship in distress about five hundred feet north-northeast. All that's there are those cannons. They probably slid off whatever ship the crew boy saw and the ship kept going."

"And made it to its destination where no country has a tax record of the riches she carried?" Bogus. The ship is down there. Somewhere.

"Or more likely the ship was shredded up so much from a storm that fragments are spread over a wide enough area to not give off an impressive sonar signal. Pieces are probably buried in the muddy seabed. I think she's gone, Ruby."

I shake my head. "If that's the case, why is Marco willing to kill me to find her? Obviously he believes she's out there."

"Oh he does. Most do. You do. This is just my opinion." He takes another drink of his water.

"How long have you thought this?"

"Just the last few days. The boys and I had a lot of time to think and talk when Marco held us hostage in the water."

"Why does Marco hate you, hate all of us?"

For a second I wonder if he's going to answer me at all, but after he coughs into his shoulder, he looks at me. "In Marco's words, I've spent my whole life showing him up. Business owner. *Esposo*, husband; your *abuela* did choose me over him," he says with a grin that lightens the mood. He opens his mouth and then stops short.

"I, uh, know about Brett. *Tío* Brett."

His weathered face shows surprise, but then he nods and says, "I raised Brett when Marco refused to be the father."

I nod. "Is that all?" I mean, sure it makes sense. But is that really the fuel behind Marco's hate?

Abuelo scratches the skin around the IV in his hand, fiddles with the tube, then meets my eyes. I raise my eyebrows. He clears his throat. I count four seconds on the wall clock. He speaks in a rush, like he has to let out some steam. "Marco wanted *El Enrique*. Searched for her like you and Tanner searched for *Dos Hermanos*. The boys and I beat him to her."

No wonder he's ticked! I can totally relate. I nod. "So I'm not the only one in this family who is as greedy as Marco?"

Abuelo shakes his head. "It isn't like that, Ruby. I didn't steal then and I don't steal now. We just happened to win the race and Marco took it as *un ataque personal*, a personal attack."

"So I *am* the only one in this family as greedy as Marco?" My anger bubbles up, my voice raising with my heartbeat.

Abuelo puts his hand on my forearm. I think he'll probably tell me that part of the dive log entry was for Marco's benefit and that he thinks I'm the most selfless individual in Florida. But he doesn't. His silence speaks loudly. He does think I'm as greedy as Marco and since he can't talk me out of it, he'll have to wait for me to calm down. To figure this out on my own. To fall on my sword and overcome my own stupid cross. I take a huge breath and watch the clock. Ten seconds tick by. I swallow my anger. Swallow the acknowledgement that I'm a seagull. The truth sucks the wind out of my lungs. I'm just like Marco. *Querido Dios, Dear God, please no. No quiero ser igual como Marco, I don't want to be like Marco.*

Abuelo senses my inner battle and whispers, "You'll get through this. You can change."

I nod, like agreeing will bring his words to fruition. I focus on my breath for a minute and close my eyes. Finally I look at *abuelo* again. "Why didn't you ever take me to *El Enrique*? I think I found her, by the way, when Brett and I landed in the sea."

"What's this?"

"When Marco was kidnapping you, I was in the aquarium plane that circled overhead. The maritime cops were a couple miles away so we were trying to get their attention to go to you. We hit some geese and had to make an emergency landing. I dove down while we waited for the Coast Guard to come. When I surfaced, Marco was pointing a gun at me. When the Coast Guard approached, he tore out of there."

Abuelo's eyebrows are furrowed. "He left us in the water right before the storm hit. He went to you at *El Enrique* and then left you with a sinking plane? With Brett?"

I shrug. "Evidently." I want to ask more about Brett, like his childhood with my grandparents, but we should deal with one dramatic event at a time.

"How did he know you'd be there?"

"He must know the coordinates to *El Enrique*."

Abuelo's eyebrows furrow deeper. "Hopefully the cops will catch up to him soon."

"So why didn't you ever take me to *El Enrique*?"

Abuelo tilts his head, his smile mischievous. "And take the challenge out of it for you? I knew you'd want to find her on your own."

I smile. Okay, okay, I forgive him. For this part. "And I guess I did, even if I thought I was finding *Dos Hermanos*." This is one of the many reasons I love my *abuelo*. He knows me, really gets me. We let all thoughts of seagulls swirl away while we talk about the ship.

"Did you like what you saw?" He's still smiling.

I nod. "Yeah, she's really something. Not as big as I envisioned, but really beautiful."

Abuelo nods. "Those old galleons aren't as big as we expect by today's standards. Every time I see her it's like the first time the boys and I laid eyes on her. I get a shiver of excitement."

I smile, but sadness soon takes over my face. I clear my throat. "I'm glad you found her."

Abuelo squeezes my arm. "Ruby, you'll find another galleon to discover."

I shake my head. "It won't be the same."

"You mean without Tanner?"

I nod, trying to tamp down the next words that need to be asked, but my hurt and anger win. "And seeing your accusation that I'm as greedy as Marco."

Abuelo opens his mouth and for the second time, I think he'll reassure me that the accusation was to catch Marco's attention in the fake entry, but then he closes his mouth, locks his eyes on mine, and squeezes my arm again. Wow, thanks *abuelo*. I do not think I'm as bad as Marco. Am I?

A sudden knock on the door causes us to both look up. Instead of a nurse, Officer Cruz pokes his head in the room. He nods at *abuelo*. "Good to see you looking more alert." *Abuelo* invites him into the room and he steps in all the way. They share some small talk for a minute and then Cruz looks at me. "Miss Salazar, can I have a word with you in the hallway?"

I look at *abuelo* with uncertainty, and he gives an encouraging nod. "Sure," I say and push off the hospital bed, leaving the fake dive log on *abuelo*'s lap.

I follow Cruz's uniformed shoulders past three rooms down the hall to a padded bench under an enormous window. Sunlight pours in, blanketing two large potted plants on either side of the bench. He sits, so I do too. "I want you to stay here tonight. At the hospital. I can bring you home for a bit if you need to shower or get spare clothes or anything."

"Sure. Are you guys getting close to Marco?"

Officer Cruz swallows and says, "We have a lead. Let us take care of it."

I nod.

"I was a little hard on you before, but I had to be. Your safety is contingent on your cooperation."

"I get it."

He shakes his head. "You get it, but you're not willing to back off."

I feign shock. "What do you mean?"

"You're still off diving and looking for trouble."

How did he know I went diving? His eyes bore into mine and dare me to deny it.

"Am I supposed to be under house arrest?"

"Not exactly, but if you don't lay off, you're going to wind up in the same situation as your *abuelo*, or worse. These criminals are serious, Miss Salazar, and they want you."

"They just want my research."

"They'll do whatever it takes to get your research."

"Unless I beat them to it and make a claim."

Officer Cruz's neck vein bulges and he takes in a big breath and faces me squarely. "I'll take you to your house. You get forty-five minutes to shower or whatever, and then you're spending the night here in your *abuelo*'s room."

"Fine." I stand, but Cruz pulls me back down.

"I'm not done."

I look at him questioningly, but before he can start in on another speech, I ask, "Is my brother really responsible for tying up Len?"

He blinks. "I can't disclose that yet. Hopefully when we catch Marco and his crew, they'll sing like canaries and the truth will come out."

I nod. "One of the guys is named Roger. Len has a new employee named Roger. Can you background check him or anything? Make sure Len is safe?"

"Already on it."

"Good."

"You have another question." How does he know?

I take a breath. "Want to go diving with me?"

"Now? Absolutely not. When all this is over? Absolutely."

"But now is when it needs to happen. Stat."

Cruz's brown eyes challenge mine. "See, you don't want to back off."

"If I dive and find *Dos Hermanos*, Marco will have no reason to get me. I'll have the protection of the nautical archaeology association, the public, the-"

"Miss Salazar, that's a big if, and I doubt that authentication can happen much quicker than sending something through Congress." He swallows and lowers his voice. "Besides, that's not how you want to find your ship."

Your ship. Again. He respects that I'm competition. That I have what it takes.

"You don't want to find her in a race against crime. You want it to be a clean, happy occasion. Not an evil race."

I blink. He's right. I nod.

"Now we can go. I brought your *mamá* home this afternoon while you were diving."

"How'd you know I went diving?"

"You're predictable."

"You're a cop. Do you have a tracking device on me or something?"

Cruz shakes his head. "Didn't need one to figure you out."

"You're watching me from the phone you gave me?"

"That's part of it."

Creepy. Sort of. "You said you weren't done. A minute ago when you pulled me back to the bench. What else do you have to tell me?"

"Are you ready to listen to an officer now?" His tone borders Reg's, but the cheeky smile fighting to fill his face hints that he's trying very hard to be stern to get my attention. I nod.

"We have to be extremely careful while we're at your house."

"So you'll guard the bathroom door while I shower?"

"Sheriff's orders."

What a relaxing shower this will be.

Outside in the scorching parking lot, Officer Cruz opens the passenger door for me. He opens his door, starts roaring the air conditioner right away, and folds up the windshield shade. It's only about a seven minute drive to our house, so I have just enough time to ask him a few more questions.

"Who's Benji?" That's the name Len asked him about. Benji. It took me a while to recall the name, but I scoured the B page on some baby name website trying to remember. I need to figure out the link between Len and Cruz.

"Benji?" Officer Cruz looks at me. "My nephew. Why do you ask?"

His nephew. "The same nephew you picked up after you left my house?"

"My only nephew," he says.

So what's significant about Benji? What's the tie? "Do Len and Tara know him?"

Cruz gives me the same sidelong glance as when Len asked how Benji was doing. Cruz inhales. "They met him." He gives a slow nod to act casual, but it doesn't work. "Once at least."

"At a restaurant?" I ask.

"That sounds right," he says, faking nonchalance. The guy is sweating bullets.

"Were you there?"

He nods. "Yeah. Benji's cool, so he invited me too."

"Why do you get all weird when you talk about him? And why does Len get weird when he talks about you?"

"Benji has had some health issues. You know how Len likes to pray for everybody." Officer Cruz gives undue attention to the stoplight. He knows how to dodge a question.

When we get home, he whispers that he needs to walk the perimeter of the house before we go in. He bobs his head and says, "Stay close to me."

Seeing nothing out of the ordinary on our silent walk around the house, he stands guard while I unlock the door and we enter. He locks the door behind us and says he's going to search the whole place. "Where should I wait?"

"Here by the door until I give the all clear."

Okay, now I'm a little spooked. What does he expect? And what do I do if something is wrong? Dart out the door and hide in his car?

Officer Cruz holds a hand on his gun and begins a walk-through of the first floor. I open the entryway closet to kick off my shoes and gasp when a masculine hand snakes out and clamps around my mouth. He yanks me into the closet, turning me and forcing my back against his chest. I try to bite the hand, stomp on his foot, twist my torso and elbow him, but the guy is huge and unfazed. "Shut up. Come with me. Or else," he threatens in a harsh whisper. He lifts me off the floor a few inches, opens the closet door, and steps into the entryway. Facing me toward the kitchen, he backs to the door. Oh no. *No puede ser*. It can't be! *This can't be happening. Come on, Cruz.* I try to scream, but the guy tightens his grip around my diaphragm and his elbow clamps onto my throat. I hear Cruz's footsteps approaching. *Hurry. Please.*

In an instant, I see Cruz round the corner from the hallway. He catches my frantic face and his eyes go huge. And just like that, I'm yanked out the door and into the blazing heat, my body protecting my captor from a potential attack by Cruz. My captor runs backward, and tires squeal, by the mailbox from the sound of it. In desperation,

Officer Cruz chases after me. If he shoots the guy's feet, he risks shooting me. I'm shoved in the backseat, presumably of the squealing tires vehicle, and the vehicle takes off before my door is even closed. I try to look out the window, but someone pushes my head down.

¿Querido Dios, Dear God, qué hago, what do I do? The vehicle is squealing around every corner, accelerating fast out of every light. "Can you slow down so I don't puke in your nice car?" It's worth a shot, right? The worst they'll do to me is kill me. I shudder.

"What'd she say?" a voice in the front asks.

"She's gonna throw up." Rather than slowing down, someone stuffs a plastic bag under my face. How thoughtful. I hear sirens behind us, and the guys swear. There must be three of them. The one who nabbed me and is forcing me down, and two up front. No way can I fight them all. More sirens, to the sides of us, I think. This is a good sign, right? They'll get pulled over and Cruz will get me out of here.

A deafening crash rattles me to the core. I'm pinned to the floorboard. The vehicle rolls, and the big guy is working with centrifugal force and his boots to keep me from flying around like a ragdoll. He must have a seatbelt on. So safety-conscious of him. Meanwhile, my head whips from side to side and I fight a pang of nausea. We're skidding, maybe on the vehicle's side, until we stop with a hard crunch. I hear moaning. "Out, let's run!" someone says. My head hurts. Pounds. I'm sick. Everything goes black.

"Her vitals are stable. I expect her to wake up in the next day or two." There's an ocean in my head. Thoughts flit in and out as quickly as little fish and nothing sticks. A hand touches my wrist. Somebody groans, maybe me, and I fall back into the deep dark.

14

Everything around me is beeping. I hate that blood-pressure cuff that tightens every few minutes. I try to swim out of it, but cold hands keep putting it back on. "We don't see any brain damage."

"Will she dive again?" August. Asking a serious question. Is he talking about me?

"In a few weeks, once she regains her strength. The concussion has to heal first."

A warm hand touches my forehead. "Come on, Ruby." *Abuelo.*

Another hand pushes hair off my face. *Mamá*'s touch, I think.

It takes focus, but I make my eyelids open. It's so bright. I want to crawl back into the dark.

"Ruby, we're here. Come on, girl, wake up." I blink. Groan. Try to swallow. A straw presses against my mouth. "Drink." I do. Water. Cold. It makes me cough.

Bad dreams and a sweaty pillow. I'm cold. Voices and noise around me, but none of it makes sense, and the same bad dream over and over. Being grabbed, lifted, shoved, and the loud crash. I'm stuck in a fog.

Beyond the fog, a voice asks how much longer. Is he talking to me? I have no idea.

A voice answers. A familiar voice. *Papá*? "I hope another year will get us out of the woods. I wouldn't have left if it wasn't desperate."

A machine beeps. Another voice. "She's close to waking up now."

Not time to get up yet. My mind settles back into the fog. I'm so tired.

"I hate seeing her like this." Janie's voice. She hates seeing who like this? Like what? Like me? "Can I play her favorite music?"

"Yes, please do. That would be very beneficial as she recovers."

A guitar strums. A gentle voice sings. It sounds familiar, but the lyrics don't come to my mind fast enough to sing along. "It looks like she's responding!" Janie's voice. "It's her favorite indie band."

"She does seem to be responding. Keep playing it."

Footsteps and a hand on my forehead. "How's the patient today?"

I open my eyes. See a doctor. "Hi." My voice sounds like a croak.

He smiles. "Ah, here's a good sign. She's up and talking. How do you feel, Ruby?" He studies machines, looks at my hands and feet, shines a light in my eyes, asks me my name and birthdate and if I know what day it is. No clue on the date. My voice still sounds like a frog's.

"You've been asleep for two days, Ruby. You were involved in a car accident and got a minor concussion. Do you remember any of it?" The doctor gives me a drink. I swallow.

"They threw me on the floor of the vehicle. Lots of skidding. Squealing tires. We crashed."

The doctor nods and looks behind him. "These are good signs."

"Thank you, *doctór*." *Papá*'s voice.

The doctor turns back to me, pokes me more, looks in my ears, and presses a stethoscope to my chest. "Ruby, your family is here and is glad you're awake. Do you have enough energy to talk to them for a few minutes?"

I nod but close my eyes. "Where's *abuelo*?"

"Staying at our house on the Gulf." *Mamá*'s voice.

My eyes are still shut. "Marco has criminals at our house."

"That's why *abuelo* left town."

I drag my eyes open and peer around the doctor to see *mamá* and *papá*. "Alone?"

Papá steps forward and squeezes my forearm. "With the twins."

Mamá holds my hand and nods. "You're safe now. So is *abuelo*."

"The twins?"

"And the twins."

"But the criminals are still on the loose?"

A pause. "Yes. But hospital security is working extra hard to keep you safe."

"What do we do now?"

"You need to rest."

"They'll get the glory."

"Let them get it, Ruby. That doesn't matter!"

"It matters to me." Because I'm as greedy as Marco. I clench my jaw.

Mamá purses her lips and looks at *papá*, then back at me. "Just try to rest and get better."

Another day has passed. Maybe two. I've lost count, but I'm feeling better. If someone doesn't let me out of this hospital soon, I'm going to break myself out. The sun is shining, the clock is ticking, and I'm more rested than I've been in weeks. I study the nurse's dry erase board on the wall. August eleventh. So I was out of it for about three days, I think. Or maybe four. I hear a knock on the door.

"Come in," I croak. I feel better, but my voice needs some warming up.

"You're looking better," Officer Cruz says. He looks at the machines to the side of my bed and nods approvingly.

"Can you break me out of here?"

Officer Cruz laughs. "I'm not a doctor, but rumor has it you're getting discharged today."

"Did you have to bring in a criminal for treatment?" I ask, noting his uniform.

"Just came to check on you."

"On duty?"

"On a short break."

"Is Marco locked up yet?"

Cruz shakes his head. "Not yet. They got away after the car accident."

"How many are there?"

"Four altogether, from what we can gather."

"I'm sorry I was stupid."

"We'll talk about that later."

"Is Len okay?"

"Len's fine. He visited you twice a day while you were out of it."

"He did?"

Officer Cruz nods. "It looked emotional for him. He prayed you through the worst of it."

I meet Cruz's eyes, seeing more than he's saying. "You did too?" I whisper.

Cruz nods. "Yeah, I did too."

I reach up and touch his hand. "Thanks."

He squeezes my fingers for about a tenth of a second and steps back when he hears someone approaching. A nurse walks in with paperwork and asks Officer Cruz if he's taking me home. "No, I believe her parents are accompanying her home."

"They are?"

"We are," *mamá* says, and she and *papá* hurry into the room.

The nurse turns to them and starts rattling off a speech of do's and don'ts. The nurse helps me change into clean clothes that *mamá* brought, and Cruz and *papá* help me get in the front seat of *papá*'s car. At home, *mamá* gets me settled on the wicker sofa on the patio.

"Who's running Ruby Sunset?"

Mamá sits by me and says, "Your *papá* and I have been trying to keep it afloat, taking out a couple tours each day. Len and Tara are helping too. *Abuelo* and the twins are keeping up on the bookkeeping and scheduling remotely from our house."

"Why aren't you and *papá* at home working?"

Mamá looks a little taken aback, then embarrassed. She stretches her feet and cracks her ankles. "You need us."

I don't know what to say. I've needed them since they moved. I just nod, then turn my attention to Cruz, who is still standing sentry at the door. "I'll let you settle in now. Keep getting better, Ruby."

He waves and walks out the door, the same door that *mamá* and *papá* will walk out in a few more days. I sigh, loneliness already settling in.

"Can we call Len and ask him and Tara to come over after work?"

"Sure," *mamá* says. "Do you feel like eating? We could invite them for dinner."

"That sounds good."

Still sitting by me, *mamá* calls The Dive Shop and talks to Len. The plan is made. They'll be over at six for dinner.

"It's sure good to see you up and on the mend," Len says. "Up and on the mend" means me sitting in a cushy rocking chair pushed up to the table. But he's right. This is better than in the hospital. Tara hugs me. I hold her for a minute, relishing the smell of the laundry detergent from their house. For a split second I'm smelling Tanner's shirt.

Once seated at the table, Len prays and we begin eating fish tacos. I love having my parents here and I wish it could always be like this. Well, I wish *abuelo* and the twins were here too. Before anyone finishes their first round of tacos, Len addresses *papá*. "How's work on the Gulf? You still like it over there?"

"We do," *papá* says. He looks at me and adds, "But it's good to be here for a while too."

"When do you plan to go back?"

Papá looks at *mamá* with a little uncertainty. "Probably by next Monday."

Mamá nods. "It's hard to be away from work so long." I knew it was coming. And it's okay. I'm almost nineteen. I don't need *mamá* and *papá* holding my hand anymore. Besides, Jerome will want me back at work next week too. The bouquet from the aquarium came with a note that said so. "Get well soon, Ruby. We hope to see you back on your fins next week. Warm regards, The Aquarium and Baby."

Len nods and says, "Well, Tara and I will keep looking out for Ruby." Tara squeezes my hand. I'm so thankful for them.

"Will you go with your parents, Ruby? At least until Marco is locked up?" I'm pretty sure Tara is asking this as a formality, but I guess it could be an option.

I shrug. "I guess we'll have to see how I feel by then, and whether Marco is still at large." I turn to my parents. "Will you guys ever move back here?"

Papá exchanges a look with Len and turns back to me. "Someday. Soon, I hope."

"Meaning?"

Papá blanches, fork in midair. He looks at *mamá*, then Len and Tara, and then me again. "Meaning, I hope to come back here someday. Soon." He smiles August's winning smile, dark eyes bright. "I miss being with my kids every day."

I let out a huff. "How can you criticize me for chasing treasure when you're doing the exact same thing? You say you miss your family, but you moved away so you could make more money. Now you say you want to move back *someday*. Why wait? If *familia* is really as good a treasure as you say, why are you trading us in for a bigger paycheck?"

Papá's mouth opens, then closes, and he sets down his fork. *Mamá* eyes me and gives an apologetic smile to Len and Tara.

I shake my head. "Sorry. I shouldn't call you out like that. I just hate that you and *mamá* left so soon after Tanner died."

Tara reaches across the table and squeezes my hand again, and *mamá* turns her apologetic smile my way.

Len stirs his iced tea and gives *papá* some secret society-looking nod and rapid conversation with his eyes. I watch them and raise my eyebrows.

Papá nods at Len and then faces me. He takes a big breath and *mamá* pats his shoulder. "I'd rather tell you with the boys here, but," he pauses and I see the wheels in his head turning. "Well, no, this will be fine. Maybe it's better we can tell you alone."

My eyebrows are still raised. "Are you having another baby?"

Mamá laughs and assures me that's not what *papá* is having such a hard time saying.

"Maybe we should do this with Francisco," *papá* says. He pulls his phone off his belt holster and dials *abuelo*, setting the phone in the middle of the table.

Abuelo answers on the second ring. "*Hola hijo*, hi, son." *Abuelo* has always called *papá* son. I guess he's a natural at bringing in new family members, with partially raising Brett, and then calling his daughter's husband his son. I smile. It's good to hear *abuelo*'s voice.

Papá explains who all is crowded around the table and where our conversation led. *Papá* takes a breath again. "I think we need to tell Ruby."

"Probably so," *abuelo* says. "I'll stay on the line to keep her calm."

"Thanks, *abuelo*," I say, wondering what news is coming that they expect me to get upset about.

A hush falls over us as I wait for whatever bomb *papá* is going to drop. Finally he says, "I made some poor business decisions with Ruby Sunset. Not on purpose, and nothing criminal." My eyes are locked on his face. *Mamá* holds his elbow. Len and Tara's sympathetic faces show that they know it all. *Papá* continues. "Your *mamá* and I had to file bankruptcy to cut the losses. We transferred the shop's ownership onto your brothers so they could start at zero rather than negative fifty grand."

My jaw drops. Negative fifty-thousand?

Papá says, "We always planned to pass the business to all three of you, but when Tanner died and the shop was sinking as fast as my debt was piling up, everybody agreed that we couldn't saddle you with the burden."

Everybody but me agreed. Somehow this makes me feel even lonelier.

Papá swallows. "The boys are doing a good job, and your *mamá* and I are getting some traction. I want to be here with you, Ruby. We hated leaving you. We only left because we had to."

I nod, feeling like I just got knocked off a boat by a rogue wave.

As promised I work on Labor Day for Len. It's a full day and I take out three tours on the colorful reef close to the shop. When the last customers leave and Len turns off the Open light, he turns to me and says, "Have you thought about diving for *Dos Hermanos* soon?"

"I think about it all the time," I admit. "Do you and Tara want to be there?" Tara doesn't dive, but she might want to be in the boat. And Len likes to dive, but has never loved treasure diving like Tanner and me.

Len thinks about this for a minute. He looks past my head at the photo of Tanner and me on the gallery wall. Finally he takes a breath.

"If you want me to come down, then yes, I'll go with you. But do what you need to do. Don't bring me just because I'm Tanner's *papá*."

I wish my own parents understood me this well. Before I head home, I stroll past the counter and sneak a picture of a handwritten list of phone numbers next to Len's cash register. I hurry home because I have a plan.

Abuelo and the twins have been back home for a couple weeks now running the shop. Marco and his cronies are either hiding out somewhere, or they fled the country, so we've returned to life as close to normal as we can. I'm doing way better from my minor concussion and can dive again, and getting back to my routine and working at the aquarium is helping me. When I saw the list of phone numbers, including the AWOL criminal employee Roger's number, I had a stroke of genius.

Nobody will like my idea, which is why I'm not telling *mamá*, *abuelo*, or the twins. Cruz will find out, in time, and he'll probably be irate, but at least it'll solve the problem. I've given it a lot of thought, and even a decent amount of prayer, and I believe it is the answer to catching Marco and his crew. For once, my plan is fully baked. The moon is full, the tide is high, and the time is perfect for my plan.

I pull up the picture of the phone numbers at Len's. Everybody on the list has the same area code and most of the employees even share the next three numbers. Totally plausible that I could text the wrong person, especially since Roger's number is right under Len's. Very carefully, I draft a message, bound for Roger's phone.

> Hey Len, it's Ruby. Got your number from the list at the shop. Finally found Dos Hermanos. Thought about your deal and I accept. Meet me at midnight tonight. 26.65, -79.86. Under our nose the whole time! We'll dive and

> share the claim, and you'll follow through
> on your end of the deal.

I press send, take a deep breath, and imagine the look on Roger's face as he reads this message. It's seven o'clock now, and my stomach does a flip. In a few minutes I get a response from Roger's number:

> Sounds good. See you then.   -Len

Officer Cruz will be so mad. If all goes well, my *familia* won't know until it's all over. I scribble a note to *abuelo* and leave it on the table: *I'm out with your boat now, and I'm going to try to catch up with Officer Cruz later tonight. Be home soon! XOXO Ruby.*

Next I take my backpack, full of water bottles, food, and a phone charger and walk to the marina. The twins are teaching their once a month evening scuba class, and *abuelo* is on a date with his lady friend, Teresa. *Mamá* and *papá* are back at the Gulf, so I'm on my own tonight. It's just me and God. Earlier this afternoon I loaded my diving gear, but if this plan works, I won't do any diving. It's too soon to leave if I want to arrive at midnight, but I'd rather be gone when the guys get home, so I check over *abuelo*'s boat, double-check that I have more than enough fuel, and back out of the slip.

The sun is a blazing orange low on the horizon, and I see some dolphin fins hopping in the distance. The blue stretches ahead of me, and I can't imagine my life without the ocean. It's a peaceful cruise to the coordinates I sent to Roger, which are a bust and are close to the marina and help. When I arrive, I lower the anchor and listen to the waves lapping against the boat. I click on a cabin light and read a Psalm. Psalm 62:1-2. "Truly my soul silently waits for God; From Him comes my salvation. He only is my rock and my salvation; He is my defense; I shall not be greatly moved."

He alone is my rock? Unfortunately I don't think I can say that about my life. Not honestly. I've decided to devote more time to God, which should be a lot easier once this mess with Marco is over. I breathe another prayer and again feel guilty that I've prayed more during distress than in times of peace. Lame daughter, I know. But I'm motivated to do better.

I see a handful of messages on my phone and take a few minutes to reassure *abuelo* that I'm perfectly safe and *mamá* that I'm not diving with sharks. I realize it won't take long for *abuelo* and *mamá* to contact Cruz directly and find out that he doesn't know he has plans to hang out with me tonight.

It's 10:30 now, so I review my plan to call for help. I plug in my phone to keep it charged and I pray that the strong cell signal continues. I make sure the boat's radio is ready to go, but obviously I can't call for help on that ahead of time or Marco will hear. I sit on the deck and flash my light at the dark water, teasing jellyfish to come. Being this alone is kind of eerie.

At 11:45 I hear a large boat approaching. My heartbeat pops up and my stomach lurches again. This is it. Using the zoom on my phone camera, I can just make out Len's boat. Ah, so they hijacked *The Dive Boat* so I wouldn't get scared and take off. Clever. I wait two more minutes until there's no doubt, and then I dial Cruz's number. I step into the cabin of the boat and listen to his phone go to voicemail. This hasn't happened before. He always answers. After the beep, I tell him my exact location. "26.65, -79.86. I'm on my *abuelo*'s boat, and Marco is almost here. Can you send help?" Outside I can hear Len's boat pull up next to me. I lay down on the bunk and pull a blanket over me. I'll pretend to be asleep. That'll buy me time, right? I call the sheriff's number and he answers on the second ring. I rapidly whisper that the at-large criminals led by Marco Gonzalez are hot on my tail and I rattle off my coordinates. "Come fast, but be stealthy so he doesn't get away again. Please!"

I hear footsteps on the deck and tell the sheriff I have to hang up. "Miss Salazar, no, stay on the-"

I hang up. If Marco knows I've called for help, it'll all be over and he'll get away again. I shove the phone into my pocket and curl up under the blanket, trying ever so hard to make my face look asleep. *Please God, make this work.*

The cabin door creaks open and a light shines in. The person flicks on the overhead light. Footsteps. "Ruby?" It's Len's voice. Wait, what? This wasn't part of the plan. But of course Marco would use Len like this. Duh. Marco has proven that he'll use an innocent person to do his dirty work.

Len's voice almost makes me open my eyes, but I'd bet Marco is behind Len with a gun to his head. I don't stir, not yet. *Act asleep.* Put off the fight until closer to help's arrival.

"Ruby," Len says again. He pushes my shoulder. I crack my eyelids open.

"Oh, hi Len. Glad you're here." Not glad you're here since that means you've been abducted, but I'll improvise. I sit up, glancing behind him. I don't see anybody, but I'm sure they're out there. Probably standing on the deck of Len's boat with guns aimed right at us. Probably listening to our conversation with some detective microphone.

"Ready to dive?"

I push the blanket off my legs and fake a yawn. I roll my shoulders and rock my head from side to side, pretending to wake up, but I focus hard on Len's eyes, looking for any sign of betrayal. He's looking at me the same way. He's terrified. Like me. Okay, I'm glad he's here. "Yes, let's look at this beauty. Glad you got my message." As I stand, I ask, "Did you tell Tara?"

He shakes his head. "No, I thought it best to keep quiet for now." Good, he's playing along.

"Probably for the best. I'm glad we came to an agreement. For Tanner's sake," I add, trying to sound normal. Len nods and squeezes my shoulder. Roger and Marco must've believed the message I sent and told Len to act it out. I'm sure they're just out of sight, under the cover of darkness, ready to attack if one of us goes off script. Their script, that is. Len and I could act on Broadway. I silently pray that law enforcement hustles like never before. I need to get Marco to let down his guard, and the best way to do that is to act like Len and I really are going to dive. Keeping myself directly in front of Len, I try to convey this with my eyes and hope he understands.

I yawn again. "I can't believe I fell asleep. Is it midnight now?"

Len looks at his watch. "Just about."

"Where's your diving gear? Mine is in the back." I'm shaking on the inside but I lead the way out of the cabin and to the rear of the deck, ignoring the hairs rising on my neck and the eeriness of knowing we're being watched. The sharks are biding their time, but I can't help but wonder at what point Marco will strike. Is he waiting for us to emerge victorious? Is he waiting for us to get in the water so he can subdue us? And how long will law enforcement take? I could tell from the Sheriff's voice that he took me seriously.

My phone vibrates but I resist the temptation to check it, knowing it would make Marco suspicious. I step into my wetsuit, toss my phone over to the steering console, and ask Len what seems like a reasonable question if this was actually happening. "We'll go together to the nautical archaeology association first thing in the morning?"

Len nods as he pulls up his wetsuit over his torso. "That's what I figured. I'll ask Tara to open the store for me and you and I can meet at the nautical association. My employees won't think anything is weird if I tell them I made a morning dive, so we can keep it quiet until the press hears."

I force a grin. "I can't wait." I shake my head and put on my mask and headlamp. "Can you believe we actually found *Dos Hermanos*?" I pick up my phone and slide it in the expensive diving case. A string of notifications appear on the screen but I ignore them, praying that this will work out.

"Well, you and Tanner found her. You're just honoring him by letting me in on it."

I put on my fins and shrug. "It didn't feel right to only put my name on it. And this way The Dive Shop can benefit from it just like Ruby Sunset does with *El Enrique*. If Tanner were still alive, we probably would've had a deal like this anyway." I get a faraway look in my eye, acting as authentic as possible. It isn't that hard, really. I notice the lights of a vessel in the distance, hope it's law enforcement, and then return to the act. I sigh. "*Gracias.*"

Len nods and holds up my air tank. "You got enough air in your pony tank?"

"Yup." He holds up my gear while I buckle it in place. I hear an approaching vessel. It sounds like a helicopter is coming too. The Coast Guard. They're far enough away that I doubt Marco will realize what's up until the chopper is right on us. This might work after all, as long as they can swoop in before Marco disappears again. If I survive this, Cruz and my *mamá* can kill me. "My headlamp has a full charge. Yours too?"

"Always. Full headlamp, flashlight, and pony tank." He squats down to shoulder his gear that's propped on the bench seat. Len clicks the buckles and stands. "Sure you're ready to do this, Ruby?" I know he's stalling for time.

I look at him. "Tanner always prayed before we went down. Can you pray?" This isn't me acting. We need prayer now more than ever.

Len nods and says, "Father, Ruby is so close to this treasure that she's wanted to find for so long. Please give her success and safety."

I know there's far more meaning behind the brief words, and at the conclusion of the prayer I smile at him. "Now I'm ready." I plaster on another wide smile. "More than ready." If we wait any longer, Marco will get suspicious.

Len nods and tells me to go in first. "I'll come right behind you."

I flip over backward and let myself sink. I grab onto the anchor line and descend. I point my spotlight toward the boat and can see the splash when Len flips in. I wonder how long it'll be before law enforcement steps in. How long will it be before Marco kills us?

Even in the full moonlight and with spotlights, visibility is practically nonexistent. I assume we'll descend into the dark to stay safe, but Len grabs my shoulder. He points to the side of *abuelo*'s vessel and gestures that we should swim over there. I hesitate. I'd rather stay on the anchor line so we don't get lost in the dark. He writes on his dive slate, "Crooks will look by anchor line. Hide."

Illuminating his message with my light, I nod and we stay near enough to the surface to have a shred of moonlight as we swim toward the boat. Near *abuelo*'s boat, I feel fully vulnerable because of our lack of depth, but also comforted for the same reason. Len is probably right that if Marco sends a perpetrator after us, he'll assume we did the routine safe practice of staying with the anchor line.

I take the dive slate and write, "They kidnapped you?" Len nods and I grimace behind my regulator and mask. I hadn't thought the seagulls would take the time to drag him into it. Very clever of them, though. I hate that Len has been pulled into this entire mess with Marco, but I'm thankful for his steady presence through it all.

Under water we can't hear what's going on above the surface. However, we see an approaching vessel and a flashing blue light catches our attention. Law enforcement. My stomach lurches again and I wonder what the scene above is. A bright searchlight circles to the left of us. Len and I slowly make our way left, staying in the shadows of the vessel. More blue lights and white searchlights. Is it safe to get a better view? Like a mosquito drawn to a porch lamp, I drift toward the blue lights, but Len pulls me back. *Sure, let's wait.* No reason to pop up in harm's way. Good thinking, Len.

The water bubbles into a whirl by *The Dive Boat*'s motor. The rudder whips back and forth. The propeller changes direction. Forward, backward. It rams into *abuelo*'s boat and Len yanks me lower. Oh that could be bad. Forward, backward. It rams *abuelo*'s boat again. Oh no.

Another vessel joins the scene, along with another set of blue lights. A splash to our right. Somebody jumps in the water. A rescuer, or Marco's accomplice? The swimmer descends along *The Dive Boat*'s anchor line, and a headlamp sweeps the whole area. We're far enough away that it would be hard for the swimmer to see us, but at this shallow depth, the moonlight feels like a spotlight. At about fifteen feet down, the headlamp stops descending and makes a wild scan. Looking for us.

The light slowly ascends, and Len nudges me back toward *abuelo*'s boat. I try to be graceful, but I move too quickly and the swimmer's light hones in on us. The swimmer approaches us with uneven, choppy strokes. I squint. The swimmer's arm is extended toward us. Len pushes me around the boat. I grab onto *abuelo*'s anchor line and peer around Len. A strange looking gun is aimed at me and the swimmer gains on us. Do guns work underwater? Or is this some type of underwater firearm? Is it a cop, thinking we're the bad guys? Len shoves me below him and we pull ourselves down the anchor line, and I focus on staring at our anchor line.

Don't look at his gun.

I'm going to die.

It'll be quick. I hope.

Wait, the guy wants *me* dead. Probably Marco's orders. Len shouldn't die. Tara shouldn't have to lose her son *and* her husband. I grab Len's ankle and yank him down, pulling myself up at the same time. He's confused, I can tell, as he struggles to put himself between me and the swimming gunman. I fight back, and we inadvertently move toward the surface in our tussle. Len should not die in my place. I wriggle out of his gloved hand and get above him, back into the light of the moon and law enforcement lights. Back into the visibility of the gunman.

The armed swimmer has an air tank and is five feet from me. Behind his mask, his eyes show no emotion. Not even victory at being so close to shooting his target. Apathy. No feeling. What a waste of a life. He aims right at my chest. This is it.

A splash directly to our left distracts the gunman for a split second. Maybe this isn't it. Len tugs me to the right. I look back at the gunman, whose eyes are again lasered on me. A jellyfish-like cloud explodes in front of the gun.

I've been shot at.

It doesn't happen in slow motion, and I'm not acutely aware of all my surroundings. I just know I've been shot at. Two seconds go by and I'm not dead.

Above the gunman, another diver comes fast. Another gun. *Please be a good guy.* Another explosion in front of my gunman's firearm and my stomach drops. Len grabs my wrist, and we cling to each other, frozen.

The second swimmer overtakes my gunman, and the gunman's gun falls into the depths. The gunman is forced to the surface. I think my heart is going to stop. Len hauls me to *abuelo*'s anchor line.

For ten minutes, I cling to the anchor line, shaking, while we watch a show of blue and white lights and pray that nobody else is getting shot at. Finally a diver swims down to us. Afraid it might be another criminal, Len and I descend, eyes glued on the visitor. The diver shines a light on a badge. An officer badge. A good guy. We ascend to the officer. He writes on a dive slate, "All souls safe?"

Len gives the OK hand signal.

The officer holds up two fingers, presumably taking a headcount.

Len and I nod.

"All clear. Go up," the officer writes on his dive slate. He sends Len first, then me, and the officer comes last. We emerge in a spotlight and hear at least two helicopters above. I'm blinded by the light, and a megaphoned voice tells us to get on the deck and put our hands on our heads. As if *we're* the criminals. I sigh. *Sé obediente*, just obey.

I squint from the helicopter's searchlight and raise my hands, stepping next to Len. I'm still shaking. Another officer steps up to us and holds up a badge. Reg. I don't have to like him to appreciate his service. In the distance I see a couple Coast Guard boats heading back toward the marina. I spit out my regulator. "Did you get them?" I blurt.

"We got 'em," Reg grunts. His glare conveys the message that I should've stayed out of it. A minute later he says it's time for us to give statements. For the first time all summer, I can finally breathe. My knees become wet noodles beneath me, and when I collapse, Len sinks down next to me, his breath shallow and fast. Reg puts hands on our shoulders and tells us the criminals are apprehended.

I look up. Marco is still here.

"Marco!" I feel like I'm shouting, but my voice is more like a whisper, like when you have a bad dream and are powerless. He's about ten feet away from Len and me, handcuffed and held by two officers. "Marco!" I try again.

He turns his head my way and his eyes harden when they meet mine. I glance at Reg. "I need a second." I force my wobbly knees to obey and I stand. *I almost died. Don't think about it*. Reg reaches out and tries to grab me, but I dodge him and stumble to Marco. I have to do this. All these years of tension and animosity. He plotted to kill me. I remember Len's words from the day after the plane sank. *"But wreck diving, the obsession with the treasure, it sometimes goes to people's heads. Makes them greedy. And greed is the root of so many heinous crimes."*

I wobble to a halt in front of Marco and lock my eyes on his. I gulp. His face curls into a snarl. "Marco. You wanted to prove yourself by finding *Dos Hermanos*?"

His eyes are beads of fire. His mustache twitches. "I'm not the only one." His eyes and tone reek of accusation like *abuelo*'s statement in the dive log. I stare at him, taking it in. I've spent a lot of time wanting to find a big one too. My throat goes dry. Marco is in handcuffs. His shoulders are gripped by two cops. Blue and white lights illuminate his scowl. His eyes are black with hate. At *abuelo*. At me. He arranged to have me killed. I swallow again. This won't be my future. There's more to life than greed. I will not be a seagull. I will not value sunken treasure over life.

I don't notice Reg approaching until his voice startles me. "Miss Salazar, I need you to give your statement."

I'm not trying to be rude, and I hope he'll understand why I'm ignoring him. I swallow my pride, still staring at Marco. "Marco, I'm sorry."

"For what?" he growls.

That you're going to die from bitterness and hate, I think. *That you have to leave the sea.*

He glares at me, and the cops swivel him away. I watch them cross the deck and board a police helicopter. He's busted. I'm free of him. But it could've been me. I almost chose greed over life too. I don't know if I'm going to throw up or cry.

15

"So you're mad, but not super mad?"

"I'm pretty ticked," Officer Cruz says. It's five in the morning and nobody has slept. Marco and his crew are detained, Len and I are safe, and the location of *Dos Hermanos* is still unknown. Officer Cruz is begrudgingly giving me a ride home. Sheriff's orders.

"At least it's over now," I say.

"At least you didn't get killed."

"But I helped you guys."

Officer Cruz clenches his jaw. "I have nothing nice to say to you right now, so I'm going to keep my thoughts to myself."

"Tell me how you really feel." The rest of the drive is quiet, besides the occasional dispatcher's voice on the radio. Cruz parks in the driveway and I wait for him to open my door. "You can come in for eggs."

"I'm on duty."

"It takes five minutes to make and eat eggs. You can take a five minute break."

"Can you even cook eggs?" His voice is edged with vexation. Boy, he is in a bad mood.

I hesitate. "I've watched *abuelo* cook eggs before."

Officer Cruz lets out a little laugh, finally. He opens the rear hatch and grabs my backpack and an armload of still damp diving gear. I grab the rest of the gear. Nobody felt like going into the dive shop at this hour, considering everything else that's happened overnight, so I suggested we bring my gear to the house. It wouldn't be the first time *abuelo*'s entryway has been cluttered with diving gear.

I walk up to the door a few paces ahead of Cruz, and *abuelo* swings the door wide open. "You have some explaining to do."

Officer Cruz steps up next to me and says, "Yes, she does."

Abuelo's eyebrows lower. He takes in the diving gear and Cruz's uniform and steps aside, motioning us to come in. *Abuelo* and I hang up my regulator and mask on the hat rack, Officer Cruz sets the tanks and fins on the rug, and then *abuelo* tells us to sit down.

"Coffee, Officer?"

"No, sir," Cruz says, holding up his hands.

Abuelo's eyebrows go low. "Don't tell me you like energy drinks."

Cruz gives a sheepish smile.

Abuelo's face shows as much disgust as if Cruz had said he picked me up for illegal drugs. I can't help but laugh. "You both like caffeine, just in different flavors."

Abuelo's coffee pot is already starting to brew, and he opens the cupboard and tosses a container of August's protein powder to Officer Cruz. "I don't have energy drinks, but here's a little something to finish your shift." He fills a shaker bottle with milk and hands it to Cruz, who pours a scoop of protein into the milk and mixes it. "Ruby, what do you need? Electrolytes, if you've been diving."

"Not a full dive, but I am thirsty." I walk to the cupboard. While I mix the electrolyte powder with water in a shaker bottle, *abuelo* says, "Give me a minute to piece this together." I return to the table, open the lid, and *abuelo* snaps his fingers. He looks back at the diving gear, eyes Cruz's dry uniform, studies my messy ponytail and nods. He walks to the coffee maker and fills a mug. Looks at the clock, nods to himself, returns to the table and rereads the note I left him. He raises his eyebrows at Officer Cruz and says, "You didn't know this was prearranged, did you?"

"No, sir." Officer Cruz takes a long swallow of his protein shake.

Abuelo holds his mug to his mouth and points at me. "Which means you set up a scene for Marco to meet you in the middle of the ocean. Then you called the cops."

I close the lid on my shaker bottle and nod.

Abuelo continues. "And I'm willing to bet you got Len involved too."

I swallow. "Not on purpose."

Abuelo looks at Officer Cruz with an expression that says, "Can you believe this girl?"

Officer Cruz still looks frustrated with me, but surprisingly he says, "To her credit, the plan worked. Marco and his whole ring have been arrested. And caught in the act of taking Ruby and Len hostage at gunpoint, which will work in our favor in trial."

My legs go weak again. The whole gunpoint part was awfully unnerving.

Abuelo shakes his head at me. "Well I'll be." He sips his coffee. "I suppose my boat needs an oil change by now."

Officer Cruz chuckles and I lower my head. "I didn't know how else to do it, so I took your boat. You always let me borrow it when I ask. And I'll pay for the damage Marco caused when he rammed into it."

Abuelo grimaces and he nods slowly above his coffee mug. He looks back at Cruz. "Is everyone safe, and is she in trouble?"

"Everyone is safe, and I don't think Ruby will get in trouble. Unless you want to press charges because she took your boat without permission."

Abuelo shakes his head.

Officer Cruz speaks again. "It was risky, and I don't condone her decisions tonight, but it did work."

"Can you stop acting so surprised every time I do something that works out?"

Abuelo and Cruz both face me, their weary expressions telling me to zip it.

Abuelo reaches across the table and shakes Cruz's hand. "Thank you, Officer."

Cruz stands, finishes the protein shake in a gulp, and says, "Thanks for the protein. I should get back to patrolling the neighborhood now. I hope you have a good day, Francisco."

Abuelo takes his empty mug to the coffee pot, presumably for a refill, so I walk with Officer Cruz to the door. "Thank you for your help." Insufficient, I know, but what else can I say?

Cruz looks at me, his mouth clamped tight, like it takes all his willpower not to say what he's thinking. He nods and steps back into the night.

I tiptoe my way to the shower. As I'm easing the bathroom door shut, *abuelo* calls from the living room. "Ruby."

Here it comes. My deserved lecture. "Yes, *abuelo*?"

"*Te quiero.*"

I smile, even though he can't see me from his place on the chair. "*Gracias. Tú también.* I love you too." His words remind me of clinging to the anchor rope to get to safety.

For two weeks we make statements to the cops and the press, work our tails off at Ruby Sunset, and finally get the sleep we need. Getting back to my routine is good, and tonight is Pilates. Most people shower after our Pilates class. Me? I have to shower before and after. Before to hose off the fish guts and saltwater from work, and after to wash off the new layer of sweat. The library is open late on Tuesdays, and I have a couple books ready to pick up from our interlibrary loan. All the sales tax from tourists around here means we have a beautifully stocked library system. My still wet hair rides on top of my shoulders, an even match for the early evening humidity. I skip up the wide brick steps of the main entrance and step to the side while a father and his passel of kids fill the doorway.

I shiver when the air conditioning hits me. At the front desk, the librarian greets me and grabs a short stack of books from the shelf behind her. Not even needing my library card, she checks them out to my name and smiles. "I know how you feel about small talk, so I'll just say hi."

I smile my thanks at her and head straight for my favorite settee tucked in the corner. I kick my sandaled feet onto a footrest and get comfy in the seat. Two nonfiction books about ecotourism and a new mystery novel. I'll flip through them for ten minutes before I need to meet Janie for our Pilates class. As usual when I'm reading, the time flies and all too soon my phone vibrates. I turn off the alarm and walk toward the door.

On my way, I see none other than Officer Cruz at the circulation desk, dressed in civilian clothes. He does a double take as I walk by and I wave when he registers me. "Hey, Ruby."

"Officer Cruz." My voice comes out high-pitched and awkward. I haven't seen him since the night I played vigilante, and I know I'm on thin ice, so I keep walking, thinking that if I don't add any pressure to talk, it will decrease the awkwardness for him. That and I don't have time to talk if I'm going to meet Janie on time.

In the parking lot, my phone vibrates again. I adjust my books and car key and answer on the third buzz. "Hey, Janie, I'm on my way."

"My stupid car broke down."

"I'll pick you up and we'll still make it in time. Where are you?"

"In the 'hood."

My stomach sinks. "No. Really? Why are you there?"

"Because my roommate Claudia decided to buy an ottoman online for ten bucks. When she found out the neighborhood of the seller, she wimped out and decided my life was worth it. So here I am stuck in the sketchiest neighborhood of Florida with an ottoman and no cash."

"Next time tell Claudia you'll meet the seller at a gas station in the touristy part of town." I try to sound chill, but Janie's probably in her yoga pants that look way too good, and picturing her in that neighborhood freaks me out on the inside.

"Um, oh, oh-" Janie's voice stumbles.

"What's wrong?" I demand.

My ear fills with the sound of shattering glass and a scream.

My heart instantly thuds. "Janie!"

I hear angry, muffled voices. Janie's screaming for help, screaming to not hurt her, shouting that she didn't see anything and to please let her go.

My hands tremble and I fumble to unlock my car. "I'll call 9-1-1!"

I toss the library books into the passenger seat and behind me I hear Officer Cruz's voice. "Ruby, do you need help?"

I spin to him, my phone still connected with Janie. "My friend does. She broke down in a bad part of town. I told her I'd come pick her up and then I heard shattering glass and she screamed."

I shove my phone to him and he listens a minute, wide eyes narrowing.

"I'll call dispatch. Do you know exactly where she is?"

I shake my head.

"Can you track her location from your phone?"

"Not anymore."

He squints at me while relaying the bare bones description of the emergency to dispatch. If there was time, I could explain that we used to be able to find each other's lost phones until her previous phone drowned in a tank at work. Even the techs at her carrier's phone store can't convince the program to forget the drowned phone and locate her new phone. They said it's an anomaly and they don't know what else to try, which really hasn't been a big deal until now. I hear her scuffling on the line and wish the drowned phone was the worst of our worries.

"Lock your car. Come with me." Officer Cruz sprints across the parking lot and I follow. "The blue Charger. I'll unlock it. Get in the passenger door." He opens the driver door of a hot car that would totally make me fan my face under different circumstances. We buckle up at the same time and he flies out of the parking lot toward the bad neighborhood.

"Janie, we're coming!" I shout into my phone. The call is still connected, but I don't hear any voices now. A distant car alarm comes over the line, and a squeal of tires traveling further away.

"Tell me everything you know about where she might be."

"She's picking up a ten dollar ottoman that her roommate bought online."

Officer Cruz mumbles something under his breath. I can't catch it, but his tone suggests that it's similar to my scolding that she should've met the seller somewhere safe. "Do you have the roommate's number? Or can you log onto the site and see if we can find the address?"

Claudia doesn't answer, so I type and scroll fast, looking for the ten dollar ottoman. I click a few times, reading fast. "Try Heron Avenue and 62nd Street."

Cruz mutters to himself again, making me think the neighborhood is worse than I imagined. He instructs his phone to call dispatch again and gives an update on where we're headed. He makes a fast right turn and I almost bump my forehead on the window. We're on Heron Avenue, up around 50th Street, when a black sedan tears through the intersection in the opposite direction as us. "Hang on." Officer Cruz checks his mirrors and does a high-speed whip around like in the old school good guy versus bad guy shows. I'm never going on a carnival ride again. After my kidnapping and now this, I'll be dizzy for life. I swallow bile and think about Janie. *Keep her safe.*

In five seconds we're on the tail of the black sedan and Officer Cruz is talking to dispatch. He's reading the license plate number and announcing every cross street as we pass it. My right hand clutches the edge of the bucket seat so tightly my fingernails hurt, and my feet push against the floorboards. My left hand is bracing the dashboard. This wouldn't be so bad if not for the car accident I was in with my captors. Bile rises in my throat again. Janie is probably in that car. Where are the rest of the cops?

Cruz is in constant communication with dispatch, and in four more blocks, a police cruiser joins us in the chase. Cruz doesn't back off, and his Charger and the police cruiser take up the width of the road. Approaching the next intersection, I can see at least two more cop cars approaching Heron Avenue. The sedan flies through another intersection and the police cars form a tight box around it. Cruz backs off to let another squad car into the tight box position. I glance at the speedometer. It's slowing down from eighty. On a residential road in the city. I touch my forehead with my left hand and try to take some deep breaths, because I really don't want to throw up in this nice car.

The police cruisers begin to slow, forcing the black sedan to follow suit. It takes about three blocks, and finally the cars are all gloriously still. My head rocks back and forth. "You okay?" Cruz asks.

I hold up my pointer finger. "I will be. Give me a minute."

Cruz nods and tells me to stay put, then grabs a bulletproof vest from the tiny backseat and exits the car. Cruz flashes his police badge to a few officers and inches his way closer to the action. I crane my neck, making out about four officers wrestling the driver out of the car. Another officer helps Janie out of the backseat. When I see her stand on limp legs, I push out of Cruz's car and make a wobbly run to her. "Janie!"

Janie finds me in the crowd, her face white and her eyes welling with tears.

I squeeze my way between some cop cars and Janie and I hug. The cop who helped her out of the car stays close but doesn't stop me from talking to her.

"Don't ever do that again." I can't watch another friend die.

"Worthless ottoman. I'm not going into a bad neighborhood with my hunk of junk car again." She's shaking. Or maybe it's me. Flashbacks from Tanner's death crowd my attention. He and I were ascending, close enough to each other, but about a body length apart. We popped above the surface at the same instant. Half a blink later the jet ski ran him over. I'll never forget the *thunk*. And now Janie, getting forced into the backseat of that car. I feel so helpless. My legs collapse under me, and someone grabs my elbows and holds me up.

"Ruby, I'm okay," Janie says. "Scared to death, but okay. It's okay."

I realize that the officer who helped her is supporting me from falling. I sob. "But you almost weren't." I squeeze my eyes shut. "And the jet ski killed him."

Tears force their way through my eyelids, and Janie hugs me again. She holds me while I cry.

16

"You're sure nobody is coming after her?" I ask Officer Cruz for the third time.

"She's safe now." Apparently while waiting for the ten dollar ottoman, Janie accidentally witnessed a messy drug deal. When the dealer and buyer realized she saw the whole thing, they freaked out and kidnapped her.

"For now. But will all their customers come after her for uncovering their drug ring?"

"It's a possibility, but it's more likely that other dealers will just step into the shoes of the guy in custody and the users will stay out of it."

I nod, hoping he's right. "Would they have killed her?"

"Probably. Or they might've paid her to be quiet. I can't always predict what druggies will do. They're a weird demographic." He shrugs. "I can't tell what their motive was. If they were going to kill her, they would've been better off to do it then and there and flee the scene, rather than to abduct her."

Right. They took her. They wanted her for something. My stomach coils. My head is spinning. "Pull over!"

The instant Cruz's car stops by the curb in front of the post office, I dive out and stumble to the trash can on the corner. The flashbacks are a hurricane in my mind – the *thunk* on Tanner's head and the light going out of his eyes, being kidnapped and the dizzying car ride, the sound of shattering glass over the phone. It overwhelmed me and it's all coming out now. My stomach heaves with such force I think I'm losing my throat. Strong hands sweep my hair into a ponytail at the back of my head. I clutch the metal ring around the trash can and wonder if this is what death feels like. When there's nothing left to lose, my tears drip down my cheeks and stomach acid coats my lips. I wipe my eyes with the back of my hand and stand upright. Cruz drops one hand from my hair and gives me a paper towel. I wipe my mouth. He hands me a water bottle. A glorious water bottle. I take a cautious swallow, then another. So refreshing, but scary to introduce to my angry stomach. Cruz lets my hair fall back to my shoulders. Then I stumble back to his car and collapse onto the passenger seat, my feet on the curb and my elbows on my knees. "*Gracias,*" I mumble.

Cruz squats diagonally in front of me. I don't blame him for keeping out of the potential line of fire. "Still dizzy?"

"No."

"Food poisoning?"

"No."

"Fear?"

"Yes. And flashbacks."

Cruz nods and offers to walk me into the grocery store so I can wash up in the bathroom. I scrub my hands and face with soap and running water and examine my pitiful face in the mirror. My eyes are puffy and sunken at the same time, and I look anemic. I shake my head at myself and leave the bathroom.

Officer Cruz drives me back to my car at the library. "You feel strong enough to drive?"

I nod, trying to convince myself. All I want is a shower and my cool pillow right now. "I think I'll be okay."

Officer Cruz sizes me up for a few seconds, like he's a paramedic assessing my sorry condition. He says, "I'll follow you home. If you get queasy again, just put on your flashers and pull over."

"Okay."

True to his word, Officer Cruz made sure I got home safely and gave *abuelo* a brief explanation of what happened. Before he left, he looked at me and said, "I'll check on you in a few days."

A hot shower never felt so good, and what really feels good is resting my wet head on my cool pillow. The dizziness is gone, but the flashbacks are still coming. The sun is going down and I'm afraid to fall asleep for fear of what nightmares I'll have.

Thunk. Tanner's body bulldozed underwater. The spray of the jet ski racing away. Him floating back up, neck at an impossible angle. The deep gash in his hairline. Grabbing him, crying out. His busted mask and his eyes with that gone look. The fisherman motoring over to help, pulling both Tanner and me onto his boat. The blood in the boat, on my lap, forever coloring my view on life and death.

Shatter. Janie's scream. Thrown into a drug lord's car, racing off. My breath hiccups. She's never had a shortage of guys interested in her. Would they have sent her off for sex trafficking? Cruz's words that if they only wanted to protect their drug ring, they would've killed her and left the scene haunt me.

My heart races, taking me back to my abduction and concussion. *Papá*'s confession about the business. Bankrupt. Fifty-grand in the hole. I hug *abuela*'s *manta*, quilt, and wish I could push it all away. The fear, the danger, the financial losses, the blood, the jet ski.

A knock on my door startles me. *Abuelo* sticks his head in, concern etched in his features. "Janie's here to talk to you."

"Send her in," I say without even sitting up.

Abuelo opens the door and Janie steps in and sits at my desk. Her wet braid hangs past her shoulder blades, and she changed out of her Pilates clothes. "The shower helped me feel better too," I say.

Janie nods and whispers, "The cops wanted the clothes I had on anyway. Fingerprints and stuff."

It's my turn to nod. I sit up and lean against the wall, my legs tucked under my chin, my pillow still close. "Did they hurt you?"

"Yes, but it hurt you worse, didn't it?"

My swollen eyes give me away.

Janie nods and is quiet for a minute. "Yeah, I'm sure I'll have freaky flashbacks." She sniffs. "It reminded you of Tanner, didn't it?"

I've talked with *abuelo* lots and with Janie some about the effects of losing my boyfriend. But the instant of his death? I haven't talked about it. Maybe I wouldn't be so messed up now if I had.

"Yeah. It all came back. Tanner. My kidnapping." I look at her. "I didn't want you to die."

One thing that makes Janie such a good friend is that she doesn't say or ask too much. She could tell me one of a million things right now, affirmations that fill Pinterest boards, inspirations from the wrappers on the protein bars the twins eat, tombstone stuff telling me to live my best life. But she doesn't say anything. She lets the silence settle and is content with being present. And right now, that's exactly what I need. I'm sure she'll leave me with a Psalm or other Bible verse, but for now, she is nothing more than here, and that is nothing less than a best friend.

After several comfortable minutes of silent contemplation, Janie looks at me. "Officer Cruz seems cool."

"Yeah, he is. He was pretty ticked when I planned Marco's arrest, but I hope he'll get over it."

Janie laughs. "I'm just glad *you* didn't get arrested that night." Then she says, "Do you like him?"

I shrug. "Do you?"

She smiles. "You know he's not my type, but I could see you two together."

I wring a corner of *abuela*'s *manta*, quilt, through my hands. "I could see myself liking him, but it feels weird to think of another guy besides Tanner."

"Of course it'll feel weird. You'll always have a special place in your heart for Tanner." She wiggles her eyebrows. "You can just make a new place for Officer Cruz."

I laugh and throw my pillow at her. "What's happening to your car?"

"The cops said there will be some hullabaloo and their report will convince my insurance company to replace the windshield, but it'll be at least a week. And it'll still need work to fix whatever made it break down. Can you pick me up for Pilates and work?"

"Yup, and Claudia should take a turn too. Natural consequences for online auction shopping in the 'hood."

Janie laughs. "Oh, she will take plenty of turns. Her days of online shopping are over."

"Where's the ottoman?"

"That's the worst part! The drug lord kidnapper guys chucked it out of my car and tore it open looking for a camera. They thought I was filming their deal with a hidden camera and reporting everything over the phone when I was calling you for a ride. So the ottoman is ruined."

"All that and Claudia still doesn't have her stupid ottoman."

Janie laughs and then her face gets serious. She must be replaying the scary scene. Thankfully *abuelo* pokes his head back in. "You two need some comfort food. Come on."

We follow him to the dining room, and his lady friend Teresa carries in a pan of tamales. Yum. How did I not smell those cooking? The twins, carrying more delicious smelling food, convene at the table.

Teresa gives me a warm hug and greets Janie by name. Teresa and *abuelo* met a couple years ago and "enjoy each other's companionship," to quote my *mamá*. Nobody wanted a replacement for *abuela*, and *abuelo* insists that's not what Teresa is. At first I was quite opposed to the idea of Teresa hanging around, but she's so nice I can't help but like her. She sure doesn't force her way into our lives, and we know she's not after the shipwrecks because the sweet woman knows nothing about galleons or diving. The longer I know her, the more I believe *mamá* that she and *abuelo* are just after companionship.

As usual, *abuelo* prays over the meal and then we start sipping our iced tea. The coolness soothes my sandpapery throat. Teresa passes the tamales and August passes the rice in the opposite direction, just to confuse everybody. Axel passes the beans across the table to Janie, and *abuelo* laughs and says it's good to have such a nice group at his table tonight.

We all listen rapturously as Janie recounts the story of her evening. When she gets to the part where the cops took her out of the car, I look at the clock. 9:00 p.m. All this happened since 4:30. I let out a shuddery breath. *Abuelo* squeezes my hand and August says, "Come on, Ruby, could you start staying out of crime scenes? Now you're even dragging Janie into it." Even I chuckle.

From there conversation is pleasant and easy. Teresa's interactions offer the perfect combination of asking questions and listening, nodding understandingly and smiling. During a brief awkward moment where Stacia is mentioned and Janie looks a little sad, Teresa is the one to move the conversation forward. Watching her treat all of us so lovingly catches me off guard. She isn't any different than she was before tonight, but I'm viewing her differently. Tonight I see that Teresa is exactly who our *familia* needs right now. She'll never replace *abuela*, and now I see that isn't her goal or *abuelo*'s wish. She's a perfect fit for us at this stage of life.

Janie's words about making a new place in my heart for another guy come to mind. I watch *abuelo* and Teresa with a gratitude I haven't felt before. I look between them, glance at their grazing shoulders at the crowded table, and then at the framed picture of *abuelo* and *abuela* on the wall, and I see what Janie was getting at. I swallow a heap of emotions and look at Janie. I can tell she's reading my mind because of the knowing nod and smile she gives. The one that says it's okay to love Teresa and never forget *abuela*. A look that says she's happy to see August happy, even if there's a bit of sorrow that he's happy without her. The look that says it's okay for me to have a crush on Officer Cruz.

"Hey, *mamá*, can I come over for dinner tonight?" I thought I was going to have to leave a voicemail, but she answered. I can practically hear her open jaw on the other end of the line. I wait a full nine seconds before saying, "*Mamá*?"

"*Sí, sí*, yes. We'll be at home. I mean, here, after work. We'd love to have you. Any special occasion?"

"Just some stuff to talk about."

"Is it about your cop friend? The cute one who makes you blush?"

In the background I hear air traffic control, so I wait until *mamá* finishes her radio response. "I want to see you and *papá*."

"I haven't been this excited for a weeknight dinner since after your accident when we stayed with *abuelo*. Granted, I don't know what I'm cooking yet, but now I have a reason to make a menu." Now I hear her smile over the phone. More like *mamá*.

I smile back and hope she can hear it in my voice. "Cool. I'll head your way as soon as I get off at 2:30." It'll be a lot of driving and a late night, but it needs to happen.

My parents' faces are frozen in a mix of relief and regret, and their eyes are glued to me. I smile, and it's a real smile and happens much easier than it had for the last year and half. A swirl of smoke catches my eye. The grill on the small deck of the tiny apartment looks like it's ready to explode. "Do we need to cover it with a wool blanket?" I ask.

"The grill!" *mamá* shouts.

Papá jumps up and turns off the propane, giving the grill a good five minutes to cool down before he bravely opens the lid. The charred burgers look like fossils.

"Maybe we can convince the Smithsonian they're volcanic ash from the moon," I say.

Papá scratches his jaw, mumbling under his breath. Of course this talk and dinner didn't go smoothly, and now the meat is burned because I tried to settle the awkwardness that has pushed us apart for way too long now.

Papá scrapes the grill and *mamá* offers to warm up water for *maruchanas*, store-bought noodles. "Not yet," *papá* says gently. He bobs his head, indicating that *mamá* should return to us. He sits across from me at the table that's almost big enough for two people, and *mamá* perches on a garden stool between *papá* and me. "What did you say, before I burned the meat?"

I swallow. "I said I forgive you. For leaving me out of important family news. For leaving me when I needed you." I swallow again and shrug. "I understand now why you moved away, and I'm sorry for all the times I resented you."

Papá's muscular shoulders lower and he stops wringing his hands on top of the table. His eyes meet mine. "I hated leaving you. I hated not telling you, but Tanner had just died. It would've killed you to tell you about the state of Ruby Sunset."

Mamá says, "We didn't mean to heap more pain on you. We had to start paying off some debt. We were desperate enough that we hurt you more."

"It's okay," I say. "You did your best in a bad situation."

Papá and *mamá* stand and we have the sappiest group hug, but it's such a relief that I don't care what the neighbors on the other side of the deck partition think.

"How's Officer Cruz?" Janie asks me in the locker room before our shift. She zips up her sleek black wetsuit.

"I haven't heard anything from him."

"Really? I thought he said he'd check on you in a few days. What's it been? Three weeks now?"

My terse nod shows how much I want to be reminded of this.

"Maybe he's working on a tough case. An undercover assignment."

"Maybe." I reach behind myself and grab the long zipper leash between my shoulder blades and pull up. "Or maybe he realized there's too much drama in my life to want to spend any off duty time with me."

Janie twists her long ponytail into a bun shaped like a cinnamon roll. She glances at me in the mirror and says, "I'm sorry, Ruby. I shouldn't have asked."

I shrug, trying to act like it's not a big deal but totally wanting to change the subject. Thankfully Janie catches the hint and talks about a long list of dolphin behaviors that she plans to reinforce to teach a new trick as she finishes getting ready. She hops up the stairs and I go down the hall to weigh fish.

Fifteen minutes later Brett leans his head in the doorway. He looks around the fish-weighing room, which we affectionately call the kitchen, like he's never seen a walk-in refrigerator full of dead fish. "Jerome said I needed to come over and see you?"

"Yeah, thanks." I look around the room, making sure nobody else is around at the moment. "I was pretty irrational, getting you involved with my Nancy Drew shenanigans. But you helped anyway." I smile. "*Gracias.*" I swallow. "*Tío* Brett."

Brett's mouth gapes and he stares at me for a minute. "I didn't know you knew."

"I didn't until a couple months ago. I don't know if that's why you helped me or not, but thank you."

"I might've helped you anyway, but when I saw him pointing a gun at my niece, secret or not, I couldn't let him shoot."

"Even though he's your *papá*?"

Brett clamps his mouth shut in a tight line, then speaks curtly. "Some DNA is the only thing tying me to Marco. Your *abuelo* is much more my father than Marco."

I smile. "*Abuelo* is the best."

Brett nods. "He really is."

Robin walks in and greets me. "Hi there, Brett. What brings the pilot down to the kitchen?"

"Ruby is finally thanking me for saving her life when she sank my plane," he says with a hint of humor trying to peek out from his gruff facade.

"He's real appreciative of my gratitude," I say, tossing a fish on a scale. Brett's eyes give the slightest twinkle and I know we're finally friends.

17

"How are you?" Officer Cruz asks. I step onto the cement steps and close the door behind me so the air conditioner doesn't have a stroke. "I know I said I'd check on you in a few days, and it's been nearly a month. I owe you an explanation and an apology. And I am concerned with how you're doing."

I adjust my sunglasses, shielding my eyes with my hand from the direct rays that shine through the millimeter wide gap between my shades and forehead. "Were you working undercover on a tough assignment?"

"No." He pauses, then rushes on. "I don't have a good reason for ignoring you. But now I want to introduce you to my nephew Benji." Cruz turns around to face his car and gestures with his hand. Two of the doors open, and a skinny young boy and Len approach me.

"Len?" I hear the question in my own voice.

Len hugs me and the skinny boy holds Cruz's hand. He looks at me with the same wide-set eyes as Cruz. Len steps back but keeps a hand on my shoulder and turns to Cruz, who nervously gives me a sidelong look. "Benji, this is Miss Ruby, the nice lady Mr. Len told you about. Ruby, this is my ten-year-old nephew Benji."

"Hi Benji," I say, wondering what the big deal is. Skinny little Benji is not the crime lord I was imagining who linked Len to a supposedly dirty cop.

Len says to me, "Benji developed a rare bone infection. Two years ago."

Pobrecito, poor little guy.

Len speaks again. "His condition was serious. He needed bone grafts." Len swallows hard as his eyes lock on mine. He speaks deliberately. "Pieces of Tanner's bones were grafted in and saved his life."

My breath hitches. A dam inside me is breaking. My heart races and Len's supportive grip on my shoulder keeps from falling. *Respira, breathe. Stay calm.* Good came out of the bad. I make myself face Benji. "I'm so glad you feel better now."

Benji gives me a shy smile, leaning his body against Cruz's leg. My eyes scan Benji's skinny body, numerous scars visible below his shorts and t-shirt sleeves. Tanner's bones. In this little body, this young life. I blink fast, willing the stubborn tears to wait until later. This kid is alive, healthy, and that's a good thing. A very good thing. Tanner left a wake that will forever touch more than just Len, Tara, and me.

My hand is shaking, but I reach out and shake Benji's hand. I wonder which bones of his were patched up with Tanner's? Benji's little smile grabs my heart and soaks up my unshed tears. My shoulders relax and I determine that the broken dam will not crumble in front of everyone. I lean into Len, whose arm now supports both my shoulders, and I smile at Benji. Cruz encourages Benji to give me a picture of himself in a soccer jersey, and I tell him how good he looks in the blue jersey. He hands me a piece of paper with game dates and locations, saying they always get frozen yogurt afterward and I can come with some time if I want.

I smile and tell him I'd like to see him play. I clutch the picture and game schedule and promise him I'll come cheer him on.

Another week passes without hearing from Officer Cruz. I decide that meeting Benji was the capstone to Cruz's and my friendship sproutlet. I guess he just needed to clear the air about Benji before going back to his regular life before I messed up his routine with my impulsive decisions. I sigh. I thought I liked him, so it's sad to see that he doesn't care about me, but it's probably for the best.

Tonight I'm going to ride with Len and Tara to Benji's soccer game. I have forty minutes before they're picking me up, so I make a fruit and yogurt parfait and sit on the patio, my just-washed hair twisted in a towel on top of my head.

The doorbell rings but *abuelo* says he'll get the door. A minute later *abuelo* leads Officer Cruz into the patio. "Here she is." *Abuelo* walks back into the kitchen.

"Oh, hey Officer Cruz," I say. I start to stand but he gestures that I can keep sitting. I scoot over and he sits next to me on the wicker sofa. He's in his work uniform. "I'm going to Benji's game tonight. With Len and Tara."

Cruz beams. "Thanks for doing that. He'll love having you there. I can't make it tonight." He points to his uniform. "Just on a short break."

I nod, uncertain why he's here and hoping I don't need to make another statement. "Would you like me to make you some eggs before you get back to work?" In the kitchen, I hear *abuelo* snort, probably because he's seen me try to cook eggs. Yeah, I know it's supposed to be easy, but I haven't been successful yet.

Cruz gawks at me for a second and just when I think he'll shake his head and say he never wants to see me again, he says, "Can I get a rain check?"

Really? I nod. "Sure. It'll give me time to watch a couple videos on how to make eggs."

Cruz laughs. Maybe I shouldn't have said that out loud.

Cruz swallows and looks over my shoulder, then back at me. "Obviously we have each other's numbers. Can I call you sometime? When I'm off duty, that is. To hang out?"

So I didn't completely sabotage our chance of friendship? I nod. "Yeah, that'd be cool." I smile. "I'll uh, make you eggs."

Cruz smiles down at his feet and then back at my face. "Maybe we could dive. I'm pretty much a beginner, but it would be fun."

It would be fun to have a dive partner again. I nod and then smile. I meet his eyes and say, "Yeah." Then I blurt out, "I thought you'd hate me."

Cruz scratches the back of his neck by his shirt collar and thinks for a moment. "No, I don't hate you. At least not yet." He smiles. "We might have to spend some more off duty time together to find out for sure."

I laugh and the tension is gone.

18

"Five more feet." I'm staring at the GPS. "Here," I say.

Abuelo cuts the motor and Len lowers the anchor. This is it. The last coordinate Tanner and I needed to search. Len's longtime, trusted employee and Tara are running The Dive Shop and the twins are running Ruby Sunset.

"You're ready?" *abuelo* asks. A seagull squawks overhead.

I meet his eyes and hug him. "*Gracias* for being here."

He nods and says, "It's your turn."

"But what if this isn't it?"

Abuelo and Len share a knowing look. *Abuelo* looks into my eyes. "Ruby, listen closely. No matter what's down there, you have what matters most. God always keeps His promises, and the Bible is full of promises. These treasures," he points his arm out over the water, "will decay, the ships will rot, the coordinates will be wrong, and sometimes the gulls will beat you. But God is faithful. If you have a Kingdom mindset, you'll ride through the disappointments of treasure diving. The disappointments of life."

"A Kingdom mindset?" I ask.

"Seek first the Kingdom of God. Everything else is temporary and doesn't really matter," Len says, sounding so much like his son. "Tanner loved the challenge, but he knew the sunken treasure wasn't the real treasure."

I nod, letting it soak in. "A Kingdom mindset. He held onto the real anchor line."

Abuelo squeezes my shoulder.

We go through all the safety checks and double-checks and I flip backward off the boat. Len follows, as requested in honor of Tanner. Down into the dark. Only seventy-three feet down this time. The coral is beautiful, the fish are bright. And then I see it. A vessel. It's upside down, but it's here. Len and I nod at each other. Even knowing it could take months or years to authenticate, I'm bubbling over with excitement. All those days we spent staring at the sonar reader, the evenings we scoured maps and documents, the times we imagined what the captain and crew endured, and all the naysayers who ridiculed us for wanting to find *Dos Hermanos* flood back to me. The rush of emotions makes my forehead hurt. We did it. We really did it!

Tanner and I correctly identified the location of this legendary ship. The fact that he's not here at my side burns worse than a jellyfish sting, but I know he'd want me to make the most of the find. *This one's for you.*

I fin my way around the ship, taking in the size. She's in better shape than I expected, especially after *abuelo*'s prediction that she was destroyed.

In dreaming of this moment, I always imagined that I'd begin by taking pictures of everything, but this baby is completely upside down. The deck is buried in the sand all the way around. Len shrugs but swims around with me. We swim up to an anchor and shine our headlamps on it. Covered in coral, as expected. A barracuda swims past. The ship is buried deep enough that portholes aren't visible. Its treasure is sealed inside. I frown, thinking about all *abuelo*'s wisdom about treasure and what really matters.

There's a debris field trailing behind the stern, as if the upside down ship skidded along the seabed for fifty feet or so before settling into its grave. The fractured remains of the masts point to the vessel like the needle on a compass. Len points to the debris field and I nod, so we both swim over to it. Remains of what look like three masts and other hefty pieces of timber are scattered. There are some wooden crates and a couple cannons. I take some pictures, not able to take my eyes off the vessel.

The Spanish coins spilling out of the crates will be telling, so I take several pictures of the few that stick out of the mud. I don't see any visible dates on the coins, but the archaeologists can better determine that. If the pictures entice them, they'll request we retrieve a few.

Len gives me a high-five, and I'm glad for his optimism. I click a few buttons on my dive computer to record my GPS coordinates. If technology works in my favor, this record will link to my laptop. The proof on my watch and the laptop that I was here will hopefully be enough for us to claim *Dos Hermanos* as our discovery. Plus the pictures. Not for exploitation though. Not to laugh at those who laughed at us. Not to get rich. But to prove that a legacy can endure, to show what two friends can accomplish. To honor the lives lost in the wreck. To solve the mystery for their home country.

I take a slow breath from my regulator, wishing we could get inside. Len looks at me as if reading my mind. He writes on the dive slate, "Go in?" I nod. Together, we swim the perimeter of the ship again. There's no way in. Len writes, "Sorry." Me too. There are a lot of emotions to unpack with this.

I know, I know. I've always said it's about the search, not the treasure. But still. It'd be nice if there was one little ruby poking out of the mud. One fragment of a Vulgate. I never asked to get rich like Mel Fisher. Frustration wells inside me. It's just that we worked so long and so hard, and this is it. Len senses my attitude and gives me a minute to stare. The whole treasure is unattainable. Sealed off. *Abuelo*'s words echo. A Kingdom mindset. This is one way to keep my focus off the worldly *tesoro*, treasure.

I blow a kiss to *Dos Hermanos* and take a few pictures of the whole view, then look at Len. He gives a thumbs-up, the universal sign to ascend, and I nod. We've seen it all. We begin our ascent. I cling to the anchor rope and suddenly remember what Tanner had on his phone's wallpaper: Hebrews 6:19 – Hope = sure and steadfast = anchor of the soul.

That never meant anything to me until now.

"This is it!" I say the second I spit out my regulator and climb onto *abuelo*'s boat. Len follows and lifts up his mask. *Abuelo* grins and Len squeezes my shoulder. I gulp. "We found her." My voice feels weak and airy. "We really found her."

"Well I'll be," *abuelo* murmurs. "Good work."

I smile, but the emotions are welling up. Tanner should be here. I meet Len's eyes. "If Tanner's Vulgate is in there, it'll stay safe."

Len's eyes tear up and he grips my shoulder again. *Abuelo* pulls me into a hug and whispers his congratulations.

I try to be happy, but it's hard. It's about the Hide-n-Seek, not the fame. And now I've got *abuelo*'s and Len's advice to focus on God's Kingdom. Tanner's sure hope that is the anchor for my soul. But still.

One little ruby and one Vulgate parchment would've been icing on the cake.

That very day, Len and I contact the nautical archaeology association. They'll send a team to try to confirm that the wreck is in fact *Dos Hermanos*. They won't say a word, and neither will Len or I. Even if the archaeologists verify her, I don't want the news to hit the press. It inevitably will, which in a way will be good to keep other hunters away. When the diving community hears that she's been found, fellow treasure divers will move their sights to another wreck. That will be good, but it makes it feel less personal when the whole world knows. Less like our ultimate scavenger hunt. But no matter what the public thinks, I'll know that Tanner and I were in it for the challenge. Okay, so maybe I got carried away with the desire to strike it big, but I'm learning. I'm working on having stronger faith, like *abuelo* and Tanner and Len.

One warm November evening, the doorbell rings and *abuelo* opens it. "Hi Officer Cruz." Cruz steps in and smiles at me. *Abuelo* looks between the two of us. "Is this the date, or another secret, undercover operation?"

Cruz shakes his head. "Definitely nothing undercover. I'm off duty."

Abuelo clears his throat. "Well, have a good date."

Cruz and I share awkward smiles. Him because he knows my criminal record. Me because of Tanner and my vigilante behavior from the summer.

"I'll keep the light on. Are you planning to take my boat?" *Abuelo* sounds serious, but I know he's forgiven me. After all, Marco is behind bars because of it.

Cruz pretends to think. "I think we'll take my car tonight. We'll wait to take your boat until you've changed the oil next."

Abuelo cracks into a grin. He hugs me goodbye and shakes Cruz's hand.

I'm excited, but torn too. This is a weird thing about grief. For a long time after Tanner died, I lost all interest in relationships. I didn't think I'd ever date again and certainly never love another guy. That would feel unfaithful to Tanner. But the bad news is, he's gone. Our relationship is over. And just because his race is done, mine isn't. I'm still alive, even though I felt so hollow after he died. For months I wished I had died too. What was the point of life without my favorite person? But *abuelo* prayed for me every day, and based on the flutter in my stomach at seeing Cruz shake *abuelo*'s hand, I know his nonstop prayers are helping with the grief.

We step outside and I recognize his blue Charger that looks like it could win races. "Cool car, by the way."

Cruz grins and holds the passenger door for me. "I wanted something fun for my spare time." He gets in the driver's seat and backs out of the driveway. "I made reservations at a steakhouse that is famous for salads."

I laugh. "That sounds perfect."

During dinner, Cruz devours his side salad, baked potato, dinner roll and steak in the time I eat my salad and roll. "After we eat, do you want to stop by an outdoor concert in the city square?"

"Sounds fun. What type of music?"

"Reggae, from what I heard. There's going to be some law enforcement there, which is how I heard about it in the first place."

"Reggae music in a park. I'm in. Wait, your cop friends are going to be there? Will they give you a hard time? Ya' know, since we're…" I hesitate, but finally say, "together?" Maybe not the best word choice. "Together" sounds so together. I quickly add, "On a date, I mean." That's not much better.

Thankfully Cruz lets the moment pass without so much as a beat. "Oh, they'll give me a hard time, I'm sure. I'll take it." When I'm part way through my small steak, the waitress offers dessert, and Cruz orders the date night dessert special. Wow. This guy can eat. Cruz snaps his fingers. "Before I forget." He pulls out his phone. "I need to show you this."

He holds the screen to me and I read the heading. "US Coast Guard, Maritime Enforcement Specialist. Request Information."

He gives a wry smile. "Reg insists that I tell you to try it."

"Reg?"

He nods.

"What do you think?"

"It seems like a pretty good backup business plan to me." We both laugh, and then he takes a breath and grows serious again. "I'm not telling you to change your career. If you want to be a cop, you already proved you have guts." He lets out a short laugh, thinking back to my vigilante attempts. "I keep meaning to ask you, what happened to my spare handcuffs you stole?"

I swallow and brush back my bangs. "Handcuffs, handcuffs…"

He smiles and shakes his head. "If you're able to return them, please do. If not, forget it. But don't ever steal from an officer again." He gives me a little smile, a truce flag.

I give a tentative smile back. "Marco's accomplice Roger cut through them with a tool. I'm sorry."

He looks at me for a minute and says, "Like I said, you have guts. So if you want to be a maritime officer like Reg, then go for it. You'll definitely have to start obeying laws though. If the cops don't obey, it sets a low standard for civilians."

I swallow. "Wow. That's a lot to think about. Thanks for the idea."

"Sometimes Reg has good ideas."

We both laugh. The two pieces of chocolate cake topped with whipping cream and cherries arrive and loom larger than my meal. I laugh. Cruz resembles a racehorse in the starting gate but politely waits for me to finish my steak. The instant I swallow the last bite of steak, he straightens up. "Ready for dessert?" he asks eagerly. I laugh.

Cruz lets me take the first forkful of cake, but he's right behind me. He swallows a bite and says, "This is delish." I eat until I'm totally full and Cruz doesn't mind finishing the rest.

On the drive to the concert, Cruz clears his throat. "Hey, um, before Marco got arrested, I was a little stern with you."

"I deserved it."

"Yes, you needed to be careful. And I was worried about your safety. But I was too rough. It's one thing to be diplomatic and firm. It's another to be, uh-"

"Like Reg?" I offer.

We're stopped at a red light and Cruz turns to me and bobs his head in an apologetic way, like he's admitting to the comparison.

"I needed to hear it. The treasure thing, and the threat from Marco, it made me pretty competitive. I know from a safety perspective I shouldn't have done what I did." I sigh. "Now that it's over, I'm glad I did it."

Cruz reaches over and squeezes my hand, briefly, and returns his hand to the steering wheel. Ten and two. Very safe. "Thanks for understanding."

"Thanks for being chill." I elbow his rock-hard bicep, and he chuckles. I notice a dark line by the hem of his shirt sleeve.

"You have a tattoo?"

Cruz sighs. "Yeah. If it didn't cost so much to remove, I'd do it."

"Changed your mind after paying for the indelible ink?" I hate tattoos, something I inherited from *abuelo*, but I won't tell him that.

"Yeah. As soon as my *abuelita* saw it, I knew I'd disappointed her. At least the police department still let me on with it, but I regret it."

"Why?"

He looks at me and whispers, "Because I let down *abuelita*. And, this might sound really weird." He swallows.

"Try me."

"I feel like I graffitied God's creation." His eyes go back to the road. After a moment in which I feel even more like a *mensa*, dork, for not knowing what to say, he asks, "What do you think?"

"I think that's a good reason to want to undo a tattoo. What is it of?"

With his left hand, he pushes up his right shirt sleeve and I study the black marks. It's like a six-pointed cop badge with a Bible verse and an American flag wrapped around it. "At least you quoted the Bible and showed patriotism on your bicep bumper sticker. That counts for something."

He chuckles. "The only good part of a dumb decision."

"Don't beat yourself up over it. It looks cool on you. You like being a cop?"

"I like helping people. The action and danger are fun. Keeping treasure divers alive is a pain though."

I laugh. "The blue in the tattoo goes with your car's color."

Cruz shakes his head. "From you, I can't tell if it's a compliment or a jab."

"For you, it's a compliment." Conversation hasn't been this easy since Tanner died.

At the concert, three different cops come over to talk to Cruz, and he introduces me to them as "Ruby, the one who helped stop the crime ring among the treasure divers." The cops are polite to me, and the way they each look at Cruz, I can tell they're going to razz him later. Poor guy. I find it hard to believe I'll be worth that. This might be our first and last date. Bummer. He's really fun off duty.

The Reggae music is catchy, and we walk around the park, amused by the concert goers. It looks like every demographic is represented here. I love the drumset and the relaxed feel of the music. We each sit on a swing and take off. "The guys are gonna razz you about me."

"So?"

I go higher and get butterflies in my stomach. "So," I pause. "I might not be worth it."

"Says who?"

I'm silent, swinging back and forth.

"Says who?" Cruz asks again, gently.

The drumset and guitar keep a steady beat in the background. I look over at him. He seems sincere. "I come from a long line of treasure hunters. It drives my *mamá* crazy that I inherited the gene, but obviously she has it too. Right after Tanner died, my parents moved to the Gulf to make more money. Well, I thought it was to make more money, but it turns out the shop was in major debt. Anyway, look at the lengths I went to to find a sunken ship. I'm kind of a mess."

We listen to the music for a minute and then Cruz says, "You're passionate. And we all have things to work through."

"Why are you so nice?"

Cruz smiles. "Because *abuelita* insisted her little southern boy behave well."

I laugh and we listen to the music for a minute. "I've been reading my Bible. Every day."

"That's cool. I try to keep up on Bible reading too." We keep swinging. Cruz smiles. "Just so you know, I'm not perfect either."

"Oh? What's your biggest vice? A parking ticket when you were sixteen?"

Cruz laughs. "I wish." He thinks for a minute and says, "I've got stuff to overcome too. And I think you're pretty cool."

We're swinging in unison right now, so I reach over and offer him a high five. Our palms meet and I grin.

"You excited?" I'm talking Cruz through the BWRAF buddy check that's second nature to experienced divers.

"A little nervous," Cruz admits. "This will be the deepest I've dived."

"You're surrounded by experts." I double-check his regulator, then mine.

"And God," *abuelo* adds.

"And Ruby's twin brothers who will take care of anyone who hurts her," Axel says.

"Don't threaten a cop," I tease.

Axel extends his fist and August and I stack ours on top. Cruz glances at me and I give him a nod, so he adds his fist to the stack. Axel counts and on three we say, "*Conquistadores.*" Cruz raises his eyebrows and grins.

Abuelo triple-checks us all and says, "Down you go. You'll be shallow enough to have two hours of bottom time. Have fun. I'll read a book and update my dive log. The real one." For safety reasons, *abuelo* will stay in the boat. That's the one safety rule Tanner and I didn't strictly adhere to, mainly because we couldn't convince anybody to ride all over the ocean with us and bake in the sun while we dove.

The twins flip backward into the turquoise water first. When they're down a safe distance, I ask Cruz if he's ready. He's nervous but nods, and with enough athleticism to make up for his lack of experience, he flips off the boat. I look at *abuelo* through my mask and he nods. I check over my shoulder that it's clear for me to hop in, and down I go.

We all hold the anchor line and descend into the colorful coral reef. As my eyes adjust to the blue and the creatures, something becomes clear to me, something that *abuelo* probably knew all along. The reef is kind of like life. Like the fish darting in and out of my sight, highs and lows will come in, capture my attention, and move out. Like the coral, all these experiences work to shape the tapestry of my life. Individual pieces of coral might not be beautiful, and some are ugly up close, but they're part of the whole. Tanner's death will forever be a dark spot in my life, and its effect will always be with me like a scar on the coral. But the coral recovers after injury, and I need to grow stronger and live with purpose and value. I can live every day to prepare my character for what matters most. The real treasure is *El Reindo de Dios*, God's Kingdom.

About the Author

*Photo Courtesy
Krista Swanson,
©Simple Wonder
Arts*

Liz is a moonlighting author, the wife of a climbing arborist, and the homeschooling mom of three energetic and laundry-producing children. She dove into an adventurous life when she spent a summer in Colorado teaching rock climbing, which has paved the way for many more adventures, from California to Kenya. Liz resides with her family in Wisconsin, where they enjoy hiking and rock climbing. She writes wholesome stories with heart to encourage others to find adventures, expand their comfort zones, and grow in the process.

Discover more at https://mlizboyle.com/

Acknowledgements

This story has had a lengthy journey to publication, and I'm stoked to finally be able to share it with you. Seeing the end product is very rewarding, and it's possible due to a devoted team, my supportive family, and a patient God.

A sincere thanks to JPC Allen, without whom this whole story would never even have been brainstormed and certainly not fanned into a flame. Thank you for helping me work through some of the trickier aspects of my first attempt with this style of story, for giving valuable feedback, and for believing in this story from the moment it was a comment on a blog post;

I am very grateful to my beta readers for pointing out obvious and not-so-obvious errors and for helping the action scenes be believable: Emeline Halsted, William Halsted, and Cynthia Saladin;

Allyson Kennedy, your editing refined all my characters and dialogue so much! And, phew am I glad that you helped Officer Cruz's wide eyes convey a range of emotions beyond just shock. He's come a long way, thanks to you. Your friendship in the authoring journey is such a blessing;

Leslea Wahl, my fellow adventure writer, thank you for fine-tuning the dive scenes and helping me get the night dive just right;

I spent more time researching the flight scene with Brett than anything else in this book (and there was a lot to learn!). Many thanks to my knowledgeable pilot connections for ensuring accuracy: Jack Young, Private Pilot since 1991, and Ross De Kraay;

Thanks to the Crime Scene Writers forum for helping me work out the law enforcement details;

Muchas gracias to my sensitivity reader Charlotte Muñoz for eagerly helping me transform this book into a powerful story of a beautiful Hispanic family;

Dr. Corey Malcom, Director of Archaeology, Mel Fisher Maritime Museum, for answering my many, *many* questions about treasure diving, shipwrecks, and Spanish galleons.

Readers, thank you for joining the adventure! I hope you loved this story!

ALSO BY M. LIZ BOYLE

Off the Itinerary

WHERE FAITH MEETS ADVENTURE

1	2	3	4
Five friends. One moonlit summit. An unforgettable journey.	Five friends. A paranoid treasure hunter. A flood of danger.	Five friends. A spark of hurt between them. "A must-read for Christian teens." -Allyson Kennedy	Five friends. One search dog. Seven suspenseful short stories.

Sign up for my newsletter at https://mlizboyle.com and receive a free short story titled "Right Where I Need To Be."

The adventure Kinsley dreams of does not involve hours of community service, thanks to her irreverent friend Griffin. While working extra hard to reclaim the promise of a scholarship, Kinsley finds an adventure in an unexpected place.

www.ingramcontent.com/pod-product-compliance
Lightning Source LLC
Chambersburg PA
CBHW021220220726
48287CB00015B/1911